The Adventures Of Dougal and Derry

Rupert the Scourge of Connaught

Michael Pierson

To Jez, Ben, Alex

Enjoy The Magic

Bloomington, IN   authorHOUSE®   Milton Keynes, UK

AuthorHouse™
1663 Liberty Drive, Suite 200
Bloomington, IN 47403
www.authorhouse.com
Phone: 1-800-839-8640

AuthorHouse™ UK Ltd.
500 Avebury Boulevard
Central Milton Keynes, MK9 2BE
www.authorhouse.co.uk
Phone: 08001974150

This book is a work of fiction. People, places, events, and situations are the product of the author's imagination. Any resemblance to actual persons, living or dead, or historical events, is purely coincidental.

First published by AuthorHouse 12/19/2006

ISBN: 1-4259-4833-2

Printed in the United States of America
Bloomington, Indiana

This book is printed on acid-free paper.

Contents

Cead Mile Failte
(One Hundred Thousand Welcomes)

Glossary Of Leprechaun / Fairy Names

Name	Pronunciation	Meaning	English version
Aedan	AY-dan	Fire	Hugh
Adam	A-dam	To Be Red	
Amber	AM-bur		
Brianna	bree-ANA	Powerful	
Balor	BAY-lor	Dumbfounded	
Cait	Coyt	Pure	Kate
Connor	CON-or	High Will	Cornelius
Desire			
Ceallachan		Strife	Callaghan
Dougal		Dark Stranger	
Derry	Der-ee	Red Hair	
		Oak Grove	
		Town/ County in Ireland	
Egan	EE-gan	Little Fire	
Lorcan	Lor-can	Fierce	Lawrence
Liam	LEE-am	Protection	William
Neave	NEEV	Bright	
		Lustrous	
Padraig	PAW-drig	Noble	Patrick
Seamus	SHAY-mus	Trips By	James
		The Hill	
Sinead	shin-AYD	Gift of God	Jane
Turloch	TUR-lock	Broad	Terrance
		Shouldered	

Key Players

Adam   A fairy soldier and Dylan's brother

Amber   A fairy princess and heir to the fairy throne

Arthur A pixie solider

Cameron A brownie rebel leader

Derry   A leprechaun and twin sister of Dougal

Dougal A leprechaun and twin bother of Derry

Dylan   A fairy soldier and Adam's younger brother

Finn   A fairy prince and captain, Amber's cousin

Izzy   The leader of the brownie rebels

Sir John A pixie knight

Liam   A fairy forester

Neave   A fairy wizard

Phil   A flying fairy dragon

Rupert Evil king of the pixies

Strahan King of the fairies and Amber's father

Shadow Master of disguise, a pixie spy

William Powerful pixies wizard and Rupert's advisor

PROLOGUE

As the two men climbed the seemingly endless stairway they joked and laughed happily, content with the knowledge everything they had worked for was falling into place. One of the men was tall by pixie standards and thin, almost skeletal. His shoulder length hair was jet black as was his long waxed mustache and goatee beard. The man's eyes were dark and just a little too close together. Behind his back they called him 'the weasel' not just because of his looks but for his cunning as well. He always dressed in black leather and was never seen without his long sword and rarely without the other man currently at his side.

This man, William by name, was short and over weight, his features were rather nondescript and he looked quite harmless. Looks however can be very deceiving, for William was anything but harmless. He was the most powerful wizard in the pixie kingdom maybe even in all of Connaught.

Rupert, king of the pixies, was about to achieve something his ancestors had dreamed of for hundreds of years. For centuries pixie kings had systematically conquered most of Connaught but none had dared to take the fight to the fairies, the only race capable of resisting the pixie conquerors. It would not be long however before the fairy kingdom would be his, followed closely by the remaining nations of Connaught.

Soon, very soon, he would rule an entire world.

As the two men finally neared the single door at the top of the staircase, the highest point in the castle, the two guards heavily armed and armoured, bowed in a mix of servitude and fear. The guards parted and the king took the only key to that door from his pocket, then unlocking the door he and the wizard entered the small room.

The woman sitting on the small bed did not even look up when the two men entered. William waved his hand and from out of thin air a platter of food and a pitcher of wine appeared on the table in the centre of the room.

'Have you changed that pretty little mind of yours yet?' Rupert asked mockingly as he looked at the woman.

She looked him in the eye rebelliously and answered, 'marry you, a pixie,' adding defiantly, 'never!'

CHAPTER 1

CAER GORIAS

As Dougal pushed his little wooden barrow that was filled with flour for his mother, he wished the flour mill was not on the opposite side of town to his house or at the very least his friend Phil was there to help him, but he wasn't, so Dougal headed for home by himself.

As the sixteen year old leprechaun travelled on he looked about the picturesque little town, a town founded by his famous ancestor Seamus O'Farrell many hundred of years before. Most of the little houses were made of old brick of various shades of reds and browns and all had thatched roofs. The houses were mainly single story, about three feet tall, but there were a few two story houses for the more important families of Caer Gorias. In all the windows hung brightly coloured curtains, reds, blues, greens, yellows and every colour you could imagine. All had neat little gardens growing beautiful roses (that would be miniature to a human but to a leprechaun they were huge) and many other flowers. More importantly the leprechauns grew their own vegetables, which they stored to get them through the long cold winters.

Dougal continued along the cobbled lane greeting many of the town's locals that he passed on his journey and even on occasions stopping for a conversation or two.

One of the leprechauns he stopped to talk to was his friend Fearghus Murphy. Both friends wore traditional leprechaun clothing that consisted of black hobnail boots (Dougal's were made by his father, the towns best cobbler), knee length emerald green pants, matching knee length socks and a thick black leather belt with a gold buckle. Their vests and coats were made from the same emerald green material and had little golden buttons and like all leprechaun males neither would be seen dead without their hats, wide brimmed (to keep out both the sun and rain, more of the latter if the truth be told) the same emerald green colour as the rest of their clothing but for a black band and a big golden buckle.

'Top of the morning to you Fearghus,' called Dougal.

'And a good day to you Dougal,' Fearghus replied.

After a brief discussion about how each other's families were and what they had been doing, Fearghus asked Dougal, 'Now Dougal, do you still play that fiddle of yours?'

'Of course,' replied Dougal, 'why do you ask?'

'Well, my band is playing at The Harp and Hare tonight and Sharon's mother won't let her play in the tavern at night. I thought you might like to take her place, after all, between you and me you're a better fiddle player than she is,' said Fearghus.

'Yes I am,' laughed Dougal, 'but I'm nowhere near as pretty as that girlfriend of yours now am I. So what time should I meet you tonight?'

'About eight o'clock outside The Harp and Hare, 'answered Fearghus.

'Right,' said Dougal, 'I'm off home, see you at eight sharp,' and with that Dougal lifted the handles of his barrow and headed for home.

Dougal decided to stop for a rest and a wee drink when he reached the town centre. He looked for and found an outside table overlooking the square, ordered a dandelion tea and relaxed.

As he looked around the square his eyes came to rest upon the town church. Just the sheer size of the building had always amazed him. The church was at least twenty feet tall and twice as long.

It was made from huge grey bricks as long as he was tall and half as high. The windows were stained glass each made from dozens of individual panels. According to legend the windows were not made of glass at all but of diamonds, emeralds, rubies and many other rare gems.

Statues of famous leprechauns, real and legend were carved into the church's walls. Dougal hoped one day his image would stand beside them.

Two huge five foot polished wooden doors marked the entrance to the church and down the far end of the building stood two turret topped towers. From these towers it was possible to see the whole town and all of the surrounding area all the way to the woods.

The church was supposed to be nearly as old as the town itself and apparently had taken over a hundred years to build. Dougal did not believe this. He could not see how leprechauns could have ever built a building of such immense size. His theory was that the big people built it for them. He keeps the theory to himself these days because in the past whenever he mentioned it everyone he told laughed at him. All the same he still believed he was right.

With his tea almost finished he turned his attention to the building that stood next to the church. It was dwarfed by the church, only one story high, but where most buildings in Caer Gorias were built from brick, this one was made from pure white marble. It was always kept so clean that you could see your reflection in the polished marble surface.

A six foot tall statue of Seamus O'Farrell stood on the cobble stoned courtyard in front of the building and a two foot tall white rung iron fence surrounded the courtyard itself. At present the gates were open but two leprechauns in full armour, armed with pikes, stood guard.

This building was infact the Caer Gorias council chambers and the two guards (only there for show) meant that the council was in session. The council met on the first Monday of every month and mainly settled disputes between neighbours, decided whom the town would trade with and other such matters. However, in times of emergency the council would convene for special meetings. The council was made up of about twenty councillors all direct decedents of Seamus O'Farrell and council word was law.

Dougal's father was on the council as was his father and his father before him. Infact there had been an O'Shea on the council since the day it had first formed. Dougal knew that one day he would be expected to take his father's place on the council. This thought alone was enough to make him shake his head and sigh. Dougal was nothing like his father. He neither wanted to be a cobbler or a councillor, which was already beginning to cause tension between father and son. Dougal's father liked to be the big fish in a small pond. As for Dougal he believed that a big fish in a small pond was still a relatively small fish and more than anything Dougal hated the thought of spending his entire life in such a small pond with such a vast ocean to explore. So with this unhappy thought, he finished his dandelion tea and headed for home.

Finally Dougal turned the corner into the street where he lived and as he did he looked up and saw Cait O'Shaunessy.

Cait had always lived in the same street as Dougal. She was a couple of months younger and a little bit shorter. She had shiny light auburn hair in long ringlets that fell down around her shoulders, eyes as blue as the ocean and the face of an angel. The instant Dougal saw her he felt his heart start to race, his face flush and his breathing quicken. Cait was looking more lovely than ever thought Dougal. The long blue dress she wore (where leprechaun men tended to where traditional emerald green clothing, leprechaun women had a fondness for bright colourful clothing) highlighted the eyes Dougal always found himself lost in. By Seamus she's beautiful he thought. Then before he had time to compose himself, there she was almost next to him.

'Hello Cait,' mumbled Dougal looking down at his feet as he spoke, trying desperately to breathe and clear his head.

'Hello Dougal and how are you today?' she replied giving him one of her most dazzling smiles, the type of smile she reserved for Dougal alone.

Breathe and don't look into her eyes he told himself.

'I'm very well,' he answered starting to feel more composed. Then he asked Cait how she was and they chatted away for a while. He told her about his playing the fiddle later that night at The Harp and Hare and she promised to come along and watch.

As they went their separate ways he risked a quick glance into her deep blue eyes and smiled. He had taken about two steps before he froze in panic. She was going to be at the tavern tonight. He didn't know if he could play with her watching. Dougal then forced himself forward on towards home only a couple of doors away.

It was with relief when Dougal finally wheeled his little barrow through the gates of his house. It had been a long trip to and from the mill and had taken him most of the morning.

His younger brother Aedan, who was weeding the garden, poked his head over a rose bush and said, 'You took your time didn't you. Come and give me a hand with the garden.'

'I'll be out soon,' Dougal replied.

Aedan was fifteen months younger than Dougal and already an inch taller. This upset Dougal but he would not admit this to anyone, especially Aedan. Dougal and Aedan looked nothing alike, where Dougal's hair was red like his father's his brother's was jet black. Aedan was of slight build compared to the stockier Dougal but if Aedan looked like his mother it was fair to say it was his father's personality he had inherited.

Dougal found his mother Brianna in the kitchen making Curach. This delighted him, as Curach (a dessert made from fresh raspberries, oatmeal, heavy cream, a little whiskey and runny honey) was his favourite. His mother was a short, slight woman even by leprechaun standards. She now had the odd grey hair showing which seemed only to highlight even more just how black her hair really was. She had one of those ageless faces looking neither young nor old and always wearing a smile. Her dark piercing eyes revealed both her intelligence and zest for life. It was from his mother that Dougal inherited his love of music and thirst for adventure and knowledge.

Dougal left the kitchen after discussing his morning with his mother. He was encouraged by his mother's interpretation of why Cait was coming along to the tavern that night. Somehow the thought that Cait was only going along to be with him warmed his heart. He knew now that he would play his fiddle better than ever before just to impress her.

On his way to the garden to help his brother, Dougal heard his sister playing her tin whistle. Dougal couldn't help but to applaud as Derry finished her first tune. He truly believed his sister was the only person he knew who was more musically talented than himself. Dougal and Derry were twins and as close as twins could be. Derry was fourteen minutes older than Dougal and loved to play the part of the big sister. He on the other hand considered himself her protector. Although she was a pretty girl, there was unfortunately not a male under twenty who was not scared of her father, so Derry had plenty of spare time to practice her music.

Although short and slight like her mother, that was were their physical likeness stopped. She had the same bright red hair (which is why her parents named her Derry meaning redhead) as Dougal, just longer and slightly curlier. Her eyes were the same bright emerald green as Dougal's and they were as alike in looks as any male and female could be.

But if they inherited their father Connor's looks it was definitely their mother's personality they possessed. They both believed that one day they would out grow Caer Gorias, it was a large world and they both wanted to see it all.

There were no secrets between them. Derry even knew about Dougal's friend Phil and infact she had even met him a couple of times. She really liked Phil but could see why they had to keep him a secret even from Aedan and their parents.

They decided that Derry would go with Dougal to the tavern later that night. This was to make sure that when Dougal and the band were playing no one else tried to dance with Cait. If they did, Derry would scare them off making sure no one came between Dougal and Cait because that was what big sisters were for.

Dougal spent the next few hours working in the garden with Aedan. The O'Shea garden was one of the largest in Caer Gorias and without doubt the finest. Leprechauns from all over town would invent reasons just to walk past the garden to see the colours and smell the fragrances of its hundreds of flowers. Behind the house were their vegetable garden and fruit trees. In the vegetable garden grew baby new potatoes, peas, beans, carrots and other plants that they needed. They also grew apples for cider and pies and various other fruits including strawberries and of course Dougal's favourite raspberries.

As well as having the finest garden in town, the O'Shea's house was a mansion by leprechaun standards. It was two stories high with a thatched roof and white walls. Both the front and back doors were bright red as were the entire window trimmings and shutters. There was a chimney at each end of the house both currently unused as it was the height of summer, had it been winter they would have been smoking merrily away.

Not long after Connor returned home from the council meeting the boys were called inside and told to wash up for dinner. Brianna had prepared Colcamon, a dish made with potatoes, cabbage, butter, salt and pepper. The Colcamon was a side dish made to accompany the Cheesy Fish Toss she had also prepared. Cheesy Fish Toss is a salad, made from smoked and white fish, traditional salad vegetables, cheese just for good measure and finished off with zippy green sauce. There was also Irish farmhouse loaf, still warm enough for the butter to melt into the bread. The meal was accompanied with cider that Brianna had made herself using apples from their own garden. For dessert they ate the Curach that Dougal had seen his mother making earlier in the day. It was the first time the whole family had been together all day so they used this time to catch up with each other's comings and goings. This was a common practice for the O'Shea's during their main meal.

Later that night after The Harp and Hare had closed Dougal and Derry headed home. Musically it had been a very successful evening. Dougal didn't think Fearghus was too happy though when Derry joined in with the band playing her tin whistle (far better than Fearghus). Turloch, the bands singer, on the other hand, encouraged her to sing duets with him and even do a couple of solos. Although the O'Shea's didn't realise it they were the patrons' favourites. Fearghus had noticed and couldn't make up his mind whether to never ask Dougal to fill in again or to ask Derry and Dougal to join the band full time. The problem with latter was with their talent and Derry's looks it wouldn't be his band for long.

The only thing that stopped it being a perfect evening as far as Dougal was concerned was that Cait had not been able to come. Her parents had gone out and she had to look after her younger brother Lorcan and Sinead her younger sister. As much as she wanted to she knew she could not take a five and nine year old to the tavern. So just after supper she had gone to the O'Shea's to tell Dougal she couldn't make it.

As the twins walked home they talked about how much fun the night had been. The conversation had been light hearted until Dougal said hesitantly, 'Derry.'

'Yes Dougal,' she replied when it looked like he wasn't going to say anything else.

'Derry, tonight was fun, *but*,' he paused for a few moments, 'Derry, I need to get away for a while, a temporary change of scenery. I can almost feel the walls of Care Gorias closing in on me and if I don't get away from our father I might say or do something that might destroy our relationship permanently. So I'm going to spend some time in the woods, maybe with Phil.'

'You know I'm going with you, don't you?' said Derry, who like her brother longed to see more of the big wide world.

'I hoped you would,' answered Dougal, 'we'll leave first thing in the morning and try and find Phil. It could take us a couple of days this time of the year as he tends to live further from the town in summer to avoid the extra people in the woods. He'll most likely be in the caves to the southeast. We'll have to leave a note for Ma and Da so they won't worry.'

'Dougal,' Derry cut in, 'let's go tonight, I'm not tired are you?'

'No,' he replied.

'Good,' said Derry continuing, 'it's settled then. We'll go home, pack some food and clothes, a lantern and some oil because there are no streetlights where we are heading. I will write the note to tell Ma and Da we are going a roving for a while. Ma will understand, Da won't be too happy but he can't stay mad with his little girl for long. He'll think you are coming along to protect me so that should keep you out of trouble for when we get back.'

With that the twins excitedly hurried home. A few of the homes they passed still had lights on but most were in darkness with their owners tucked up in bed asleep for the night. They both stopped dead in their tracks when several downstairs rooms in their house were glowing with light. If their parents were up it would delay their departure until the morning.

When they crept through the front door and went room by room it was with sheer delight that they found that their mother had left the lights on for them and infact no one was awake.

They quickly went to their rooms and packed the clothing that would be needed for the journey. Derry changed out of the clothes she wore to the tavern earlier that night and into more appropriate travel clothing. By the time Derry came back downstairs Dougal was already packing food for their adventure. Derry wrote the note to their parents explaining their need to get away for awhile and how they would return before winter set in. With the note finished they walked through the front door and into the lamp lit street beyond. Their adventure had begun.

'Derry, have you got your whistle with you?' asked Dougal as he pulled his out of his pocket and began to play an old Irish tune.

'Of course,' she answered joining in with his tune.

They walked for the next half hour, sometimes talking, sometimes playing but passing no one as they arrived at the southern exit of the town. Both stopped while Dougal put his whistle back into his pocket and unhooked the lantern from his belt and lit it. They both took a deep breath as they left the safety of the city lights behind them. Dougal lit the way with his lantern while Derry continued to play well-known tunes from famous bards of the past. Dougal even sung along to some of the more heroic songs, the ones he knew the words to anyway.

After a couple of hours and at least a mile travelled they left the road and looked for a campsite for the night. It was not long before they found a small cave on the sheltered side of a small grassy knoll. They soon realised how cold it had become so Dougal collected some twigs, lit a fire and there they stopped for the night.

Once warmed by the fire they pulled out their travel blankets and settled down for what was left of the night. Both were asleep in an instant neither realising how tired they really had been.

CHAPTER 2

THE SEARCH FOR PHIL

Dougal woke to the smell of frying quail eggs, mushrooms and bacon. Derry, who had been awake for about half an hour by this time, had been shocked by how late she had slept. It was the sun streaming into the little cave that had woken her and by then it was after ten in the morning and that was the latest she had ever slept. So it was with some guilt she got up and set about making breakfast.

'Good morning Derry,' said Dougal, 'breakfast smells wonderful.'

'Hi Dougal, I can't believe we slept so late can you?' she asked.

'It must have been four before we went to sleep last night, so I'm amazed we woke so soon, so you can stop feeling guilty,' he answered, 'anyway Derry,' he continued, 'we have nowhere we have to be with nothing we have to do and two months before the first of the winter storms arrive. This time of the year we'll have no trouble finding food with all the wild fruit, wild vegetables and edible fungus as well as all the wildlife in the woods.'

'You're right,' she said, 'it will just take me a couple of days to get used to all this extra freedom. Go wash up for breakfast, there's a small stream just through the trees to the right. By the time you get back the bacon will be crispy, just the way we like it.'

When Dougal returned from the stream they ate what was more of a brunch than a breakfast and if anything it tasted better than it smelt if that were at all possible. Once they had finished eating Dougal took the pan and eating utensils to the stream and washed them. He then filled the pan with water and used it to douse the fire Derry had used to cook their meal. He then helped Derry clean up the campsite and repack their packs and get ready to continue their journey. They decided to avoid the road and keep to the woods. They did this for a couple of reasons, firstly, it would be more fun and secondly, it would be far easier to forage for food as they would eventually need to replace what they consumed on their adventure.

With the campsite clean, they headed off on their search for Phil at a leisurely pace. Dougal found himself thinking about when he had first met Phil. It was about three years before, he could still to this day vividly remember that high pitched cry for help. It was really more a screech than a cry but if you asked Phil about it he remembers it as a manly, staunch request for assistance. Dougal had followed the cry for about twenty minutes before he came to the little clearing. He looked up in the direction the noise was coming from and saw the trappers net swinging from a tree branch about fifteen feet above him. From this distance he couldn't tell who or what was in the net. He remembered climbing the tree and out to the branch. It had been both frightening yet exhilarating so high above the ground it had almost made him dizzy. All that had been forgotten though when he had seen the occupant of the net.

When Dougal had seen what was in the net he nearly fell out of the tree. The creature looking back at him, pleadingly, was like nothing he had ever seen or heard before. It had golden eyes, red scaly skin and gossamer wings. Four powerful legs with large claws that if it had had enough room it could have freed itself because they would have been easily sharp enough to cut through the net. It also had a long tail and the body the size a large domestic cat. The creature's head was shaped like a cross between a dog and a crocodile with long sharp teeth.

It had taken a few moments for the creature to convince Dougal that he wouldn't eat him if he freed it. So Dougal had freed the creature by cutting through the netting with the little hunting knife he always carried with him when he was in the woods, letting the creature fly to the ground. The rest as they say is history. From that day on Phil (who is actually a fairy dragon) and Dougal have become very good friends.

'Dougal,' Derry called which shook him from his thoughts, 'look what I've found.'

Derry had found a quail nest with four eggs in it. There was tomorrow's breakfast sorted. They packed the eggs away and were about to carry on when Dougal decided he wanted quail for dinner. It took about an hour for a quail to step into the rope trap he had set but when it did that was dinner taken care of.

They continued on for a couple of hours until they came across a small pond. As it was now very warm, Derry suggested that a swim would be a good idea, so the two of them dove into the inviting water, clothes and all.

They decided after the swim that although it was only around three o'clock they would try and find a campsite close to the pond. They settled on a small clearing just to the southeast of the pond. Dougal again gathered wood for the cooking fire while Derry set up camp for the night. Dougal lit two fires that afternoon, one to spit-roast the quail for their dinner and the other to roast the vegetables to go with it. They were both really starting to enjoy themselves and the freedom of the road. The spit roasted quail, roast potatoes, roast shallots and fried mushrooms, which they had gathered from their little clearing, were delicious.

After dinner Derry and Dougal sat by the fire (not because it was cold but just because they liked the feeling of the hot flames against their faces and hands) drinking Dandelion tea. Derry asked Dougal about how much of Phil's history he really knew. After a short pause (in which he fondly remembered his and Phil's many little adventures together like the time the pair had convinced Fearghus there was a ghost living in the northern woods. To this day Fearghus never went there unless Dougal went with him) Dougal explained that apart from the last three years he really knew very little. What he did know was that three years ago Phil had had a fight with his father and decided to leave the place he lived and go into a voluntary exile from his people. Phil had always been very vague about the reasons for the fight and also about where it was he had actually lived.

Dougal told Derry that he'd never pushed Phil to give him details of his past for a number of reasons. The first being whatever Phil had done before they had met was none of Dougal's business unless Phil wanted it to be which brought Dougal to his second point and that was Phil would tell him about his past when he was good and ready.

Dougal did have his own theory however (as he did about everything) and that was that Phil's father was an important fairy dragon and he was pressuring Phil into taking on responsibility. When Dougal told Derry she just laughed (a common response to one of Dougal's theories) and asked if he was talking about himself or Phil, but he believed that was why the leprechaun and the dragon got on so well. Although very different creatures they had very similar problems and expectations being placed on them by others. But at least Dougal had Derry and his mother at home to help him through, where as he believed Phil had no one to support him and that he had no choice but to leave his troubles behind him. Dougal knew that one day these troubles would catch up to Phil and he was determined to be there for his friend and help him through when that day came.

After their tea was finished the twins turned in for the day deciding on an early night so they could start out bright and early the next morning.

They woke in the early hours of the next morning. Derry cooked the quail eggs she'd found the day before for breakfast while Dougal washed in the pond. After they had eaten it was Derry's turn to spend some time in the pond by herself while Dougal packed up camp and got everything ready for their departure.

Soon they were off on their way again firmly believing that today was the day they were going to find Phil. The hills to the southeast were in clear view so they were sure they would reach them in two or three hours and then they would start searching the caves one by one until they found Phil.

It was not long after they began their day's journey that things started to take a turn for the worse. They arrived at a river that was both too wide and flowing far too swiftly for them to attempt a safe crossing, not only that but the course of the river turned back in the opposite direction taking them away from the caves. It took three hours before they finally came across a small swing bridge and were able to cross the river. The bridge was old and in a state of disrepair, which meant it was very slow crossing, so one at a time and with great caution they finally crossed the bridge reaching the other side. After three hours the pair were now further from their destination than they were when they had set out earlier that morning.

Once on the other side of the river Dougal and Derry refilled their water bottles and headed back into woods. It was not long after that they heard the first but still distant howls of a wolf. Unconcerned they carried on as they were now making good time and were quickly closing in on the hills before them. Around mid day they stopped for a cold lunch. It was then that they realised the howls of the wolf were much closer than before. Still not overly concerned, they did though decide it would probably be better to carry on and keep moving just in case.

However the faster Dougal and Derry went the closer the wolf sounded. It was not long before panic started to set in. It now sounded as if the wolf was right behind them. Derry looking over her shoulder as she ran caught the first glimpse of the wolf. It was huge, with long mattered grey fur and running straight for them. Derry alerted Dougal to the wolf's presence and they franticly searched for a tree with branches low enough for them to climb. By this time they could almost feel the wolf's breath on the back of their necks. Then Dougal saw a tree with bark rough enough for them to climb. He grabbed Derry by the arm and dragged her to the tree and forced her to climb it first. With Derry safe in the tree Dougal followed and only just made it as the wolf threw itself at him as he franticly climbed. The wolf hit the tree with such an impact that Derry nearly fell from her sanctuary.

With the wolf showing no sign of leaving, the O'Shea's settled in for the night, uncomfortable but safe. They were forced to eat a cold meal consisting of the last of their stale bread and cheese that they had brought along in case of an emergency and this seemed like an emergency.

It was an uncomfortable night for the twins, neither daring to sleep in case they fell from the tree to the wolf waiting below. The wolf finally left in the early hours of the morning about the same time as it started to rain. So by the time dawn broke the twins were tired, irritable and cramped from sitting in the tree all night. They were also soaked to the skin because although the tree had given them some shelter it had not been enough to keep out the torrential rain. To top it all off they were still further from their destination than they were at the start of the previous day.

Their mood improved somewhat as the rain cleared, the sun came out and the temperature increased. It was not long, however, before they had to stop and rest as the lack of sleep had finally caught up with them. When a suitable site was found they stopped to have a couple of hours sleep before they carried on. It was decided that one would keep watch while the other slept as they were still worried about the wolf's return. Dougal took the first watch while Derry slept. He gathered some wild berries, a few root vegetables and mushrooms that seemed to grow everywhere at this time of the year. He didn't have to venture more than fifteen feet from Derry to gather these things which was the main reason they had chosen this spot for their campsite. That and the fact that there were plenty of trees which appeared easy to climb just incase the wolf returned. Dougal lit a fire and started to cook a vegetable stew. While Dougal slept Derry finished the stew adding some dried lamb and herbs to give it some flavour.

Derry woke Dougal around midday and after their first hot meal in over twenty-four hours, their spirits raised, they set out again feeling much better.

They reached the caves just after nightfall. It was too late to search for Phil so they found a small sheltered cave and set up camp. With only two hours sleep since the previous morning, it was little wonder the twins were asleep before they had even set a fire or eaten.

It was the sun streaming into the cave that woke them the following morning. Both felt refreshed and eager to continue their search for Phil, who if he was in these caves, could not be far away. They ate the berries Dougal had picked the day before for breakfast then headed off in search of Phil. Derry and Dougal searched the caves one by one but found no sign of him. Phil however had heard them call him early that morning and thought it would be fun to hide from them for a while.

Dougal and Derry were starting to believe they were wrong in thinking that Phil was anywhere near these caves. They were stumped and did not know what to do next. Dougal could not think of anywhere else Phil spent his summers. It was decided that if Phil could not be found then they would have to go home, the only alternative they could think of was to become travelling bards. They weren't sure however if even their mother would be happy with that. Deep in discussion they both jumped a mile as a shape materialised out of thin air infront of them and shouted, 'boo!'

CHAPTER 3

PHIL - THE FAIRY DRAGON

'You know I hate it when you do that,' stormed Dougal when he had recovered enough to talk. He looked over at Phil who was still laughing. Dougal shook his head and muttered, 'I should have left you in that net.'

Derry, who had also been shocked, was already seeing the funny side of it and laughing said, 'you'll give someone a heart attack one day. Dougal told me you could make yourself invisible but I didn't really believe him.'

'I can only do it for about an hour a day so I try and make the most of it when I can. I've been right beside you for over half an hour and I think you'd make great bards,' Phil joked.

Dougal, still annoyed said, 'we've been searching these caves all morning trying to find you.'

'I know,' Phil answered, 'I heard you calling first thing this morning but it was far too much fun watching your mounting frustration. Anyway, you would never have found my lair, it's too well hidden. Follow me and I'll show it to you.'

With that he disappeared again.

'Just kidding,' Phil said as he reappeared and led them to his lair. Dougal and Derry followed Phil who was flying ahead. After fifteen minutes they stood at the foot of a very high and very steep hill. The twins watched in amazement as Phil seemed to fly straight into the side of the mountain and disappear. After a few moments Dougal decided Phil had made himself invisible again and he was starting to lose his patience. Dougal was stunned when Phil stuck his head out of the side of the hill and asked them if they were coming or not.

When Derry and Dougal made no attempt to join him Phil flew back out to find out why they had not followed him.

'How did you do that?' asked Dougal.

'Do what?' answered Phil.

'You just flew into the side of a hill,' Derry cut in, 'the solid, sheer rocky side of a hill. That? How did you do that?'

'Oh that, it was nothing,' explained Phil, 'there's a very large opening half way up.'

'No there's not!' shouted both Dougal and Derry simultaneously.

'Phil,' Dougal continued, 'it's a solid wall of rock.'

'If you let me get a word in,' said Phil, 'I'll explain. There is an opening but it is masked by an illusion spell. The only reason I can see it and you can't is because fairy dragons are immune to all magic. So come on up and let's get something to eat.'

So with a little more prompting Dougal and Derry followed Phil up the hill and through the illusional rock face into the cave beyond. To the leprechauns the cave seemed impossibly large and they noticed an immense golden mound glowing in the torch lit cavern. It was not until they were closer that they realised what the mound was. It was a twenty foot long, ten foot high pile of coins, gems, jewellery and other treasures.

Dougal stared at the treasure stunned, he had never dreamed that so much wealth existed in the world. He finally composed himself and asked the two questions that had formed in his racing mind, 'where did you get all this from?' and, 'what causes the illusional wall?' He blurted almost unintelligibly.

'It was all here when I found the cave earlier this summer,' Phil answered. 'This cave was once a dragon lair and it's common for intelligent dragons to use magic to disguise the entrances to their homes.'

'You mean a real dragon,' gasped Dougal in dread, 'a huge, red, fire breathing monster with very large sharp teeth and claws and did I mention fire breathing. What if it comes home with us still here?'

'Dragons aren't always red you know,' huffed Phil indignantly annoyed like most dragons were with this common but misguided generalization, 'they come in all sorts of colours and they're not all evil. But in thinking about it, in your world they were, evil that is, not red. This one must have been quite young and only about ten feet long judging by the size of his bed.'

'The size of his bed,' asked Derry puzzled not even seeing a bed.

'The treasure,' exclaimed Phil, 'don't you two know anything about dragons?' Not waiting for an answer he continued on, 'all dragons any colour, good bad and yes even fairy, like to sleep on a nice horde of treasure. And if you did know anything about dragons you'd know that, that George character killed the last one in your world well over a thousand years ago.'

'Phil,' Derry asked because she knew Dougal wouldn't, 'you keep saying our world, what do you mean?'

'Well,' Phil paused, thinking about how he should answer, 'your world is one of many. These worlds are connected by a series of doors. In mine everyone knows about the doors and certain people know the location of a few of them. In every world there is probably hundreds of doors and even in mine, an enlightened world, most are still undiscovered. As far as I know, no one in this world has any idea about any of this and you can't tell anyone.'

'We won't,' both replied not sure whether they believed him but both wanting to hear more, 'tell us about your world.' Derry urged.

'My world, are you sure you want to here about it?' asked Phil. Although they both detected a hint of sadness in his voice they nodded eagerly.

So Phil told them about his home, 'let's see, where should I begin. I know, firstly, I'll tell you about the people who live there. Obviously there are fairy dragons but I'll get to them later so who else is there. Connaught has many races, some magical, others not but the most powerful are the pixies and the fairies. The pixies are about six inches tall, their skin is a leathery tanned brown. Most pixies tend to have brown or blond hair and their eyes are mostly green or brown. As a rule pixies wear clothes that are hard wearing and tend to be dull earth colours. They live in a woodland kingdom most making their homes among the trees. The king however lives in a huge castle surrounded by a very wide and extremely deep moat. Some say the moat is full of some very nasty and always hungry animals. Most pixies possess no magical power but there are some who do and they are taken from their families at the first sign of magical ability and sent for wizards training. There is no choice given to the child or family and any parent who tries to hide their child's power is put to death. Anyone with magical powers belongs to the king to use as he sees fit. The rewards for a powerful wizard are many with riches, possessions and power there for the taking. The most powerful wizard heads the wizard's council and is always the king's chief advisor. The pixies have already overrun many of the smaller kingdoms and believe it is their destiny to rule my whole world. Their current king is Rupert IX, a particularly nasty and ambitious man even by pixie standards.'

'Now the fairies, they look very similar to you leprechauns, their ears are a bit pointier and like the pixies they're only about six of your inches tall. Fairies tend to have pale freckly complexions with red or black hair being most common but there are a few fairies with blond hair. Where only female leprechauns wear bright colours all fairies do. They live in a mix of small villages and large towns and they farm the futile soils of the kingdom. Like the pixie king, the fairy king lives in a large castle but it has no moat and its gates are open at all times to the citizens of the kingdom. Again like the pixies only a small number of fairies possess magical ability. Fairy wizards are not taken from their families.'

'The fairy king is Strahan IV, a just and kind man and his only daughter Amber is heir to the throne. Fairy dragons guard the fairy royal family. With our size and our ability to make ourselves invisible and the fact we are totally impervious to all magic, makes us perfect bodyguards. The relationship between fairy dragons and fairies goes back to the time when the fairies first united into a single kingdom. Even before the fairies first arrived we were there. In fact we are the oldest race in our world, maybe any world. A bond was formed between Padraig I, the first fairy king and Lord Piaras who was the ruler of the fairy dragons at the time. The oaths sworn all those years ago have been kept til this day. Their only real enemy is the pixies who see them as the only major obstacle in their plans to conquer and rule the entire world.'

'Connaught is a very small world with only one major landmass and a few small, uninhabited islands. It has two main mountain ranges, the Drogheda Mountains in the west and the Saharsa Alps in the northeast. It's a beautiful green land covered with numerous forests, woods, lakes and rivers. The plants and animals are very similar to those of your world just much smaller.'

'You miss it don't you?' asked Derry.

'Yes, I do, very much,' Phil answered with a tear in his eye.

'Why don't you go back?' Dougal asked.

'Although I would love to look upon the two suns and four moons of Connaught again Dougal, I have sworn an oath never to return. An oath I fully intend to keep no matter how home sick I become,' explained Phil, an edgy bitterness now in his voice.

Phil's tone and abrupt finish left the twins in little doubt that that was the end of the 'Phil going home' topic.

Phil lapsed into silence as he began to think about the events that lead to his self imposed exile. Phil, the second son of the fairy dragon king had always been a disappointment to his father. Phil's father had never approved of his sons close relationships to his fairy friends. Although the dragon king honoured the centuries old arrangement between the two races he believed that his people were superior to all the other races of Connaught and would one day have it all to themselves once more. This was not a view that was shared by Phil and only heightened the tension between them.

Things had come to a head when Phil was supposed to go hunting with his elder brother but had decided at the last minute to spend the day with his fairy friends instead. His brother had gone off alone and when he didn't return a search party was dispatched. The dragon prince's body was found five days later. Phil's father held Phil totally responsible for the death of his favourite son and heir. His father, who was determined to turn his poor excuse for a son into an heir that would not be an embarrassment to his ancestors, forbid Phil to leave his private caves telling him if he did he would never be allowed to return. Phil was not sure whether it was his father's heavy claw or the guilt he felt for not being with his brother when he died that made him decide to leave his home. All he knew was that he had to go and never return.

Phil was shaken from his reverie when Derry in an attempt to end the now uncomfortable silence asked, 'so with all the gates in Connaught why did you come here?'

'To be honest Derry,' answered Phil, 'it was the closest gate to home. But I must admit now I'm here I'm glad it was. Especially now I've found this cave, it's the perfect home for a dragon of any type, good, bad or fairy. In case you didn't know the only difference between a real dragon and a fairy dragon is the size. Even before I found this cave I really liked it here, as I love the green meadows. Its forests are really wonderful but most of all I've got a couple of really great friends as well. The only thing I would change about this place is the amount of rain. Why does it have to rain all the time?'

'How do you think we keep those meadows so green?' joked Dougal and then he asked, 'have you ever been to any other worlds Phil?'

'Only one other, Mor Sliabh we call it,' Phil answered, 'a mountainous world where the south has no summer. It's a land of continual storms, lightning, rain, hail and snow. In the north there is no winter, hot, arid temperatures never falling below thirty-five degrees celsius. The lands in between are a pleasant temperate climate almost like a year round spring. Fairy dragons believe that Mor Sliabh is the birthplace of all dragon kind. From the south came the white, silver and other dragons who favour colder climates. From the north came the blue, brass and fairy, red and others came from the central region.'

'Phil why do you call it Mor Sliabh?' asked Derry, 'in our language that means large mountain.'

'It does in ours as well,' Phil answered and he went on to explain, 'we call it Mor Sliabh not for all the mountains but after one mountain that stands all alone in its centre. It's a huge mountain at least forty thousand feet high. Dragon legend has it, that Slevin Gofraidh, the father of all dragons good and evil, lives in a lair very close to its summit. No dragon has ever found his lair but there are accounts throughout our histories of his appearing to dragons in times of great importance to our kind. To this very day every dragon prays they are the next to see Slevin Gofraidh for it the greatest honour we can ever receive. Slevin Gofraidh has also decreed that no dragon shall harm another anywhere on Mor

Sliabh. So it has become a safe haven for us all, in fact some good and evil dragons even have strange friendships, which would be impossible in any other world. Anywhere else the best relationship between good and evil dragons is a grudging respect of each other's skill, bravery and honour. Nothing is more important to any dragon, even an evil one, than his or her honour.'

'My father took me to Mor Sliabh on my eightieth birthday, a coming of age tradition of my race. All dragons are brought to Mor Sliabh to see the home of our founding father and the birthplace of all dragon races.'

'Did you say eightieth?' asked Dougal, shocked as he always took it for granted that Phil was only a year or two older than him.

'Yes, I did, I'm eighty two years old. Dragons age much slower than leprechauns. In your years I'm about nineteen. We also live for hundreds of years. Some of the larger dragons like the reds and blues can reach one thousand years, that is, however, fairly rare even for dragons. We fairy dragons normally live to about four or five hundred years, a short life for a dragon but I think it's long enough don't you?'

The twins both mumbled a 'yes' struggling to take in all they had learned, both still finding it hard to believe that Phil was eighty two years old. It was now getting quite late so while the twins prepared the camp for the night Phil went hunting, returning with a brace of plump rabbits that were promptly cooked by Derry. Phil was not happy about his rabbit being cooked as dragons eat their meat raw but he ate it without complaining not wanting to upset Derry.

As they talked over breakfast the following morning, Dougal asked Phil to show him and Derry the gateway to Connaught. Phil agreed to show them but he made it very clear that they were not going to Connaught. He explained that it would take the best part of two days to get to the gate, so they decided to pack and leave as soon as possible. In less than an hour they were back on the road.

From time to time Dougal and Derry would have to call out to Phil, who was flying ahead, to slow down. It was hard for them to keep up due to the unevenness of the terrain that they had to cross. It was becoming clear that in a day Phil could travel far greater distances than the twins. Not that any of them minded because they had nowhere else they had to be and nothing else they had to do. So for the next three days the trio travelled the countryside, heading for the gate.

During the journey Dougal and Derry took turns telling Phil leprechaun legends including the story of Seamus O'Farrell and the founding of Caer Gorias. In return Phil told them more about his home and its people, in particular Strahan the current fairy king. His family had ruled the fairies for over a thousand years. Strahan had ruled the fairies for nearly thirty years and was approaching his fiftieth year. He had always planned to abdicate on his fiftieth birthday and retire to the country to enjoy his latter years in peace and quite.

Strahan's only child Amber would turn eighteen, fifteen days before he turned fifty, which meant she would be old enough to rule by herself. Any fairy monarch under the age of eighteen must follow the guidance of a regent until their eighteenth birthday. Phil had described Amber as being strong willed and feisty but deeply loyal with the good of her people being her main concern.

Next in line to the throne was Amber's cousin Finn. Finn, according to Phil, liked nothing better than a good party. He was rather fond of food and ale and anything else with an alcoholic base. He was also the most eligible bachelor in the fairy kingdom, not just because he was rich and of royal descent but was also dashingly handsome as well as brave and fearless. Finn, for all his love of the good life, also cared for his people dearly and would fight any enemy to keep them safe.

They set up camp at the end of the third days travel in a small clearing on the banks of a rather large river. While Derry and Dougal set the fire and started it burning, Phil went fishing. The first fish he caught he devoured on the spot, glad at last to get hold of some raw meat before Derry ruined it by cooking it. It wasn't long before three more fish lay in a small pile on the riverbank. Phil nearly cried when first he watched Dougal fillet and then Derry fry his beautiful fish but he did admit to himself how tasty it really was. It didn't stop him eating the fish heads however when he was suppose to be burying them. Dinner finished, dishes done, the trio turned in for the night, Phil having assured the twins that tomorrow they would stand before the gate to Connaught.

They set out mid morning on the last leg of their journey. The sun was beaming down from the cloudless blue sky. The twins were both in good spirits and highly excited about seeing a portal to another world. It was not long though, before they realised that the closer to the gate they got, the more subdued Phil became. When Phil's mood became down right surly Dougal suggested that they turn back (much to Derry's disgust) and maybe come back some other time when Phil was more mentally prepared. Phil, touched by Dougal's concern, insisted they carried on, his mood improving somewhat.

And then there they were, standing at the gate. Derry and Dougal stared in abject disappointment at the very normal tree standing before them. They were just about to complain to Phil when a door appeared out of nowhere in the trunk of the tree and out stepped a small male figure not more than six inches tall. As soon as the little man exited the tree he yelled, 'Philproinnsias Tuatha De Danan,' Dougal and Derry turned to Phil who was nowhere to be seen.

CHAPTER 4

THE FIVE FAIRIES OF SARASIDHE

𝕿he twins watched in absolute disbelief as four more of the little people emerged from the tree all calling Philproinnsias Tuatha De Danan. It was then the twins realised that they had backed away and hidden in some bushes. They must have done this subconsciously when the door first appeared. So although they could see what they believed must be fairies, the fairies could not see them. There was still no sign of Phil and the twins were starting to think he had flown off and left them. It was then they heard a female voice speak.

'Philproinnsias Tuatha De Danan, although I can't see you I can sense your presence. Show yourself,' she said sternly. But then in a much softer, gentler tone she said, 'Phil we need you, you know we wouldn't come for you if there was any other option, we are all your friends. We understand and accept your reasons for leaving but Phil we are desperate, really desperate.'

The twins watched as Phil materialized inches from the woman's face and said, 'Neave I can't go back. I won't go back. How can any of you ask me to, you're supposed to be my friends.' He looked each fairy directly in their eyes as he spoke their name. 'Adam, Dylan, Liam, Neave, Finn how can any of you ask me to go back, you all know why I left.'

Dougal and Derry both gasped out loud when they heard the name Finn realising they were looking at a fairy prince. They decided it was time to give Phil some support so they left the safety of the bush to stand at his side.

The fairy, Phil had called Dylan, saw the twins first and putting both hands on his head while at the same time covering his eyes and bowing his head wailed, ' arrrgggghhh nooooo, giants.'

'We're not giants,' said Dougal (who would be lucky if he was tall enough to look a human directly in the knee) indignantly, 'we're leprechauns, the little people.'

'Not from where I'm standing,' pouted six inch tall Dylan.

'And we're friends of Phil's,' continued Dougal.

' Dylan enough,' snapped Adam, 'we're here to get Phil's help not to discuss the differences between giants and whatever these giants think they are.'

Dougal looked appraisingly at each fairy. Finn although of similar height to the other male fairies, was far more muscular than the others. He wore a suit of chain mail, a long red cape and blue pants. He was heavily armed with a bow over one shoulder, a sword in its scabbard hanging from the right side of his belt and a dagger in a sheath on his left side. To complete his armament he had a throwing knife in each of his little black boots.

Next his attention turned to Dylan and Adam standing together. The pair had to be related, Dougal guessed brothers. Adam looked to be the older of the two, both had blond hair and Dylan was slightly shorter. Like Finn the brothers wore chain mail, a long red cape and blue pants. Dougal was starting to think it might have been some sort of uniform. Both were armed with a sword and dagger.

Then there was Liam who stood out from the other fairies. Unlike them, who were all fair skinned, Liam had a rich brown tan, the kind you get from spending long periods of time in the sun. His hair was jet black and he wore brown leather armour, a green cape and pants. Dougal had no doubt that if Liam did not want to be seen in the woods he wouldn't be. He carried a bow, a sword that was shorter than Finn's or the brothers' and what looked like a smaller version of Dougal's hunting knife.

Lastly there was Neave. Although Finn was the prince Dougal got the distinct impression she was in charge. Red headed, fair complexion and very pretty thought Dougal. She was about half an inch shorter than the boys. She wore a long red robe with blue velvet trim and appeared to carry no weapons except for what looked to Dougal like a small tree branch. Maybe it was some sort of staff he thought. He wondered what five fairies wanted with his friend. Dougal looked up when he heard Phil talking again.

'What reason could you possibly think would ever be good enough for me to return home? You all know what led to my leaving and how I swore a dragon's oath never to return.'

'I know Phil,' said Neave, sorrow evident in her voice, 'the last thing any us want to do is cause you pain but you're our only hope. Phil, Amber's missing! Nine days ago she vanished without a trace. We have searched the whole city and found nothing. We have questioned all the city guards and no one saw her leave the city. I searched her room for magic and detected the faint residue of a spell casting. Phil it wasn't fairy magic.'

'I can see why you're worried,' Phil said, 'and yes Amber is my friend but finding her is the responsibility of the dragon guard, where were they anyway? They should have detected any use of magic and gone in to find out what was happening.'

'The fairy dragons have left Connaught Phil,' Neave explained, 'three months ago your father went to King Strahan and told him the fairy dragons were departing. When the king asked him why and where they were going your father refused to answer. So all the king could do was thank your father and all the dragons, past and present, for all their years of service to the fairy nation and its people. The next morning the fairy dragons had gone, it was almost like they had never existed. Now do you see why we have come for you Phil, you're our only hope if we are going to find Amber.'

Phil looked at Neave in speechless disbelief, his brain racing trying to think of what would cause his father to take such drastic action. He could think of nothing.

'It's true Phil,' Finn said softly.

'I believe you,' Phil said after a moment and continuing after a short pause, 'I can think of no reason as to why my father has done this. It does however make things easier for me. My problem is with my father not with the fairies who are my friends, the five of you and Amber in particular. With my father gone there is nothing stopping me going home for a short time. So let's go and find Amber.'

'Phil we want to come too,' said Dougal almost pleadingly.

Before Phil could answer Dylan said, 'I think they should come. How can we turn down an offer of help from two giants? If we get into a fight while looking for Amber they could really come in handy, even the girl.' He cried out in pain as Neave clipped him on the head with her staff and called him an idiot.

'I was only joking about the girl bit,' said Dylan rubbing his head.

'Are you sure,' Phil asked, 'if there is magic involved it could get dangerous.'

Dougal looked over to Derry who nodded in approval. 'You couldn't stop us coming even if you wanted to,' he said.

'Thank you,' said Phil sincerely and then went on to properly introduce the leprechauns to the fairies. He explained to the fairies, Dylan in particular, that the twins were not giants and in fact in this world they were sometimes called the little people. Neither Adam nor Dylan however seemed overly convinced.

Phil sent Dougal and Derry out to gather some wild berries and vegetables telling them to collect enough to feed them all for at least three days. While the twins did that he went hunting, catching a couple of rabbits and pheasant and four quails, one of which he ate before he returned to camp. He had explained to the twins that without stealing food from farmers (something Phil wouldn't do) they would struggle to find enough food to feed three large specimens like him and the twins between here and their destination to the fairy capital.

With the supplies gathered Dougal and Derry said goodbye to their homeland and followed Phil and the fairies through the gate. Both were amazed as the gate seemed to grow larger so they and Phil could pass through to the other side. Although they had entered the gate through a tree, it was from the side of a hill they emerged and into what was for the leprechauns a whole new world and for Phil a return to his home.

As the twins looked around their new surroundings they each took in the scenery and enjoyed the warmth of both suns on their backs. They saw trees that were just five feet tall, at home these same trees would have been at least fifty or sixty feet tall. The small company began their journey towards the fairy capital. It was not long before they passed the first farm. The farmhouse was visible in the distance and to the twins it looked like what they had always imagined a human child dolls house would look like. As for the livestock, Dougal looked over and thought, 'if I was really hungry I could eat a whole cow and before I go home I'm going to try.'

He whispered, 'Derry we are giants.' Derry just nodded in reply.

Dylan who had heard Dougal, shouted, 'I knew it. I knew it. You all heard him didn't you, he just admitted he was a giant. I told you they were.'

'Yes,' said Dougal, 'in your world it appears we are.'

Being a leprechaun he was used to hiding from the big people on the very rare occasions he saw them. Now, here in this world, he was a giant and there was something very exciting about that.

For the first time in his life Dougal was starting to feel like a big fish and he was already beginning to enjoy it.

As they walked Finn and Neave filled Phil in on the general happenings in Connaught while he had been gone, the major events being pixie related. Just over a year ago they had conquered the Brownies and turned them into another puppet state paying huge tributes to Rupert. On the bright side, pixie raids on the fairy borders had diminished and the relationship between pixie and fairy, although not friendly, was the best it had been in years.

With the other three deep in conversation the twins talked to Adam, Dylan (who were indeed brothers) and Liam. Dougal asked Liam why he was dressed differently to the others and he explained that although the friends spent a lot of time together he wasn't a member of the Royal Fairy Infantry like the others. Liam was a tracker and scout, (some of Connaughts other races called his kind rangers) he didn't live in the city like the others but in the woods. He was always there however when the others needed him. Derry asked if the robe that Neave wore was standard dress for fairy woman because she really liked it and thought it was very pretty. Adam laughed at that and said she probably should keep that to herself because all fairy wizards wore robes and there were far more male wizards than female ones. He did add, however, that there were few with the talent and power Neave possessed.

Adam explained that although Neave was still in her early twenties she had already risen to the rank of First Wizard of the Royal Fairy Infantry. The third ranked wizard in the fairy kingdom always held the post of First Wizard. Neave was twenty years younger than any other to hold this position and she seemed to grow with power with the passing of each day. Adam was convinced that she would be the next Wizard High Lord, which was the head of their order. As First Wizard, Neave out ranked Finn in military matters.

Finn was one of three Captains in the Royal Fairy Infantry. He had reached this rank due to his talent not because of his royal birth. Finn had a brilliant military mind and like Neave he was very young to have reached such a high rank. The only people who out rank him in military matters are Neave, General Ceallachan and the King. Finn believed that the pixies needed to be taught a lesson and that the fairies were the only ones strong enough to do it, so they should. Someone had to look after smaller nations who were falling prey to pixie cruelty, many others, did not however, share this view. The fairies are a peaceful people Adam went on to explain and although they had a strong army they would only fight when they had to, to defend themselves. Adam and his little group of friends believed that day would come sooner rather than later.

By the time they reached Sarasidhe, the fairy capital, three days later, Dougal and Derry could feel a bond forming between them and the little band of fairies. They bypassed the pretty town and headed directly for the castle. Derry and Dougal were awe struck. It was massive even by their standards. It must have been at least ten times the size of the church in Caer Gorias.

Dougal asked, 'How did such a small race of people ever build such an incredible building?'

Finn answered proudly, 'With a lot of hard work.'

'And a lot of magic,' Neave added.

Phil then mentioned the fact that the fairy dragons had done all the carrying and the placing of the bricks and that may have helped a little as well. The three conceded it had been a team effort but none the less the twins were still very impressed.

The castle had been built for both fairy and fairy dragons so Derry and Dougal had no problems moving about freely once inside. Phil insisted they headed straight for Amber's room to investigate hoping the spell residue still lingered. There would be plenty of time for the formal pleasantries later.

Phil insisted on the others waiting outside as he entered Amber's chambers, he didn't want anyone getting in his way. It struck his heightened senses the instant he entered the room. He could still detect the magic and 'yes' he knew what it was. Phil knew without a doubt that a very powerful wizard had kidnapped Amber and if his kin had not deserted their post she would have been safe now.

He returned to the others with a heavy heart and said, 'We have to tell the king that the pixies have kidnapped his daughter.'

CHAPTER 5

A SHADOW LURKS

Phil and his friends left Amber's room and headed straight for King Strahan's private chambers. Strahan however was not in his chambers so the little band set out in search of the fairy king. They finally found him, a forlorn lonely figure standing on the rampart of the city walls gazing into nothingness.

Finn approached him and gently placed a hand on his shoulder and said, 'Uncle, we have found Philproinnsias.'

The king turned to face Finn and Phil and smiled for the first time since Amber's disappearance.

'Thank you Phil,' Strahan said sincerely, 'I know how hard this must be for you.'

'That's not important now,' said Phil, 'what is, is Amber. We went to her room as soon as we arrived and although I don't know who has taken Amber at least I know what has,' he looked around to make sure no one who shouldn't hear what he was saying was close enough to listen. When he was satisfied he continued, 'Amber has been taken by the pixies, or at least one pixie anyway. I detected traces of a very powerful pixie spell having been cast in her room. I got there too late to tell what the spell actually did, but I do know the mage that cast it must have been at least as powerful as Neave which probably means Rupert was behind it.'

'If Rupert wants war that much I'll give him war,' fumed an irate Strahan.

'We can't invade Tudorland,' said Neave, 'if we do and they are holding Amber prisoner they may just kill her.'

'What else would you have me do?' asked Strahan, 'how else can I save my daughter?'

'I think our best chance is to send a small party of volunteers who can creep in without being noticed and rescue Amber,' suggested Finn.

'It's our only chance,' Neave agreed, 'but I do think you should fully mobilise the army just incase, you never know what Rupert has got planned long term,' she added.

'When will you leave and how many of my guards do you need?' the king asked.

'It will take a couple days to gather enough supplies and weapons. As for personnel I don't think we should involve any one who is not here now because it's imperative we keep what we know secret. To be honest we don't know who we can trust,' advised Neave.

'Are you sure Neave?' asked Strahan, 'that one fairy dragon and five fairies can rescue Amber.'

'Don't forget us,' blurted out Dougal.

The king had been so involved in the conversation with Neave and Finn he hadn't even noticed the twins and when he did he nearly fell from the wall. He regained his composure to ask respectfully, 'who are you and why are you here?'

'They're giants your highness,' yelled Dylan more to annoy the twins than for any other reason.

'Derry and Dougal O'Shea at your service your Royal Highness,' said Derry stepping forward and then curtsying to the king. 'We are leprechauns,' she continued, glaring jokingly at Dylan who just grinned back, 'we are friends of Phil and we are here to help in anyway we can.'

'Thank you,' said the king adding, 'any friend of Phil is a friend to the fairy people. Tonight we will hold a banquet to honour Derry and Dougal as representatives of their people. If there are pixie spies about, it can't hurt for them to think we have some new friends and if they happen to think we are negotiating an alliance between our two nations even better. Neave, take our honoured guests to the rooms we reserve for our most important visitors so they can rest and freshen up for tonight's festivities. You had better make sure it's one of the rooms the dragons use to use, none of the others will have beds big enough. The rest of you, come with me, we have a banquet to organise.'

And with that, they all went their separate ways.

The cloaked figure waited several minutes before he was satisfied it was safe to leave the shadows. He was a master of disguise and could seemingly blend into any surface. To the pixies he was known simply as the Chameleon. To the fairies he is not known at all although he has spent a lot of time in Sarasidhe. The Chameleon couldn't believe his luck. He had followed the king on an impulse not really sure why, but one thing the thief, assassin and spy had learnt over the years was to never ignore a hunch. He witnessed the whole meeting between the king and the little group of friends and he knew Rupert would reward him generously for this information. He almost felt sorry them, their plan was a good one and would probably have worked. He would have to warn the 'Weasel' not to take this group too lightly, the girl wizard in particular. He was also sure there was more to the giants than just their size, what it was he didn't know, but he knew there was something, he could sense it.

Ten minutes later the stooped old peddler drove his small wagon, drawn by a single horse, through the main gates of Sarasidhe and none of the guards spared him a second glance. Yes, Wilberforce Smyth the Chameleon was, *the master* of disguise. Once out of view of the town he stopped his wagon, walked to the back and opened the cage holding a particularly nasty looking Raven. He placed his note into the pouch attached to the bird's leg, whispered in its ear and released it.

Neave opened the doors to what would be the twins' home for the next couple of days. Both twins were very happy with their temporary chambers. Each had their own bedroom, with round beds and a soft feather mattress large enough for a fairy dragon. Dougal liked the look of the dining area, especially the plates of beef and loaves of bread (more like bread rolls to the twins) that Neave had made appear out of nowhere on the rooms large table. Derry was delighted when she saw the bathroom with its bath large enough to fit several leprechauns. It had been a week since she had soaked in a nice hot tub. She had asked Neave if some hot water could be brought to her and Neave just shook her head and laughed. Neave showed Derry two buttons, one red, the other green and to her amazement hot water started filling the bath when she pushed the red button and when she pushed the green one cold water flowed. Neave had explained that the hot water was piped in from a hot spring just behind the castle. Neave then left the twins alone warning Dougal not to eat too much so he wouldn't spoil his appetite, explaining there would be a lot of food at the banquet tonight.

Two hours later there was a knock at the twins' door. When Dougal opened the door he saw sixteen fairies pushing two large trolleys. Once they had pushed their trolleys into the room they then bowed to the puzzled leprechauns and left. Before the twins had a chance to see what was on the trolleys there was another knock. Dougal opened the door and this time Neave walked in.

'Good, I see your presents have arrived,' said Neave, 'hurry up and open them, they are from King Strahan.'

Derry went to the trolley Neave indicated was for her. She pulled back the cover and saw a dress like no other dress she had ever seen before. It shimmered and sheemed and seemed to change colour before her eyes.

'It's beautiful,' she gasped.

'I hope it fits, we had to guess your size and I have to admit it's not our best work with time restraints and all,' explained Neave.

Then it was Dougal's turn. He drew back the cover and saw a black cape, pants and vest but what really caught his eye was the crest on the cape, a green shield with a golden rampant lion at its centre.

'How did you know about the crest of Caer Gorias?' he asked.

'From Phil,' she answered.

With that Neave left the twins to get ready for the upcoming festivities telling them that she would return in an hour to lead them to the banquet chambers. Both twins went excitedly to their bedrooms to change into their new clothes and to prepare themselves for what promised to be a thoroughly thrilling evening, neither quite believing they were about to share a king's table.

When Neave returned an hour later both twins were ready to leave, their new clothes a perfect fit. As Neave led the twins to the banquet chambers, she explained to them that all the guests at tonight festivities had been told that they were diplomats from another world here to discuss trade terms and perhaps even form an alliance. Strahan was certain that would buy them some time with the pixies and at the same time explain what two giants were doing in Sarasidhe.

The night flew by for the twins. The food was delicious and Dougal was very proud of himself. He had managed to eat a whole cow in one sitting during his very first 'real meal' in the fairy kingdom, not to mention half a sheep and a leg of pork as well. The twins both enjoyed being the centre of attention answering questions from many of the fairies about what life was like in Caer Gorias. They had a great deal of fun fabricating how important they were back home which was of course the reason they were chosen for such a vital mission.

After the formalities of dinner were over it was time for the entertainment to begin. To Dougal and Derry's surprise the music played by the fairies was very similar in style to the music they played themselves. Dougal excused himself momentarily and when he returned he carried both his and Derry's tin whistles. Dougal then asked the king respectfully if he and his sister could play along with the musicians. The king had been delighted because there was nothing the fairies loved more than music (apart from food maybe). Not for the first time the twins stole the show. The audience was particularly impressed when Dougal had picked up a double bass and played it like a fiddle.

It was a very late night for all concerned and the twins were thrilled with the new songs they had learnt. Dougal had already decided he was going to spent all of his free time over the next few days memorising or writing them down, that is, if he could find some paper and a pencil large enough. He had also decided that he and Derry would have to tell everyone back home that they wrote the songs themselves because even if they could tell their family and friends the truth no one would believe them anyway.

Over the next three days Finn, Neave, Liam, Adam and Dylan made all the necessary arrangements for the journey ahead. It was all done openly with the residents of Sarasidhe believing that they were just arranging a routine diplomatic escort.

While the fairies were busy with their duties Phil searched the caves that were normally home to the fairy dragons. He was trying to find some trace of them or a least a clue as to where they had gone, but for all his efforts there was nothing. He was surprised by the sadness he felt and for the first time he wondered if he had been wrong in leaving Connaught.

Dougal and Derry spent this time with Strahan. To the citizens of Sarasidhe they were locked in trade talks but in reality they spent their time eating, drinking, playing music and talking, just getting to know each other.

For his part Strahan was starting to view the twins with genuine affection. He had been deeply touched when he had given the twins a chance to back out of the mission but they refused. He explained to them how dangerous Rupert was and how the pixie would stop at nothing to get what he wanted, that this is a life and death mission. Dougal had simply replied that Phil was his friend and if Phil believed this mission was important enough to come home they had to go along to help him. Besides what Rupert had done was wrong and he agreed with Finn and Neave the pixie must be stopped. Derry just nodded her head in support of her brother. Strahan wondered whether all leprechauns were like these two or if they were something special. He believed it was the latter.

The twins had nothing but respect for the fairy king. His duty to his people was vitally important to him but he did not place his people before his family. In this situation the most important thing to the king was to rescue his daughter at almost any cost. Dougal wondered if his father would see it the same way.

By the time the twins returned to their rooms for what was going to be their last night in Sarasidhe they had almost come to see themselves as tall fairies. It was strange, they both felt like they belonged there, they knew that the friendships they had made would last a lifetime, infact, it felt as if they had been friends with these fairies all their lives. The fairy and leprechaun people had a lot in common. They looked a lot alike apart from their size, their songs were very similar and there were other similarities as well. Dougal had a theory and that was that the two races were related in some way and may even have lived along side of each other in some long forgotten time. When Dougal made this theory public over dinner with his friends they all just laughed at him with the exception of Dylan who had a 'you could be onto something there' expression on his face. The others seeing Dylan just laughed even louder.

At the same time as the twins were turning in for the night, the black raven returned, having flown night and day non stop to the castle of the king of the pixies. It sighted the king and flew down landing on his outstretched arm. Rupert stroked the birds head fondly then withdrew the note from the pouch on its leg and read it…

Your highness, Strahan knows you have Amber. He has sent five fairies, a fairy dragon and two giants to get her back. By the time you receive this missive they may have already left Sarasidhe. Do not take this party lightly particularly the fairygirl she is a powerful wizard. Watch the giants as well. Also if you hear rumours of an alliance between the fairies and giants don't worry it's not true. They believe this is a secret mission and no one apart from you, Strahan, the rescue party and me know about it. Awaiting your further command.

W S
The Shadow.

The pixie king re-read the missive and smiled. The Shadow cost him a great deal of money but he was worth every gold piece. So Strahan thought he held the advantage did he, well wasn't he in for a surprise. He did admit to himself that this situation required some thought.

He called over the nearest member of his bodyguard and said, 'Fetch William and have him meet me in my private chambers.'

The guard simply nodded to the kings back, already forgotten and set out in search of the wizard. The king went straight to his desk and wrote a note containing further instructions for The Shadow.

He then put his fingers to his lips and whistled shrilly. Within seconds, almost as if it had anticipated his call, the raven flew through the open window and landed on the desk in front of Rupert. The king again stroked the birds head fondly, he did not like many living things but he liked the raven. He considered most just pawns in the little games he liked to play. Most pixies served him out of fear, a few others like William and The Shadow did so for personal gain, although The Shadow probably would have done it just for the fun of it all.

With the obviously intelligent bird it was different, the raven served him out of loyalty. He had found it years before with a broken wing. His first thoughts were to just leave it there and watch it suffer or maybe to give it to one of the wild cats that lived in his castle to play with and torment for his amusement but something in the way the bird had looked at Rupert pleadingly made him spare it. That was the first selfless act the king had ever committed and it was also his last. He had personally nursed the bird back to full health and it had served him faithfully ever since.

Rupert placed his instructions for The Shadow into the pouch on the birds leg, stroked it one last time and then said, 'return to The Shadow and fly well. I hope to see you soon my friend.'

'I will see you soon my friend,' came the birds squawking reply as it flew out of the window.

Rupert was never really sure if the bird knew what it was saying or just mimicking him, for some ravens, like parrots, had the ability to talk and mimic. He had tried to engage the raven in conversation, sometimes it answered, other times it didn't. When it did answer him it was only with phrases he often used himself, proving nothing.

It was while the king was thinking about the complexities of the raven that William entered his chambers and said, 'you called for me my king. All is well I trust.'

'Yes of course it is,' he answered.

He then went on to tell William all he had learnt from his spy.

The pair then went to visit their prisoner in the high tower, to question her and find out what she knew about the giants and the others in the rescue party. She had said she knew nothing of the little group on its way to free her and was totally shocked by the presence of giants in her homeland. They then left the girl alone and headed back to Rupert's chambers to plan their next move.

On the way Rupert asked, 'was she telling the truth?'

'Technically yes,' answered William who had magically read the prisoners mind, 'she genuinely knows nothing about the giants and although she did not know about the rescue party, when you mentioned it to her, being a female wizard, a clear image came into her mind. The wizard is the third highest ranked of her order and her normal companions are Prince Finn, two royal guards and sometimes a hunter and tracker. If you add the dragon and the giants into the equation it is an unquestionably potent little party so we must be cautious, very cautious indeed.'

'You never cease to amaze me William. All that information from that little mind of hers and from just one small question from us,' said Rupert.

'It was nothing my liege,' he humbly replied.

It was then Rupert decided that it was too late to plan anything in detail that night so he dismissed William with instructions to meet him first thing tomorrow morning after he had given himself time to mentally digest all that he had learnt that night.

While the twins were readying themselves for the next stage of their journey, Rupert and William were mentally absorbing their newly acquired information.

King Strahan, Neave and Finn were finalising their plans for the next days departure, content in the misconceived confidence that no one, not even their fellow fairies, knew what they were doing. Finn had wanted to leave before dawn and get the next leg of their journey under way as quickly and quietly as possible. Neave and Strahan had disagreed however, believing that if Dougal and Derry vanished without a formal farewell, the fairies and more importantly any pixie spies, might become suspicious and that was a risk they could not afford to take. The only real chance of success they believed was if they had the element of surprise on their side. So the three spent the next couple of hours preparing for the upcoming mission.

Long after the twins and fairies had retired for the night, a solitary figure stood in the high tower staring into the darkness and for the first time in the fifteen days (or at least she thought it was fifteen days, she was starting to lose track of time) she felt some real hope. Her closest friends were coming to save her and were bringing some very big companions to help. Yes, for the first time in weeks, Amber felt much better, much better indeed.

Rupert

CHAPTER 6

THE SEARCH FOR THE PRINCESS BEGINS

The next day dawned fine, being sunny and warm with hardly a cloud in the sky lifting the companions' already high spirits. They had all met in the twins' chambers to have one last breakfast together in comfort before they began their journey.

After breakfast they went to attend a final audience with King Strahan who presented the twins with gifts to thank them for their assistance.

To Dougal, he gave a vest of chain mail made from a metal he had never seen before, incredibly strong, but it was as light as if it had been made from wool. He was also presented with a shield, long sword, dagger and a longbow all made to perfect leprechaun scale by the most skilled fairy craftsmen. The shield and front and back of the chain mail vest were adorned with the green shield and rampant gold lion of Caer Gorias. Dougal withdrew the sword from its scabbard and was amazed by the beauty of the blade. Engraved on its surface were a series of what looked to Dougal to be Celtic runes and crosses and just below the hilt was yet another crest of his home town. Dougal was pleased and delighted by his gifts.

Derry received a vest and sword identical to Dougal's and a green travel cloak with a full length golden lion imprinted on its back. Derry thought she looked like a sword maiden and she was thrilled by the whole idea. Neave was disappointed however because she had sensed magic within Derry, as had Phil and they had suggested to Strahan that they give Derry magical gifts and train her in the art of magic. However, the king had disagreed with this, his argument being that according to Phil, no one from Derry's world possessed magic and those that were believed to have any magically ability were persecuted. He was worried about her safety when she retuned home if she carried any magical items or could perform magical spells. Neave was still not sure whether she was going to let Derry make that discovery for herself or whether she was going to disobey the king and tell Derry she might possess latent magical ability.

Large crowds of fairies lined the streets to get one last look at the giant ambassadors. All were very excited by the connection with a new race from a new world. Everyone believed the king's story when he said that Phil had been on a secret three year mission to explore new worlds. No one questioned the fact that a fairy dragon, a prince and a high ranked wizard as well as a forester and two other guards were escorting the giants, believing the two diplomats were more than worthy of the honour.

It was a magnificent sight with Phil flying in the lead, the five fairies riding (what was for them very large, powerful, war horses) and the twins wearing their new armour and weapons, walking and waving goodbye to the residents of Sarasidhe as they exited the fairy town.

They left via the west gate and headed off in the direction of the portal that would take the twins home. The plan was to wait until they were well out of view of the city and then turn to the north and finally back to the east. After that it would be onto the land of the pixies and its capital to rescue Amber.

About ten minutes after they left Sarasidhe they passed a stooped, old peddler who was heading in the opposite direction. They exchanged pleasantries. The peddler even tried to sell them some of his goods but they politely declined and continued on their way.

The Shadow watched as the companions became specks in the distance and finally disappeared from sight. He had enjoyed his little exchange with the small group. It had been his first chance to get close enough so he could get a good look at the giants and he had to admit to himself he was impressed. It was not just the giants that impressed him but also the large prince, the pretty mage and even the three others fairies not to mention the fairy dragon, all of which looked formidable. He wanted to follow them there and then, but knew he couldn't as it would be at least two days before the raven returned with his next assignment from Rupert and he had to be here to receive it. After a great deal of self debate he decided to wait for his orders reasoning that it would not be too hard to catch up to the rescue party because they would lose a day, maybe two, circling Sarasidhe. So at most he would only be a day or two behind them and he was already looking forward to the chase.

William entered Rupert's chambers at ten in the morning (first thing for Rupert) to find it empty. So he pulled up a chair and sat down knowing better than not being there when the king finally arrived. William was powerful but he was no match for Rupert and he knew it all too well. He had learnt from his predecessor's mistakes and would not make the same mistakes himself. So when Rupert gave him a direct order he obeyed it, he always obeyed. It was his job after all to serve the king of the pixies and he really did enjoy the benefits that came with that.

It was after midday when Rupert finally arrived. He made no apology and William had expected none. He informed William that he had sent instructions for the Shadow to trail the rescue party and to keep him informed of their progress but under no circumstances to take action against them.

They then discussed what course of action they were going to take.

William wanted to send a large band of battle-experienced wizards. However, when Rupert reminded him about the fairy dragon's presence he conceded his course of action was probably not the best after all.

After a discussion lasting a good two hours they decided the best course of action was to send out small groups of highly trained hunters to ambush the fairies and their friends. The idea being to eradicate the threat they presented in one foul swoop or at least thin out their numbers rendering them ineffective. It was also decided to set up sentry points with orders not to engage the party but to send back information on their progress. This would enable Rupert and William to react more quickly to any change in the current situation.

The final stage of their preparations was to arrange an escape plan to make sure that if the fairies did reach the pixie capital and even onto the tower itself, they would find it empty. The pixie king knew that no matter how powerful the rescue party was they would be no match for the might of a fully prepared pixie army. He decided however to tell no one about the fairies except the sentries and he would swear them to silence under the penalty of death. The hunting parties would be told they were on routine patrols with orders to destroy any foreign party found inside pixie borders. He thought it would be much more entertaining to let the fairies think they still had the element of surprise on their side. He almost wished the fairies got this far and he would be there to see their faces when they found the tower empty. He ordered William to make the arrangements and then called for some food and wine to be brought to him. He was feeling very pleased with himself indeed.

It was just after midday when Finn and his companions released their horses and left the road. They entered the woods that would enable them to double back and bypass Sarasidhe in secret. It was here that Liam took the lead and the forester was in his element. He led them down trails the others could not even see. His job was made much harder due to the fact that he had to find trails large enough for the twins and Phil to pass through but it was a challenge he relished. By the time they made camp for the night in a large clearing they were due north of the city and very happy with the distance they had travelled.

While the others prepared the campsite Liam left them alone and went out into the night to explore the surrounding area and to make sure they were no unwelcome visitors. He returned half an hour later content in the knowledge they would not be disturbed this night.

After their evening meal was finished they turned in for the day. Liam had suggested that even though they were still safe in their own territory and there was very little or no chance of them being disturbed, it would still be a good idea to start setting a night watch just in case. The others all agreed and Dougal asked if he could take the first watch. No one objected as they were all ready to call it a day.

Dougal's mind raced and he doubted whether he would sleep at all that night. He drew his sword from its scabbard and stared at the blade. All his life he had dreamt of being a warrior and hero. He had never believed he would ever get the chance to be either and he knew if he was still at home he probably never would have. Deep down Dougal realised he didn't really like being a leprechaun. It was hard being one of the 'little people' in the world of big people. Even in his lifetime, contact between big and little people had diminished. The big people had their own problems and soon the little people would be forgotten altogether, left alone on their little island just off the coast of the main land. A lot of leprechauns liked the idea of being left alone but not Dougal. He longed for adventure not the boredom of racial solitude. Dougal like being a giant and he wanted to be a hero to these people (more for himself he realised than for them). He knew he should be ashamed of himself but if he was honest he knew he wasn't.

Lost in his thoughts his time on the night watch flew by and before he knew it, it was time to wake Adam who was next to relieve him. Much to Dougal's surprise once he lay his head down he was asleep in seconds.

Dougal woke to Derry's touch gently stirring him awake and to his amazement the campsite was all activity. He couldn't believe how deeply he had slept and that he had not heard when everybody had packed up camp and prepared breakfast. It was not long before they were back underway with Liam again taking the lead.

The journey got harder and harder as the forest thickened and at one point they lost over half an hour having to back track because the forest was just too dense for the twins or the fairy dragon to proceed. Liam was forced to take his companions further north than he had planned. He did eventually find a path that was far more accessible for the larger members of the party and this allowed them to increase their pace markedly.

They only stopped twice during the day. The first time for a brief rest, the second for a quick meal. The fairies all pushed themselves very hard determined to make up for the time they had lost earlier in the day. Neither the twins nor the fairy dragon had any trouble keeping up with the fairies, if anything they found the going rather slow (they did have the advantage of much longer legs).

When they did eventually stop for the night Finn and Neave were reasonably happy with their progress so far. They stopped in a vast clearing that was dissected by a large, quick flowing river.

Dougal approached Finn and asked, 'Finn, I've never used a sword, can you teach me how?'

'Of course,' answered Finn, 'when would you like to start.'

'Now.'

'How about we wait until after we've eaten because I'm starving,' suggested Finn.

Dougal agreed and they went to help the others set up camp for the night.

He found Derry and said excitedly, 'Derry, Finn's going to teach me how to use my sword properly.'

'If he's teaching you, then he's teaching me as well,' she replied determinedly.

'I'm sure he will if you ask him to Derry,' said Dougal, 'but I think it would be better if you ask him nicely rather than demand it or worse still just take it for granted.'

'Of course I'll ask nicely Dougal, you know I'd never demand anything,' she said with a slightly guilty smile on her face.

After dinner Finn wandered over to the twins, looked at Derry and said, ' I'm about to teach your brother a little about the fine art of sword play,' he then asked, 'would you like to join us?'

She simply answered, 'Yes,' and looked over at Dougal and smirked.

Dougal new the smirk meant she knew this would happen and that she had never intended to ask Finn to teach her at all. He looked her in the eye and shook his head laughing to himself.

'Dougal, do I have to teach you how to use your new bow as well?' asked Finn.

'No, Dougal's the best hunter in all of Caer Gorias,' Derry answered for him, 'pick a spot on any of those trees and he'll hit it.'

Finn looked around and picked what he thought was a reasonably tough target and said, 'how about the moss on the oak tree on the far side of the clearing this side of the river.'

Dougal picked up his bow, pulled an arrow out of his quiver, drew back the bowstring and released it. The arrow flew straight and embedded itself at the very centre of the moss. The sound of the bow drew the attention of the rest of the fairies.

'It's all right,' explained Finn, 'Dougal is just giving me a demonstration of his skill with the bow and arrow.'

'It was hardly a difficult shot,' objected Dougal, 'give me a target worthy of my talent.'

'All right,' said Adam, 'look over to the other side of the river. Can you see that half broken branch still hanging from the tree? Can you hit that?'

'Adam, no one could hit that, it's impossible,' said Neave.

'I can do better than hit it,' said Dougal confidently, 'I can sever it at the break.'

As the others looked on doubtfully Dougal drew another arrow from the quiver and fired. They watched in amazement as the arrow hit the branch exactly at the break severing it completely.

Dougal then asked, 'any more requests?'

Adam was about to point out a tiny red brown leaf when Phil said, 'well done Dougal, you've proven your point and as much as I'd like to see you show off some more of your skill, you can't afford to. Even after I retrieve both those arrows and even if they are undamaged, you only have twenty and we can't afford to lose or break any. Whether we want it or not, there could be a battle around the next corner and we need all our resources just in case one eventuates.'

Everyone had to agree with the merits of Phil's argument so they went back to what they had been doing before Dougal's little archery display. Finn, who was assisted by Adam, spent the next hour and a half taking the twins through various fencing drills. He was reasonably happy with their progress because although neither could be called 'naturals' and both lacked experience they more than made up for this with their sheer size and strength.

By the time they had finished both twins were breathing heavily and sweating freely. They had been surprised by just how much effort swinging a sword took and how much they needed to learn.

When the four joined the others, it was agreed that Dougal would again take first watch. They then all settled in for what would almost certainly be their last night in friendly territory. They knew that if all went well the following day, sometime late in the afternoon they would cross the Corrib River which was the border between the two nations.

About an hour into his watch Dougal heard a faint sound just to the north of the campsite. Although not overly concerned he crawled towards the sound and was surprised to see Liam returning from a scouting excursion. What surprised Dougal so much was he hadn't even realised the forester had left the campsite in the first place. They returned to the camp together and Liam told Dougal to get some sleep as he would take over his watch as he was not at all tired. Dougal thanked him not needing any convincing what so ever as he was very tired after his training and couldn't wait to get some sleep.

About the same time as Dougal and Derry were training, The Shadow waited impatiently for the return of the message carrying raven. He couldn't believe how much he relished his chance to match wits with the wizard and her friends and he had almost decided he would follow them regardless of the king's orders.

Finally the raven returned. He read his instructions, which were to follow the party but not to intervene. He decided to leave at once. He would ride as long as the light would permit and then set out again first thing in the morning determined to make up for all of his unnecessary loss of time.

He ordered the bird to search for his quarry knowing they could be anywhere and he would need all the help he could get to find them. The bird however had other ideas. It looked him directly in the eye and seemed to shake its head. For a moment the Shadow was at a loss, he wasn't quite sure what to do next. Then it struck him, he knew the bird was loyal to the king, he knew that the raven only travelled with him because the king had asked it to and it seemed to do anything the king asked.

With this in mind he said to the bird, 'our master would want you to do this.'

Again the bird looked at him, this time no longer shaking its head and then after a few seconds squawked and flew off in a northeasterly direction. Now it was the Shadow's turn to shake his head. He laughed as he mounted his horse, sure he hadn't told the raven where he believed their prey would be found but it was obvious the bird knew where to look.

The next day Dougal and his band arrived at the banks of the Corrib River just after midday. They decided that the best way to get across the river was to have Phil carry them over. It would be far safer for the fairies than trying to swim and far quicker than building a raft. They ruled out trying to find a ford or bridge for two reasons. Firstly, being time constraints and secondly, but most importantly, that all the known crossing points were most probably well guarded and they wanted to keep their presence secret for as long as possible.

Liam and Phil flew to the other side of the river to make sure there were no pixie sentry stations in close proximity. Dougal watched as they landed on the far side and Liam jumped off Phil's back and then vanished into the woods ahead. Phil waited on the far bank incase Liam needed to get away in a hurry.

Then out of the corner of his eye Dougal saw Finn, Neave and Adam in what looked like a deep and meaningful conversation. He waved to Dylan and Derry and they wandered over to join him.

'That looks serious,' he said to both Derry and Dylan pointing in the direction of the others.

'I think we arrived here a little earlier than they expected,' suggested Dylan, 'and if I know those three and I do, they will be discussing the merits of carrying on now, in enemy territory, during broad day light, or stopping and carrying on after dark. I'd put gold on them stopping now and resting till nightfall.'

The twins and Dylan stood together and waited for the others to finish their conversation and it was not long before they did. It turned out that Dylan was right and the leaders of the expedition had decided to stop for now and set on again after nightfall. They believed there was far less chance of running into pixie patrols at night. With Liam's tracking abilities and the bright clear star lit sky at this time of the year they should have no problem in making their way to the pixie capital at night.

Derry and Dougal were both very restless and had trouble settling so they went off together to practice their swordplay. While the twins went through the drills Adam and Finn had taught them the day before, the rest ate lunch and waited for Liam to return with his report of the surrounding area.

When Liam did return it was with news that none of them wanted to hear. He had almost run into two separate pixie-scouting parties, each consisting of twenty highly armed and armoured pixie warriors. He wasn't sure why, but he got the distinct impression they were looking for something or someone. He had followed both parties briefly but had learnt nothing from either of them so had decided to head back and inform the others.

They decided that it would be far too dangerous to cross the river here so they headed southward down stream moving in the opposite direction to the pixie scouting parties but at the same time moving closer to the pixie capital. They stopped just before nightfall and again Liam crossed the river with Phil's help while the others rested while they could.

On his return, Liam briefly spoke to Finn and Neave, who were on watch, about what he had found on the other side of the river and it was decided that this would be a safe place to cross the river in the early hours of the following morning. Liam then turned in for some much needed sleep.

CHAPTER 7

WALKING IN SOMEBODY ELSES SHOES

Finn woke the twins just before dawn the next morning and they began the river crossing. Phil firstly carried Adam and Dylan then Liam and Neave. Finn, Dougal and Derry all had to be carried separately because they were all too big for Phil to carry in pairs.

Once on the other side of the river Liam again took the lead. Dougal was surprised how much light shone through the trees. He never really believed they would able to travel through these woods at night. It was then Dougal remembered that Connaught had not one moon but four. The companions travelled in silence, no one wanting to give themselves away to any nearby pixies.

The first night in enemy territory was uneventful but the going was rather slow. As good a forester and tracker as Liam was, this was all new country to him. It was new to all of them because pixies have never allowed any fairies into their kingdom in the past and it was highly unlikely they would in the future either.

As dawn approached Liam discovered a cave big enough for even the twins and it was there that they stopped for the day. Sheltered in the cave they ate a cold meal while Adam and Dylan took the first watch. No one had any trouble sleeping that morning as they all had had only a couple of hours sleep in the last twenty-four hours.

It was during Phil and Finn's watch around midday when Dougal was woken from a deep sleep. Finn placed his forefinger to his lips to alert Dougal to keep quiet and pointed outside of the cave with his other hand. It took Dougal's eyes a second to adjust to the light but then he noticed the half dozen small figures just a short distance from the cave. Dougal knew without a shadow of a doubt he was seeing pixies for the first time. He looked around the inside of the cave and saw that all of his companions had drawn their weapons with the exception of Derry and Neave. It was then he realised that Phil was nowhere in sight. Dougal crawled over to where his bow and quiver of arrows lay and then returned to his position at the mouth of the cave. He drew an arrow from the quiver and placed it on his bowstring just incase he needed to fire in a hurry.

Dougal nudged Finn and then wrote, 'where's Phil' into the dirt on the cave floor.

Finn brushed Dougal's question out and then wrote, 'outside, invisible.'

Dougal nodded in reply and as he did from out of the corner of his eye he noticed movement and looked over to see six more pixies moving over to join the others who by this stage had started to cook a meal.

Adam crawled over to join Finn and Dougal. He surveyed the area outside and mouthed, 'let's take them out.'

Finn just shook his head in reply and wrote in the soil, 'it's too dangerous, some might get away and warn Rupert.'

Adam nodded, understanding Finn's reasoning but Dougal got the impression he was not overly happy about it.

No matter how hard he tried he could not hear what the pixies were saying. He was not sure whether he would understand them even if he could hear them. It was while Dougal was wondering whether he would be able to understand 'pixie' that Dougal saw a third group of pixie soldiers join the main group. He watched the eighteen pixies hoping they weren't planning a long lunch or that they felt the need to investigate their surroundings, in particular a certain cave more closely.

The pixie warmed his hands over the cooking fire. It wasn't that he was cold he just like the feeling of the fire on his hands.

'John,' he looked up when he heard his name and he saw his commander walking over with the second group of the hunting party.

'Any luck?' his commander continued.

'No.' John answered. 'The ground's too dry to leave any clear trails. There are plenty of signs of someone or something passing but no way of knowing who, when or even where they are travelling. I don't think we're going to find them without an actual sighting. How about you Oliver what did you find?'

'The same as you,' Oliver replied. 'Personally, I think this is all a wild goose chase but I'm not going to tell the king that, are you?'

'No,' answered John, 'I value my life far too much to question the king.'

Oliver then asked, 'Have you checked that cave out yet?'

'I'm not going anywhere near that cave, there's not going to be anyone in it during the day. Remember what happened the last time, we woke a hibernating bear. We lost two men and more importantly I broke my arm.'

It was while the two pixies were discussing the merits of examining the cave that the final attachment of troops arrived back to the rendezvous point. The leader of this group broke ranks and wandered over to join Oliver and John.

'What a waste of time,' he said, 'and why are we out here anyway, surely there are far more important things for three as highly ranked as us to do other than routine patrol duty?'

'Calm down George,' soothed Oliver, 'there are far worse places to be than out here.'

'Name one?' asked George.

'The cemetery,' answered John, 'and that's were we'll end up if we don't follow the king's orders to the letter.'

'Or worse,' added Oliver.

'Okay, we'll stay out here then,' said George, 'but why don't we just camp here for a couple of weeks and train this rabble properly. Then we can go home and report that we found nothing. Because let's face it, no matter how hard you search you can't find something when there is nothing to find in the first place.'

'Not a bad idea George,' said John.

'It won't work,' said Olivier. 'Rupert has got over a hundred troops searching these woods. He must actually believe something very important is out here and if he has this many men out now he'll be searching with magical means as well. I don't want to be the one explaining to the king why his wizards searching spells found us in the same place more than once, do you?'

Oliver looked at the two who were simply shaking their heads in reply, he laughed and said, 'let's send someone to check out that cave,' he paused, looked over to his troops, and decided who he would send. He then picked one and called, 'Purcell, check out that cave.'

When the pixie was slow to react George added, 'today, soldier, today.'

Purcell, who was there the day they woke the sleeping bear unhappily headed towards the cave.

'Arrrgggghhh nooooo,' gasped Dylan softly, pointing at the approaching pixie.

Neave gestured for everybody to retreat into the shadows of the cave walls and for Finn to get into a position to silence the pixie. Neave's lightening fast mind was already planning their next move.

The poor pixie didn't know what hit him. Finn struck him with the hilt of his sword as soon as he stepped into the darkness of the cave and then caught him before he hit the ground.

Neave then placed her hand on Liam's shoulder and whispered a few words of which neither of the twins understood. As she was doing this Phil materialised out of thin air beside Neave.

The twins were stunned to see Liam transform into a perfect likeness of the unconscious pixie.

'Will he have the pixie voice?' whispered Phil.

Neave nodded her reply.

'Good,' said Phil as quietly as he could. He pointed over to three pixies standing apart from the others then said, 'those three are in charge. John, the taller one is your squad leader but when you go back report to Oliver, he's the one that arrived second, he seems to be in command. Watch out for the other one, his name is George. He seems mean even by pixie standards so watch your back around him and be careful Liam. Oh and by the way, our sleeping pixie friend's name is Purcell. So when you hear it remember they'll be talking to you.'

Neave then said, 'Liam, first chance you get, get out of there, we'll wait here until you return before we leave. If things do start to go wrong remember Phil will be close by, even if you can't see him, he'll be there.' She then walked over to the unconscious pixie, placed her hand on his head, spoke a few words no one else understood, nodded happily and then explained to the others, 'he'll sleep until this time tomorrow and will remember nothing. He'll most likely have trouble explaining his absence to his commanders but that's his problem.'

They all watched Liam draw a deep breath then smile as he nodded to friends. He turned and exited the cave heading directly towards the pixie leaders.

John turned to Oliver and said, 'finally he returns,' pointing to the pixie returning from the cave. 'I was starting to think something had eaten him.'

'He does tend to dawdle doesn't he? Shall I beat it out of him?' asked George.

'Settle down George, he hasn't done anything wrong yet,' said Oliver.

The pixie arrived at the trio and said, 'Oliver,' before he could say another word he was struck in the face by George's gauntlet covered hand and knocked to the ground.

'What makes you, a peasant, think he can address a knight of the realm without his proper title,' snarled George.

Liam still on his knees put his fingers to his mouth then looked at the blood on his now wet fingers. He looked Oliver in the eye and said, 'I beg your forgiveness Sir Oliver' (he prayed he used the man's correct title knowing his life might depend on it).

The fairies and leprechauns watched in horror as they saw the pixie strike their friend. Adam only just managed to grab Dylan in time, stopping him from charging with blind rage out of the cave to assist his friend.

'Dylan, no,' said Neave quietly but also forcefully, 'if we attack the pixies Liam will be dead before we get half way to him. He stands a far better chance of survival if he can talk his way out of this. Don't forget he has Phil out there with him as well. Phil will be able to assist him far quicker than we can.'

Dylan obeyed the order but did not look happy about it as they all then turned their attention fully back to their friend's desperate situation.

Oliver waved his hand as if to dismiss the whole matter and then said, 'well man! Are you going to tell me about the cave or not?'

'I'm sorry Sir Oliver,' answered Liam bowing his head, now starting to feel a little more in control of the situation. He then continued his report, 'it is a large cave sir, which is why it took me so long. It's empty and has been for a long time. There's no sign of animal or any other presence in there and that's the only entrance to the cave.' Liam finished his report and waited for further orders looking at Sir George out of the corner of his eye. Liam was determined to remember every one of this man's features. He wanted to make sure he would never forget this man. He hoped that they would meet again sometime in the future in a situation different to this one, one where he could teach this man a lesson he was obviously long over due for.

Oliver dismissed Liam and sent him away to get something to eat.

'Purcell,' he looked up when he heard the name of the pixie he was impersonating and he saw a rather small pixie waving him over. He walked over to join the man who handed him a plate of steaming stew. Liam who hadn't had a hot meal in over twenty-four hours thought to himself maybe this is not so bad after all.

The soldier next to Liam noticed the way Liam glared at Sir George and said, 'don't worry about that one, he'll get what's coming to him. I bet it'll come in the way of a knife or arrow in the back in some battle in the not too distant future, if you get what I mean?'

Liam was sickened by what he heard. There was no way a fairy would ever kill another fairy and here was a pixie openly taking about a pixie being murdered in cold blood by one of their own. Liam looked at the pixie and said, 'I hope it's at the hands of a fairy (meaning himself) that George is taught his lesson. I'm sure that would hurt him far more.'

'Yes, he does despise fairies but I doubt whether he'll live that long,' replied the pixie next to him.

Liam proceeded to finish his meal in silence. He was just finishing his meal when he heard Sir John call the name Arthur. He looked up to see who Arthur was. Just then the pixie beside him nudged him and said, 'Arthur snap out of it, Sir John wants you.'

Momentarily confused, Liam got up and hurried over to Sir John. It was then he remembered that pixies often used last names. This was something fairies never did. He had presumed that Purcell was the pixie's first name but it was obviously his last. He mentally reprimanded himself. If he was going to stay alive in his current surroundings he could not afford to take anything for granted.

He followed Sir John to the far side of the camp away from Sir George and Sir Oliver.

Once there Sir John said, 'I'm sorry about that Arthur,' he handed Liam a small silver flask, 'here, drink some of this. It won't heal the bruising but it will close the cuts.'

Liam saw genuine concern and remorse in the other man's face and he realised for the first time that not all pixies were evil. The man before him was a fair and kind man just following the orders of an evil, ruthless king and doing the best he could to survive. Liam took a small drink from the flask then handed it back to the pixie knight thanking him. Within moments Liam felt the pain in the side of his face and head disappear.

Sir John patted Liam on the back telling him they were moving on in ten minutes. Liam watched John walk over and join the other knights hoping he would never meet him on the battlefield. It had never occurred to Liam (who had never actually met a pixie before) that any pixie could be anything other than evil. He knew that one day, most probably sooner rather than later, things would come to a head between the two nations and that it would lead to war. Liam knew it would be far easier to fight the pixies if they were, as he had always believed, all like Sir George. The thought of fighting the likes of Sir John left him feeling sad and empty.

The three knights moved away from their troops to talk in private. As soon as they were out of earshot of the others, Sir John turned to Sir George and stated pointedly, 'don't you ever lay a hand on of one of my men ever again. If you do, you'll have me to answer to!'

'That peasant shows no respect for his betters, he got off lightly and should be thankful I was in a good mood,' roared George indignantly.

'You're not his better, you're not even his equal,' joined Oliver moving closer and standing by John's side, 'Purcell has been with John and me for over five years. He saved both our lives during the Brownie campaign with great risk to his own safety.'

'He was also the man who saved me from the bear two years ago,' added John.

'I am a knight of the realm and he is a peasant. You, Sirs, have both insulted me and I would demand satisfaction from you both had the king not banned the dual. But rest assured gentlemen, this matter is not forgotten.'

It was then with all the self control that he could muster, Sir George removed his white clenched knuckles from the hilt of his sword and turned to rejoin his troops, seething with the contempt that he felt for the other two knights.

Liam felt a chill run through his entire body when he saw the look of undisguised hatred, aimed in his direction, on the face of Sir George as he stormed back into the camp. Liam felt sorry for the poor pixie he was impersonating and hoped that Purcell didn't suffer too much because of his actions. Sir George ordered his men into action at the same time glaring at Liam. He then afforded another glare, even more hate filled if that was at all possible, in the direction of the other knights as he turned and thundered out of the camp followed somewhat reluctantly by his men.

Liam walked over to join Sir John and Sir Oliver as they returned to the campsite (he hoped this wasn't another breach of protocol) but he believed they needed to be warned about Sir George. When their paths met Liam hesitantly began, 'I don't want to talk out of turn my Lords.'

Laughing Oliver said, 'that knock to the head has really shaken you hasn't it my friend?'

'Yes, I guess it has. I must admit I don't really feel myself right now,' said Liam, 'but I just wanted to tell you both to watch your backs. I believe Sir George has it in for all three of us.'

'Watching our backs as always, ah Arthur,' said John putting his arm around his shoulder as only a true friend would. 'Sir George is definitely a loose catapult and must be watched. Like you Arthur, Oliver and I will be watching all three of our backs. And what's with the 'my lord' business? George isn't here, you know there are no titles between us.' Liam smiled at the obvious fondness and trust that these three pixies so obviously shared, much like his friendship with those watching from the cave.

Back in the cave the companions watched as the first group of pixies broke camp and headed off into the woods. They were all surprised to see Liam wander over and join the two pixie commanders. They were now curious to know what was going on out there.

Within quarter of an hour the last pixie troops had departed. Now on their own again, Neave insisted they all get some much needed sleep but they were all too worried about Liam to sleep. Neave, however, reassured the group that Liam could take care of himself and reminded them that Phil was still at his side. She and Dougal then took the first watch while the others tried to sleep, some without much luck.

It was about half way through Dougal's watch, when what was to him a very small black bird, flew into the cave, stole a small piece of bread from the floor and flew out again.

'I hate ravens,' whispered Neave softly, not wanting to wake any of her sleeping friends.

'That was a raven? If you hate ravens here, you'd really hate them where I come from. They are bigger than you in my world. I have to admit, I'm still coming to terms with how small your animals are here. However, I'm glad they are because I have always wanted to try beef and by the way, yum, it's delicious. At home cows are so big we've never found a way to butcher them.'

Neave wasn't paying a lot of attention to what Dougal was saying, still mentally coming to terms with the thought of ravens the size of a full grown fairy.

'Are all animals that much larger in your world?' she asked.

'From what I've seen so far, yes,' he replied.

'Even snakes?' she asked hesitantly.

'What's a snake?' he asked having no idea what she was talking about.

'They're the only things I hate more than ravens,' she said, 'you must know them as something else. They are like a lizard but without legs. They just slither their way along the ground, up trees and some can even swim. A few of them are even poisonous.'

'I've never seen or heard of such a thing, they sound horrible. I'm not saying we don't have them in my world but we certainly don't have them in my small part of it.'

Dougal and Neave continued to talk about Dougal's hometown until it was time to wake Adam and Dylan. Once relieved from their watch, they then tried to get some sleep themselves.

Sir John and his pixie soldiers spent the next two hours searching for their unknown (and what they all believed imaginary) prey. They had not, which was no surprise to anyone, found any signs of anything out of the ordinary. It was then that Sir John called Liam and another pixie Eric Gillingham over. He sent Eric to the north and Liam to the south while he and the others continued in the westerly direction. The idea behind this was to cover as much ground as possible. He sent Arthur (Liam) and Eric because they were his most experienced men and the only ones capable of solo scouting missions. The plan was that the main body push west to the banks of the Avon River and then make camp. The other two would cover the flanks and join the others before nightfall. Sir John had to admit to himself that he was glad he would not be rejoining his fellow knights for another two days. He hoped that Sir George would have calmed down by then.

Once out of the sight of the pixies Phil materialised beside Liam, 'ready to join the others?' he asked.

'Yes.' Was Liam's short reply.

Phil carried Liam on his back and flew above the trees back to their friends who were waiting in the cave. Liam was amazed how quickly Phil covered the distance back to the cave. What had taken Liam over two hours on foot took Phil only twenty minutes to fly even carrying the fairy forester.

Liam insisted that Adam and Dylan wake no one other than Neave. Neave hugged Liam, genuinely relieved that he was back safe and well. The two fairies joined them and they then went outside to discuss what Liam and Phil had learnt while they were travelling with the pixies.

'All I know,' said Liam, 'is that they are looking for someone. What's making it hard for them is they have no idea who they're looking for. It has to be someone really important however, because there are another five search parties, all with eighteen pixies, scouring the whole countryside. We have to be realistic, they may be looking for us.'

'Even if it's not us they're looking for, it still means we're going to have to be extra cautious. Well done Liam, now go and get some well-deserved sleep,' said Neave.

'What are we going to do with Arthur?' asked Liam.

'Who?' asked Neave in reply.

'The pixie in our cave,' answered Phil, who had up until this point been the silent partner in the conversation.

'Leave him in the cave. We'll be long gone before he wakes up,' explained Neave.

'We can't do that,' said Liam.

'Why not?' asked Neave.

What Liam wanted to say was that Arthur didn't deserve the trouble he would get into if the pixies found him in the cave and thought he was deserting them, but what he said was, 'there would be too many questions if the pixies find him in this cave. I think Phil should find a convenient spot near where the pixies are now and make it look as if he has fallen and knocked himself out.'

'That's fine by me as long as it's all right by you Phil.' Neave replied.

'I think that's a great idea,' said Phil, who turned to Liam nodded and winked, his way of letting Liam know he believed he had done the right thing.

With that they re-entered the cave. Neave waved her hand over the unconscious pixie and within seconds the pixie's face was covered with bruises that were a perfect match to those of Liam's.

'They're only an illusion,' explained Neave, 'they're likened to yours and will fade as your ones do.'

Phil, then carrying the pixie, flew from the cave. Again he flew above the tree line until he reached the place were Arthur was to meet with the other pixies. He then faded into invisibility and landed. He walked south for about ten minutes until he found a ditch where he gently placed Arthur at the bottom making it look like the poor fellow had fallen and knocked himself out. Phil was sure that Arthur was close enough to the pixie rendezvous to be found so he then headed back to the cave.

Liam was still awake when Phil arrived back at the cave. Now satisfied that Arthur was safe he finally allowed himself to fall into an exhaustive, deep sleep.

CHAPTER 8

THE PRINCESS – ON THE MOVE

It was an hour before dusk when the raven returned to The Shadow. He removed his map from a saddlebag and showed it to the bird. The raven pecked the map at a spot well to the northwest of his current position.

He nodded and smiled to himself, 'so they have crossed the border,' he said to the bird that seemed to bob its head in reply.

He mounted his horse and rode at a gallop for what was left of the sunlight. He knew that the fairies had to be on foot as there was no way they could ride horses through the pixie woods and he also guessed that they would only travel at night and this would also slow them down. His mind racing, he tried to guess the route they would take to the pixie capital and decided it would be the most direct one.

He knew one thing however and that was he would catch up to the little rescue party and quickly, because unlike them he had a horse and could travel the open roads allowing him to cover much larger distances in a day.

Once it became too dark to ride any further that night, he took out his sleeping blanket, rolled it out and slept deeply. He was happy the hunt had finally begun and that for the first time in his life he believed he had found a worthy prey.

None of the companions felt overly rested when they set out again just after nightfall. They headed in a southeasterly direction the most direct approach to the pixie capital. Due to the unevenness of the terrain and their tiredness it was slow going. An invisible Phil scouted ahead and it was just as well he did. He helped them bypass eighteen pixie hunters camped for the night. There were also two static sentry posts each manned by a small garrison of ten pixies.

No one was surprised at the fact they had discovered yet another search party since they knew there were at least six such groups combing the countryside. What was a greater worry however, were the sentry posts. This sort of thing was common practice on pixie borders. None of the fairies however, had ever heard of them doing this this deep inside their territory before.

Neave was starting think that Liam may be onto something and the pixies might be looking for them. She racked her brain but could not think of anyway that this was possible, so she let the matter rest in her mind for now but was determined to be even more cautious in the days ahead.

They found a small deserted hut just before dawn and decided it would be the best place to stop for the night. Because of the size of the hut Dougal, Derry and Phil had to camp outside, they were simply too large to get through the door. The twins camouflaged themselves the best they could behind the hut while Phil just faded from sight. The fairy brothers took first watch while their companions all slept soundly.

Amber was woken by a pixie solider roughly shaking her.

'You have twenty minutes to get ready to leave,' he ordered and then simply turned and walked out of her small room leaving her alone. Trying to clear her head she heard the pixie lock the door after him.

It was the first time Amber had seen any pixie other than the king or his pet wizard (as she liked to call William) since she had woken in this room for the first time weeks before. She was amazed that the pixie had a key to the door because Rupert had told her he always carried the only one on him at all times.

The thing that surprised Amber most of all was the fact it was still dark outside. The whole time she had been held captive she had never been disturbed before midday. She walked over to the window looking out at the moons above. By their position in the sky Amber could tell it would be at least an hour before the dawn.

While Amber washed, dressed and readied herself to leave, she listened at the door trying to hear something of importance from the guards outside. It was almost impossible to hear anything but she thought she heard the word 'north'. Having no idea whether this was important or not, but having nothing else to go on, Amber picked up a knife and carved two words, north and Amber, into the rooms oak tabletop.

'She has been told to ready herself your highness,' said the guard who had woken the fairy princess.

'The guards?' asked the king.

'They know nothing,' said the pixie handing the key back to the king.

'Excellent,' said the king drawing his jewelled dagger from its sheath. He then stabbed the unsuspecting pixie through the heart. 'Now only you and I know,' he said to William who sat yawning in his comfortable chair.

'Would you like me to get rid of that?' William asked pointing to the crumpled body of the unfortunate pixie that lay before him.

The king nodded and laughingly said, 'make sure you get the blood off the carpet. When you've finished here, get the fairy and wait for me at the deserted hunting lodge just outside Cromwell Woods. It will take me an hour to get there.' And with that the king turned and walked out of the room leaving William alone with the corpse.

William called two pixie guards and ordered them to remove the body. Both William and Rupert liked to let the pixies know what would happen to anyone who upset them and the fate of this poor fellow would be the talk of the barracks that night.

'Have the body burnt immediately and make sure no wizard tries a 'converse with the dead' spell before the body is destroyed,' ordered William. 'Rest assured, if any do, I will know and will hold you personally responsible.' He finished threateningly, leaving the guards in no doubt what would happen to them if they didn't follow his orders to the letter.

William, content now with the knowledge that no one left in the city knew that within the hour the fairy princess would be gone, was happy to leave. Even if the fairy rescue party made it this far, there would be no one telling them where to find their precious princess.

Almost as an afterthought he waved his hand over the pool of blood. He then watched in satisfaction as the blood first dried and then disappeared. He then decided to head off and get some breakfast to fill in the time before he would escort the princess on the next stage of her journey.

After Rupert left William he headed straight for the stables, where twenty of his most experienced bodyguards waited. He had his favourite horse, a tall, black stallion named Black Lightning, saddled. Within fifteen minutes the pixie king and his bodyguards left the pixie capital. Everyone in the city (with the exception of

Rupert and William) including his guards themselves, believed they where heading out for an extended hunting trip.

Amber sat at the window watching the sunrise and waited. She had always loved watching the birth of a new day. It had almost been an hour since she had been told to ready herself and she was starting to think Rupert was playing one of the games he was so famous for, this time with her.

Lost in her thoughts and the sunrise, she didn't see or hear the wizard materialize out of thin air behind her.

William watched the princess for a moment and then said, 'good, I see you're ready.'

Amber nearly fell off her chair and out of the window in surprise. With her heart racing she took a deep breath to compose herself, she stood and turned to face the wizard.

'So, now he sends his chubby little pet. You move very quietly for such a round little man don't you?' she said. While she spoke to the wizard she tried to figure out where he had come from because she was sure he had not entered through the door.

The astute wizard seeing her slightly startled expression and subtle glances around the room chuckled to himself pleased to see the normally composed and self-assured princess rattled even if it was only slightly.

He smiled his most obvious insincere smile and then said, 'I'm sorry your highness, did I startle you, because if I did I am truly sorry,' his words, like his smile, were obviously insincere.

'Keep your apologies and just tell me how you got in here and where your are taking me?' demanded Amber.

'How I got in here you'll find out soon enough, as for where we are going, that is only for the king and myself to know and I believe that is for him to tell you when he is ready,' he answered, then added, 'actually apart from the guard that woke you this morning and he's dead, there is no one left in the city who will even know you're gone. Everyone who knows you're here will just assume that the king has left you up here to die. But don't worry, no one will lose any sleep over the thought of you wasting away, up here, all alone.'

Amber almost panicked when she heard this because it meant that when she'd overheard the guards outside her door saying 'north' they weren't referring to her. The note she had carved on the table could be sending her rescuers in the wrong direction and that thought terrified her.

It was then William grabbed her by the arm and she reflexively pulled it free of his grasp and spat, 'don't you ever touch me again!'

William just laughed, grabbed her by her wrist so tightly that this time she could not break free of his hold. He looked her in the eye mockingly and after a moments silence he spoke four words. Amber did not understand the words but she felt a strange sensation like she had become transparent and there was also queasiness in her stomach.

After a few seconds she started to feel more like herself, still slightly dizzy but the queasiness was starting to pass. Amber was shocked to find she was no longer in her small room in the highest tower of the pixie castle. She surveyed her surroundings and saw what looked like some sort of deserted run-down inn at the edge of what seemed to be a large forest. She saw several small trails and one large road leading into the woods.

'How did you do that?' she asked.

'You would not understand, nor would your inept wizards, as pixie magic is far superior to that of the fairy,' he condescendingly replied. He then grabbed her by the arm and led her into the deserted building before them.

If the building looked old and run down from the outside, the inside was a totally different story. Amber looked at the lavish furniture, extravagant china, and huge gold-framed paintings. A sword with a jewel encrusted hilt was displayed in a wall mounted glass case and giant crystal chandeliers that were obviously magically lit, hung from above. The palatial beauty of the dwelling almost took her breath away. Not even the fairy princess had ever seen so many treasures (obviously gathered from every corner of Connaught) in one place.

William shoved Amber onto a leather cushioned, high backed mahogany chair and ordered, 'stay.'

Amber determined to defy the wizard tried to stand but was horrified to find she couldn't move.

'What have you done to me?' she screamed.

'Just making sure you stay put. I don't want you trying to run off now do I?' he answered. When he saw she was about to speak again he simply looked at her and said, 'silence.'

Amber was adamant that she would make the wizard answer her, so she tried to ask another question but found to her horror and disbelief that her voice had gone. She glared at William as defiantly as she could but on the inside she felt desperate and alone.

The king and his men arrived at the lodge a short time later. Rupert dismounted and ordered his men to wait for him outside but to be ready to leave on his return. Most of the pixies present had been to the lodge many times before but none had ever been inside. Even when the king stayed over night at the lodge his guards camped in the paddock in front. No one but the king and wizard knew what lay beyond its run down walls.

The king entered the lodge and smiled when he saw Amber and William already waiting for him.

'Good, I see you have arrived safely. How do you like my little hide away?' he asked. When Amber didn't answer him he gave the wizard an annoyed look saying, 'you haven't cut out her tongue have you?'

'Of course not my lord, although she talks so much it's not a bad idea.' He waved his hand and spoke another word which Amber did not understand and then said, 'she can now speak again, but I think we will both regret it.'

The king turned his attention back to the fairy princess and repeated his question, 'so, do you like my sanctuary?'

'How could I not, it's beautiful,' Amber reluctantly replied.

'When we marry it will be my wedding gift to you,' stated the pixie king.

'How many times do I have to tell you, I am not going to marry you or any other pixie for that matter,' Amber said boldly.

'Yes you will and you will do so willingly,' said Rupert quite matter of fact.

'Why!?' asked Amber surprised by the absolute certainty in the king's tone.

'Because, if you don't, I'll invade your country like I have many others in Connaught and hundreds, most likely thousands of your people will die. Those who live will be enslaved and forced to work in the mines of Rhondda or Merthyr if they are lucky. For the unlucky ones like your family and friends, I'm sure I can think of a fate much worse, given a little time to think about it of course. On the other hand, if you marry me, when your father abdicates at a time of his choosing and we become king and queen, I still take control but this way everybody gets to live and fairies get to live in peace and as equals to pixies. This way we all win, I admit me more than most, but you must see how marrying me benefits your people.'

Amber was stunned as she looked at Rupert in disbelief. He was right. By marrying her, he would rule the fairy kingdom as her equal after her father's rule ended. She also knew that unless the fairy army was fully mobilised they would not stand a chance against the full might of the pixie war machine.

'Did you think this plan up all by yourself or did your little pet wizard here help?' she asked turning her head in the direction of William.

'The plan is the king's and the king's alone,' said William who had indeed helped dream up the scheme but knew better than to take any of the king's credit.

'It was nothing,' said the king smugly thinking their plotting had impressed Amber.

'But why should I believe you?' said Amber, 'when you say you would treat my people as equals. What's stopping you from killing me once I become queen which would of course leave you as the sole ruler of the fairy kingdom?'

'Nothing,' admitted the king, 'I guess you'll just have to trust me as the alternative, after all, is rather grim and if you don't marry me a lot of fairy deaths will be on your head won't they?'

'I'll need to think about it,' said Amber.

'You have until we reach Caledonia to make up your mind but I do suggest you think of your people, after all, their survival depends upon you.'

Then, finished with Amber, the king turned to William and said, 'we will leave in ten minutes. Make sure she's ready to travel. I have a spare horse for each of you outside.' And with that Rupert turned and walked outside to join his troops.

Rupert smiled to himself as he saw his troops mount their horses the second he walked through the door. For his amusement he decided not to tell them they would not be leaving for another ten minutes. He was too preoccupied however to enjoy their discomfort. He was not altogether happy with how his conversation with Amber had gone, she was far too clever for her own good he decided. He would have to have Strahan killed immediately after the wedding and then Amber soon after that. He could not afford to give them time to interfere with his plans for the fairies and their kingdom. The fairy realm would be his and his alone and the fairies his slaves.

Amber followed William outside the extravagant lodge to where the troops and king waited. While William and Rupert were deep in conversation, Amber thought about making a break for freedom but looking at all the pixies present decided now was neither the right time nor place for such an attempt. Still wanting to make the most of the king and wizard's distraction, Amber pulled a white silk handkerchief from her pocket and 'accidentally' dropped it on the ground. The handkerchief had her name embroidered in thread made from actual gold on one of the corners. She knew it was a long shot but she hoped that if, (and it was a big 'if'), her friends found the handkerchief, they would know she was still alive and they were closing in.

Rupert ordered Amber over to the horses and as she moved closer she felt a strange sensation which unknown to her was a magical barrier. This she felt half way between the lodge and the mounted troops who were waiting obediently for their king's further command.

Once mounted they rode off, not through the woods as Amber had expected, but to the east keeping the woods to their left. After three hours they left the woods behind them and an hour later they arrived at what looked to Amber to be a main road heading north and south. They stopped there for a short time to rest the horses and then continued on, this time taking the main road to the north.

Neither the king nor the wizard spoke to Amber after they left the lodge and none of the other pixies so much as glanced in her direction.

Much to her surprise she found she enjoyed the journey even admitting to herself how beautiful the pixie countryside was. As they rode along the highway they passed the occasional farmer travelling in the opposite direction. Everyone they came across fell to their knees as the king passed but if he noticed any of them he showed no sign of it.

Rupert decided well before dark that he had ridden enough for the day and it was time to find comfortable lodgings for the night. It was not long before he saw smoke in the distance and ordered his troops off the road and in the direction of the smoke. He smiled to himself when he saw the delightful, well kept farmhouse and smelt the delicious aroma of fresh baked bread and still cooking food.

A middle aged pixie farmer opened the door to see what all the noise was and seeing his king, fell to his knees.

'Get up and get out. Take your wife and any children and leave now,' ordered the king.

'Where will we go my king?' asked the stunned farmer.

'I don't know and further more I don't care but because I'm in such a good mood, I'll give you three minutes to pack your things and leave but don't take the fresh bread and food, leave that for us.'

Rupert saw the devastated and distraught look on the farmer's face and laughed, 'don't worry peasant, we'll be gone from here in three days and you can return then.'

Amber watched in sorrow, when five minutes later the farmer, his wife and their three children left their home. She turned to Rupert and asked, 'how can you treat your people like that?'

'Easy. Their sole purpose in life is to serve me, as it is for all my subjects. I do with their lives anything that I like. Those who serve me well are rewarded, others who don't, generally live short lives. If the food in the farmhouse is good I might leave them money, if it isn't, I'll probably burn their house down.'

Amber shocked by Rupert's callousness tried to change the subject by asking, 'why are we staying here for three days?'

'We're not,' he answered.

'Then why did you tell the farmers we are?' asked Amber even more shocked.

'Because it amuses me. I thought it would be funny to make them live in the open for a couple of days,' then turning to William he said, 'you were right, I'm starting to regret letting her talk. Shut her up for a while will you.'

'As you wish my lord,' answered William as he waved his hand while laughing at Amber.

The fairy princess turned to reply and found her voice gone again. Furious she stormed into the farmhouse slamming the door behind her still shocked and appalled by Rupert's total disregard for the welfare of his subjects.

The king then called the captain of the bodyguards over and said, 'Woodward, make camp out here. I want five men on watch at all times, two covering the front, one on each side and also out back. If the fairy princess escapes, I'll have whoever is responsible slowly spit roasted alive.' The pixie captain simply nodded and returned to his men to implement his king's commands.

Amber remained awake long after Rupert and William had retired for the night. She had washed the dishes and cleaned the farmhouse (much to her captors amusement) hoping to make things easier for the farmer and his family on their return. She watched the guards long into the night looking for any chance of escape but finally gave up knowing it would be useless and decided to get some sleep herself.

CHAPTER 9

THE FLITCH OF BACON

Dougal and Derry, who had been the last pair on watch, woke their companions just before sunset. Liam still carried the bruises he received at the hand of the pixie knight Sir George, but was now back to full strength. He had been excused from sentry duty and a full day's sleep had done him the world of good.

All in all everyone had rested well and were in good spirits, all totally unaware though that Amber was no longer in the city they were heading to.

After yet another cold meal Dougal asked, 'Neave, when we first arrived in Sarasidhe you made food magically appear out of thin air, why can't you do that now with something nice and hot?'

Neave, who would also have loved a hot meal, answered laughingly, 'it may have looked like that but what I actually did was transport food already prepared in the castles kitchen to your room. I can't do it now because I'm too far away from the kitchen.'

Dougal's disappointment was quickly forgotten as a thought crossed his mind.

'Neave,' he asked, 'if you can move food from one place to another, what about moving fairies? What I'm trying to say is, could this be how the pixies got Amber out of Sarasidhe without being seen?'

Neave thought about this for a couple of minutes then answered, 'no fairy mage has ever been able to teleport another living thing, not even a small bird. I don't think it's possible but even the thought that pixie magic could be this advanced is frightening.'

While the others were cleaning the camp, Neave headed over to the side of the camp where she could be alone for awhile. She picked up a ladybird in her right hand and sat on a log trying to think of a way to modify her transportation spell so it would work on living things. She made half a dozen attempts at moving the ladybird from one hand to the other, all failing.

She was just about to give up and join her friends when a thought struck her. Holding both hands in front of her she spoke several long phrases of magic and watched in amazement as the ladybird vanished from her right hand and almost instantly reappeared in her left hand. Stunned, Neave looked at the ladybird in disbelief. She had just achieved something no other fairy had ever done before. Now that she had proven it could be done (even on such a small scale) she had to admit to herself that Dougal may have been right and the pixies could have used teleportation to kidnap Amber. She needed time to consider this theory and what it meant.

Once the campsite was clean the rescue party set out again towards to pixie capital. With Liam scouting ahead as usual they again had to avoid several pixie sentry posts along the way. The closer they got to the pixie capital, the nearer the sentry posts were to each other, which slowed their progress drastically.

Neave spoke to no one all night lost in her thoughts trying to come to terms, firstly with what she had done and secondly and more importantly, how powerful the pixie wizard or wizards were that she would possibly come up against. If they could infact teleport a full grown fairy out of her castle without anyone knowing, what other surprises did they have instore for her and her friends.

They started looking for a place to camp well before dawn but found nowhere suitable and in the end they settled on a small hill. There was no real shelter but at least if they were spotted it gave them a good defensive position. They decided to increase the watch to three to lessen the chances of being taken by surprise.

Amber was the first to wake in the farmhouse the next morning. Still dark outside she looked out of all windows but was disappointed to find the pixies still vigilantly guarding against any escape attempt she might make.

Within the hour they were back on the road heading north.

The cloaked figure entered the empty cave around midday. The fairies had done a good job covering their tracks. They left no signs that they had ever even been there but The Shadow was far more skilled in the art of tracking than any other pixie. It did not take him long to find faint traces of their passing and he followed the trail for a short time. When he was certain of what direction they were heading he returned to the cave and mounted his horse. Unlike his prey, The Shadow knew the surrounding area well. He knew which paths and trails to take and he had a horse whereas they all travelled on foot so he was now confident that he would catch them up well before they reached their destination.

He chose a path he believed paralleled the direction travelled by the fairies and then rode off. From time to time he left the trail and searched for signs of the fairies passing. Like his prey he avoided the pixie sentry posts and search parties not wanting any unnecessary delays.

It was early afternoon when Phil who had flown off to checkout the surrounding area returned.

He woke Neave and Finn immediately saying, 'there's a pixie hunting party heading this way.'

'How many and how far away are they?' asked Finn.

'I only saw six but from what we've seen so far there's probably another dozen close by and it will take them at least an hour to reach us.' Phil answered.

Neave then said to Adam who was on watch with Dylan, 'wake the others,' and then asked Finn, 'well, do we stand our ground or make a run for it?'

'If we run, there's the chance we could run into the other pixie hunting parties of this detachment. We could then get caught in the open or even worse caught by surprise. If we hold our ground and they do stumble across us, having archers like Dougal, Adam, Liam and myself, we can take out six pixies easily enough,' said Finn confidently.

'Finn, I don't want to fight with them if we can avoid it,' said Neave firmly.

'As much as I'd like to teach these pixies a lesson or two, you're right,' agreed Finn, 'we're best to avoid a fight if we can. If we lay low using the bush and scrub for cover they may walk right past without even seeing us. Phil, we'll need you invisible in the open so you can warn us if it looks like we've been spotted.'

'I can do a sweep of the area first to see if I can find the rest of the pixies also checking to see if the others are still heading in our direction.' Before he even finished speaking Phil vanished from sight.

Finn and Neave called everyone together and explained the situation to them. They took their assigned positions with the archers laying their bows within easy reach. Dougal drew three arrows from his quiver and placed them next to his bow and tried to calm his nerves.

Time seemed to stop for the companions as they waited for Phil's return. When he finally did return he informed them that the pixie hunting party was only about ten minutes away but there was no sign of any other pixies.

'If they do find us,' said Neave, 'it's vital that no pixie escapes. We can't afford to have anyone warning Rupert or returning with half of the pixie army.'

After what seemed like an eternity Phil saw the first pixie appear in the distance still heading directly towards him and his friends.

The two women who had been in the damp, dimly lit cell for five days sat on their flea ridden straw beds. They had been there for nearly two days before either of them had been able to force themselves to eat the mouldy bread (the only food they had been given) that the pixie guards had thrown on the filthy cell floor. It was only because of their extreme thirst that they drank the stale warm water that had been left for them.

The women were both dressed in brown leather pants and woollen tunics but it was there that their similarities ended. One was tall with dark olive skin (unusually dark for a brownie) with long curly black hair. The other was a short blond woman, two years older, who had sparkling, mischievous eyes and pale skin (curiously pale for a brownie, it was rumoured that she had some fairy blood but no one, not even she, knew for sure).

'Why do I listen to you Izzy?' asked the tall brownie.

'You can't blame this on me Cameron, it's not my fault we got caught.'

'I know, but if I hadn't followed you, I wouldn't be here now would I? But you are right, someone has to fight these pixie scum and drive them from our country,' admitted Cameron.

'They knew we were coming. Someone betrayed us and when we get out of here I'm going to find out who it was and make him or her pay,' stated Izzy irritably.

'So what's you're plan?' Cameron asked.

'I'm still working on it, but don't worry, I'll come up with something soon. If they hadn't been so thorough in their search we could have just picked the locks but as it is they've got all of our tools. Those boys really enjoy their jobs don't they?'

'They sure do, the thought of the 'search' still makes my skin crawl,' Cameron shuddered and then said, 'but what I can't understand is why are we still alive, they normally execute rebels.'

'Cameron, remember we were betrayed, they know who and how important we are. They probably have no idea what to do with us and are waiting for instructions,' answered Izzy.

The horseman had ridden for the last five days only stopping for short rests, quick meals and to change his horse. When he saw the pixie column heading in his direction with the pixie king at its head, he forced his horse into a gallop and rode to intercept them.

Amber watched as the single horseman approached and wondered what his hurry was. She was impressed by the pixie's horsemanship watching in disbelief as he stopped the horse, dismounted and landed on his knees directly before the king, all in one fluid motion.

'My Lord, I have news from Caledonia,' said the pixie messenger.

'Well, what is it man, I'm waiting?' asked the king impatiently.

The messenger handed his sealed parchment to the king who snatched it from his hand.

The king turned to William saying, 'it's from General Broomfield.'

'I wasn't aware that Broomfield could write,' quipped the sarcastic wizard.

'He probably dictated it,' said the king as he opened and began to read the missive. The more Rupert read the happier he became. Amber watched the smile on has face grow and wondered what could possibly be written on the paper that pleased him so.

The king turned to William as soon as he finished reading and said excitedly, 'he's got them.'

'Who my Lord?' asked William.

'The rebel leaders. The two females who have been leading the raiding parties against our troops in Caledonia. Of course, now that that fool has captured them, he's got no idea what to do with them and is waiting for my orders,' answered the king.

'You could always make them part of the wedding festivities,' suggested William who was sure he could come up with an entertaining plan.

Rupert thought for a moment and then exclaimed, 'Yes! I know what to do. To start with I'll have them tortured to find out how many supporters they have and who they are. Then on the morning of my wedding, our wedding,' he corrected himself looking over and smiling at Amber who couldn't believe what she was hearing, 'I'll have them hung, drawn and quartered then stitched back together, tied to stakes and left for the birds. This will show all brownies what happens when you try to stand against me. I can see it now, what a perfect start to the day of celebration,' finished the king.

'What of their followers your highness,' asked the wizard.

'Without our prisoners they are just a leaderless rabble, no threat to us at all. With the help of Broomfield's spy we should have no problem rounding them up and when we do, we will just execute them on the spot. The world will see what happens to those who oppose me.'

As he made the last statement Rupert looked directly at Amber. This left her in little doubt what would happen to her if she didn't do exactly what he wanted her to do. However, the headstrong princess was determined not to be the evil king's puppet. She was now more adamant than ever that if a chance to escape presented itself she was going to take it.

The king's conversation with his advisor was now over and he ordered the messenger to join his bodyguard and spurred his horse forward. He was really enjoying his journey, throwing farmers out of their homes. Now he had two thorns in his side removed and waiting for him to deal with as he pleased. Everything, as always, was going his way. What was next he wondered smiling happily as he rode on.

Phil watched as the first pixie appeared followed by five others. They steadily approached the hill where the leprechauns and fairies hid. Without so much as a glance at the small hill the pixies marched right past and quickly disappeared from view. Finn watched as the pixies departed. He was more than a little disappointed as he was ready for a fight and starting to get impatient. It took all the self control he possessed not to take up his bow and shoot the departing pixies.

Finn's feelings were not shared by any of his friends however, they were all happy that the pixies had passed without incident. With the pixie threat gone for now, the companions, who were not on watch, tried to get as much sleep as they could before it was time to move on again.

It was late afternoon when the king and his entourage arrived at 'The Flitch Of Bacon', a small travellers tavern on the main highway. Rupert decided he liked the look of the tavern and that it would be a good place to spend the night.

'You and you,' he said pointing to two of his guards, 'clear the tavern, but leave the barmaid and cook behind to serve me.'

Soon after the guards entered the tavern, ten patrons (mainly farmers from nearby farms) and a loudly protesting landlord exited. The protests ended abruptly however when the landlord saw the king sitting on his horse looking down at him in distain.

'You can stay with us this night Colin,' said one of the farmers.

'Thank you my friend, your next drink will be on me,' answered Colin.

The king payed them little notice as he dismounted his horse and entered the tavern followed by William who led Amber by the arm.

The three walked into the now almost empty tavern and sat at a table next to a fireplace, which was currently unused.

Rupert waved a serving girl over commanding, 'light the fire now.'

When the king saw Amber's glare he said, 'I know it's not cold, I just like the look and feel of a fire.'

Once the fire was lit the king then said to the serving girl, 'bring me a jug of your best wine and it had better be your best.'

The nervous girl returned with the wine, poured a small amount into the goblet and placed it before the king. She was waiting for him to taste it and give his approval before she filled the goblet and then served his companions.

The king pushed the goblet over to the serving girl and said, 'drink.'

The confused girl lifted the goblet to her lips and drank the wine. When the goblet was empty she placed it back before the king.

Finally, when Rupert was satisfied that neither the wine nor the goblet had been poisoned, he ordered the girl to fill all three goblets and also requested three plates of venison casserole.

When the serving girl left to organise the casserole, William looked at Rupert and asked, 'why did you make the girl sample your wine my lord?'

'It could have been poisoned,' he answered.

'But you are magically immune from poison,' William reminded him.

'We know that, but no one else does and it's always fun to watch people die painfully and I was really hoping these people wanted me dead and poison would have been their only real option.'

A short time later the girl retuned with the three bowls of steaming hot venison casserole. Amber stopped listening to the conversation between the wizard and the king, instead concentrating on the excellent wine and delicious stew. She looked around the tavern looking for possible escape routes deciding that if she was given any opportunity to get away tonight she was going to take it. She finished her meal, refused Rupert's offer of more wine and stared into the fire while she waited for the others to retire.

CHAPTER 10

A BREAK FOR FREEDOM

Just after dusk the tired rescue party headed off again in search of their princess, however, after just two hours of walking they were forced to stop due to the lack of light caused by a cloudy night obscuring the moonlight. They had stumbled across a clearing large enough for a campsite and decided this place would be as good as any to plan their next move.

After what was a surprisingly short debate they decided that travelling at night was not working, the disadvantages out weighed the advantages too greatly. Travel at night was just slow and the risk of getting caught by surprise while sleeping was just getting far too high the nearer they got to the pixie capital. If they ran into any pixie hunting parties during the day at least they would all be awake and have their weapons close at hand.

With all this decided Derry, Dylan and Finn took the first watch while the others more than made up for the sleep they lost the day before.

Amber waited until she was sure William and Rupert would be asleep but she had no way of knowing for certain as she had been given her own room. She walked over to the window but could not open it (Rupert had personally nailed it shut) and knew breaking the glass would make far too much noise. She opened the door a fraction and peered out into the hallway and could not believe her luck. The messenger from Caledonia had drawn watch duty but was overcome with exhaustion from the last five days and had promptly fallen asleep.

The princess crept into the hallway, passed the guard, pausing only long enough to pick up the pixie's short sword that lay beside him, she then moved silently down the stairs into the common room below. She searched the kitchen and found a suitable backpack and filled it with water, food and wine. Amber then headed to the back door of the tavern and seeing no guards, slipped out and headed directly for the woods two hundred yards away.

She didn't stop running and didn't look back until she reached the relative safety of the trees. Once there, she did look back and was relieved to find that her escape, so far, had gone unnoticed. With that she adjusted the straps of her new backpack and headed to the deepest, least accessible part of the forest. Amber hoped that because she was smaller than any of the pixies she was leaving behind, she could go places they would not be able to follow.

Amber's spirits remained high despite her slow progress, reasoning that if she couldn't see more than two feet in front of herself at a time then neither could anyone who may be following her. She continued on for a couple more hours but finally gave in to her growing need for sleep.

Three hours after Amber's escape, the messenger was found asleep outside her door by the guard who was sent to relieve him. He ran over to and opened the door of the princess's room and momentarily froze in panic when he saw the princess was gone.

The pixie took three deep breaths and forced himself towards the king's door praying the king would not hold him responsible for the fairy's escape. He knocked on the king's door and waited.

'You had better have a very good reason for disturbing me,' said the king in a quiet but still threatening tone.

The pixie pointed to the still sleeping messenger and said simply, 'the fairy's gone.'

The king flew into a rage. He pulled the guard's sword from its scabbed then shoved the anxious man to one side. The poor sleeping pixie never knew what hit him as the king literally hacked the defenceless man to pieces.

'You!' he shouted at the pixie guard, 'wake the wizard and have him meet me outside!' The king bellowed as he headed downstairs then outside slamming the door behind him.

The pixie guard had watched the king in horror. He had fought many battles and had seen many people die but had never witnessed anything like what he had just seen. He wondered how a man who was so obviously insane had become the most powerful man in Connaught. Although he felt sorry for the man the king had just murdered, he was relieved it wasn't him and vowed to himself never to upset the volatile monarch. He woke the wizard who hastily headed outside to join his king.

William found a calmer Rupert talking to the captain of his guard.

The king turned to the wizard and said, 'all the horses are still here so she's on foot. My guess is she's headed into the woods but with this cloud cover it's too dark for her to get far. We've sent a couple of scouts out but we'll have to wait till first light before we can stake a proper search.'

Without waiting for a reply, the king turned and headed back inside.

A much revived rescue party set out just after dawn. Neave again sent an invisible Phil to scout the area for any sign of pixie activity.

They set a brisk pace finding the going far easier in the full light of day however Dougal and Derry found it rather slow going as they could go so much faster than the fairies.

Just over an hour into their day's journey they found Phil waiting for them at the side of a path that ran through the woods. Liam inspected the path and decided that no one had travelled it in at least two days. However, after a short debate, they decided not to use the path but to keep to the woods hoping to avoid any pixie contact.

Amber had been on the move since just after sunrise and was finding the going tough. She was forced to back track a couple of times due to the denseness of the woods and the unevenness of the terrain. Determined not to become disheartened she pushed herself forward hoping she was heading in the right direction.

As the day wore on Amber began to believe she might have actually succeeded in leaving her captors behind. Around midday she came across a small creek and decided to try and confuse anyone who was tracking her. She crossed the river and left an obvious trail leading into the woods on the other side. Then she carefully back tracked to the creek and entered it. It was a warm day and she found the knee deep cold water quite refreshing. Although walking with the current, the going was slow and on two occasions she lost her footing and fell, totally submerging herself in the water. Both times she simply picked herself up and carried on undeterred, content in the knowledge she was leaving no trail while travelling in the creek.

Finally after about three hours she left the water and re-entered the woods. She only did this to give herself time to dry out before nightfall.

For the first time since her escape Amber thought about her friends and wondered where they were. Also, for the first time, she was not sure what to do next. Should she search for her friends or try and find her way home which could prove difficult as she had no idea where she was. As much as she wanted to find her friends (and she really did) she knew she had to warn her father about Rupert's plans so her father could mobilize the fairy army and prepare for the imminent pixie invasion. Decision made, Amber headed in what she hoped was the right direction.

The Shadow stopped his horse and dismounted. He smiled as he examined the path before him. The tracks were faint but fresh, his prey had passed this way in the last two or three hours at most.

'So they are travelling by day now,' he said smiling to himself.

He sent the raven into the woods to see how far ahead of him they were. While he waited for the bird's return he took the opportunity to eat on the ground, a pleasant change from eating on the back of a moving horse.

The bird's quick return confirmed his belief that he was only hours behind his prey. He briefly considered setting his horse free and following them into the woods on foot but decided against it.

By this time, the day after tomorrow at the latest, the fairies and their friends would find themselves free of the woods. That would leave them a half day trip through open country before they reached their destination.

He had decided to follow the path out of the woods and then follow the tree line back, close to where he believed the fairies would break free of the trees. He would then just sit back and wait.

The day passed without incident for Dougal, his twin sister and their friends. They camped in a small clearing beside a small creek (the same creek that Amber had travelled along earlier that day, but about two days travel to the south).

It was a warm night and they ate yet another cold meal. Everyone, with the exception of Phil, was longing for the day they could risk a fire and cook a hot meal.

Despite the cold meal, spirits in the camp were still high that night, everyone had enjoyed travelling during the daylight hours.

Amber finally collapsed in exhaustion just after dark. She slept where she fell, too tired to even eat or drink.

She was woken the next morning by the sunlight streaming through the trees directly in her face. Every muscle in her body seemed to scream in protest as she forced herself into a sitting position using a tree to support her back. She ate half of the remaining cold venison casserole, now well past its best. With her breakfast finished, she tried to stand and with great effort finally succeeded.

Her progress was initially very slow but as the pain in her legs decreased her speed improved as she headed towards what she hoped was the west and her home.

The princess walked into a small clearing but just after she passed the halfway point, to her horror, she saw two pixies enter the clearing directly in front of her. She turned and ran for the woods but was not fast enough and was caught and tackled from behind by one of the pixies.

Amber was surprised when the other pixie pulled her attacker off her.

'Stay still and we will not harm you,' he said.

She looked at the pixie speaking and nodded, wondering how he received the nasty bruising she now saw on the side of his face.

A short time later four more pixies entered the clearing. One of the men ordered his three companions to watch the prisoner and signalled for the man with the bruised face to join him.

'What do you think Arthur, is this what we've been looking for?' he asked.

'I don't know John, if she is, I feel sorry her,' he paused, 'she must be. What else would a fairy be doing here and a young woman at that. Who is she anyway?' asked Arthur.

'A spy maybe?' John suggested.

'I've never heard of fairies using spies before, that's more our style really,' stated Arthur.

'Right. We are going to have to question her,' said John.

The two pixies walked over to Amber. Sir John dismissed the guards and then introduced himself and Arthur to the fairy princess who stubbornly refused to give her name or answer any of their questions.

The two pixies, now very frustrated, again stood alone trying to decide what to do next.

'We're going to have to take her to the king,' said John but he could see by the look on Arthur's face that his friend was not at all happy about that.

'I don't like it either Arthur, but what else can we do?'

Arthur thought for a moment then reluctantly said, 'you're right John, but we'll have to watch Stow.'

'Why?' asked John.

'Let's just say it was a good thing that I was with him when we found her. Enough said?' answered Arthur.

John, nodding in understanding, replied, 'I'll send him back to Oliver with a message explaining what we are doing.'

Arthur simply nodded his approval and walked over to Amber.

'Right,' Arthur said to Amber, 'there are two ways we can do this. Either you can give me your word that you won't try to escape and then you will be able to walk freely about, or I'll have to tie your hands and feet to a post and carry you like a dead animal, which neither of us want, do we?'

'You wouldn't dare,' she started but stopped when she saw the 'if you make me I will' look on his face.

'All right, you have my word,' she said.

'I'm told that a fairy always keeps their word so please don't disappoint me. Now, can I get you anything to eat or drink before we depart?' asked Arthur.

'No, but thank you for asking,' answered the princess somewhat surprised.

Amber watched the pixie walk over to the man who was obviously in command. She then looked around the clearing and for the first time noticed that the man who tackled her was no longer present.

Within minutes the fairy princess and her five new pixie captures were heading east back towards the pixie king.

Dougal and his friends were again making steady progress and everyone had noticed that the trees had begun to thin out. Then out of nowhere Phil appeared.

'Three hours, maybe sooner and we'll be out of these woods,' Phil told them.

'Any idea how long it will take us to reach the pixie capital?' asked Neave.

'No', answered Phil, 'do you want me to fly ahead and see if I can find out?'

'Yes. Fly around and see what you can find and we'll wait for you at the edge of the woods,' replied Neave.

Phil disappeared again and the others headed on with renewed vigour. In their eagerness to reach the open spaces they never saw the pixie scout, who on seeing them, turned and ran to warn his fellowmen of the approaching fairies.

An hour had passed since Phil had left the companions and they knew they soon would leave the woods. They all chattered happily until suddenly, from out of nowhere, two arrows struck and bounced off their armour.

'Take cover!' yelled Finn.

The well trained fairies were all quick to find cover behind the trees. The leprechauns were slower but their armour saved them by deflecting numerous direct hits.

'Can anyone see them?' Finn asked calmly and only loud enough for his friends to hear.

'There's two of them in the large tree to the right,' said Dylan pointing to the tree in question.

They then heard a pixie yell, 'throw down your weapons and surrender and I will let you live, if not, you die. You have two minutes to decide!'

'Finn, there's at least half a dozen pixies trying to get behind us,' Adam pointed out.

'We can't afford to let anyone get behind us. Adam, Liam, it's up to the two of you to stop them. Dougal, you and I will take the guys in the trees. Neave, keep an eye out for any wizards and if there are any, they're yours.'

'Times up!' shouted the pixie and even before he had finished the pixies sent a volley of arrows at their unseen foe.

'They're trying to keep us pinned down so they can get behind us. Liam, Adam, see if you can drop back and find a safe place to pick them off before they surround us,' ordered Finn.

Adam and Liam crawled through whatever cover they could find and were both relieved to find a dry stream bed that would provide them with excellent protection.

Finn thought about pulling back to join Liam and Adam but realised there was no way that Dougal or Derry could do this without being seen.

The pixies continued their barrage of arrows effectively pinning down Finn and Dougal making it impossible for them to return fire.

Liam tapped Adam on the shoulder and pointed to a group of eight pixies that were almost in a position where they could fire on the unprotected backs of their friends. Without a word being spoken, Liam fired an arrow that thudded into a tree two feet above Finn's head. The fairy prince spun around and noticed the arrow, then saw Liam pointing to where the approaching pixies would shortly emerge.

Finn nodded in understanding, then turned to Dougal and said, 'Dougal, there's a group of pixies about to attack us from out of the trees over there,' Finn pointed and Dougal fully understood what needed to be done.

Once Liam was sure that Finn understood the situation he turned to Adam and nodded. The pair then fired on the unsuspecting pixies. Before the first arrows found their mark both fairies sent a second arrow on its way. Two pixies fell never to rise again, another was hit in the right shoulder and fell to his knees in pain. The fourth embedded itself harmlessly into a tree.

Chaos broke out in the ranks of the unsuspecting pixies. Two of their number one men were dead and another injured and no one knew where the arrows had come from. Two more pixies fell as they tried to reach for cover but on this occasion one of the pixies saw Liam and Adam as they let their arrows fly.

Liam signalled to Finn that the pixies had pulled back.

Finn nodded. 'Dylan, watch their backs,' he ordered.

He then turned his intention back to the pixies in front of him. A short time later the rain of arrows stopped and everything went quiet.

'What are they doing?' asked Neave.

'I don't know,' answered Finn honestly.

For the next ten minutes there was no sign of any movement from the pixies. The fairies were starting to believe that perhaps the pixies had retreated for some strange reason.

Then again from out of nowhere, two groups of six pixies charged them from different directions. A separate group also numbering six pixies charged the isolated Liam and Adam who managed to drop two of the attackers with arrows before they were forced into hand to hand combat.

Dougal was the only archer in the main group to get a shot hitting a charging pixie in the shoulder pinning him to a tree.

The attacking pixies hesitated when they saw the twins up close and it was only their extreme discipline that enabled them to continue. Finn who had been waiting for the opportunity to teach the pixie people a lesson (which he believed they richly deserved) made the most of his attackers distraction cutting two of them down before they had a chance to defend themselves. Dougal dropped his sword and lifted a pixie in each hand. He then banged their heads together knocking them both unconscious. Although still learning the art of swordplay Derry's huge reach advantage allowed her to fend off two far more skilled opponents.

While the battle raged, Dylan picked out the man who he believed to be in command. He was disgusted to see him standing so far behind the battle shouting orders. Dylan crawled through the bushes until he was behind the man. He then crept up behind him and grabbed the startled pixie placing a dagger to his throat.

'You have ten seconds to call your men off or you die,' said Dylan coldly.

'Fall back now,' ordered the pixie knight not needing to be told twice.

'Tell them to drop their weapons.' Dylan ordered again, pressing his dagger more firmly against the pixie's throat.

The pixie obeyed and his men dropped their weapons in surrender. Dougal immediately turned and ran to the assistance of Liam and Adam who were struggling to hold their own against four pixies. Dougal's large legs covered the ground quickly. He picked up the first pixie he came across and threw him in the air, the pixie hit the ground and lay there unmoving.

'Drop your weapons or I will take them from you,' demanded the leprechaun.

The pixies who had seen what Dougal had done to their companion did as he ordered.

'I love being a giant,' said Dougal. Adam and Liam just laughed in reply.

'What are we going to do with them?' asked Finn pointing at the eighteen pixies that were all tied to trees. Of the twenty four pixies that had tried to ambush them, six were dead and one was dying. Another was badly hurt but would live, the rest, for the most part, were relatively unharmed.

For their part, the fairies had gotten off lightly, apart from Liam who received a nasty gash to his left arm (already bandaged by Neave). The others escaped with a variety of small cuts and bruises.

'I have no idea,' answered Neave honestly, 'any ideas, does any one have any ideas?' she asked.

'Neave, are you sure he told you the truth about not sending anyone for help?' asked Dougal.

'Yes. I cast a truth spell so he couldn't lie even if he wanted to but it was a waste of a good spell, he's too much of a coward to risk his life by lying to me anyway,' she answered.

'It's simple really,' said Dylan matter-of-factly, 'either we leave them here tied up hoping no one finds them or untie them until we're long gone, or we kill them all,' he finished bluntly.

'You're right Dylan,' said Finn drawing his dagger from its sheath and walking towards the pixie commander.

Everyone looked on in horror as Finn grabbed the pixie by his hair and pulled his head back.

After what seemed like an eternity Finn said, 'if you come looking for us or send anyone after us, I'll come looking for you and *I will find you* and when I do you'll be a dead man,' stated Finn emphatically.

The pixie, who went visibly pale, just nodded in understanding.

Adam and Dylan went through the pixie's supplies taking all the arrows and food they and their friends could carry. Finished with the pixies and their supplies the companions then headed off to meet Phil.

Although she had given her word Amber was still tempted to try and escape again. It was true that these pixies had treated her far better than her previous captors. The knight and his friend had even been courteous, respectful and kind. They were however going to return her to the king.

Her only hope if she couldn't escape was that these pixies would take her to the pixie capital. It was highly likely that they did not know the king had left his castle. As long as they didn't run into the king's men, she realised Sir John could actually be doing her a favour. The further south they headed the closer she would be to her friends.

'Finally a decent path.' Amber looked up at the sound of Sir John's voice. 'Arthur, scout ahead and see where it leads.'

Without a word Arthur headed down the path and returned half an hour later.

He walked up to John who was talking to Amber trying subtly to get some information about her but failing dismally.

'The path joins up to one main path with two forks, one heading south the other northeast.' Arthur explained.

Amber decided there and then that if they headed northeast she would try and escape but if they took the south road she would make no attempt to leave these pixies, for the time being at least.

'The south fork should have us in the capital within five days,' said John.

'Two if we can get hold of some horses from somewhere,' added Arthur.

Amber and her captors headed down the path towards the southern turnoff but before they had even got half way they heard the sound of approaching horses. Within minutes the first horseman appeared before them followed by three others.

'You've found her, the king will be pleased,' cried the ecstatic horseman as he rode forward to intercept them.

'Who *are* you?' Arthur directed to Amber.

'Crown Princess Amber Tralee, heir apparent to the fairy throne,' answered Amber and for the first time in her life she used her formal title.

Arthur tried to speak but no words would come so he found himself just staring dumbly back at the princess. Amber nearly laughed at the poor fellow despite the situation.

John, standing close enough to hear, Amber turned to look at the princess, his face she thought bore the look of a man who had just been hit by an unexpected arrow.

'Well done Sir Knight,' said the horseman dismounting and then patting Sir John on the back, 'I can tell you the king has been most unhappy since she escaped. He killed the poor blighter who was on guard where he slept, made a nasty mess I must say. Oh, forgive me, my manners are shocking old boy. I'm Sir Cecil James newly promoted lieutenant of the kings guard. Seems my predecessor had a nasty accident but mustn't dwell on such things. And you are?' inquired the bustling man.

'Sir John Loxley.' John answered wondering how such an obvious idiot had achieved such a high rank. Either it was an act or no one else would take the job. He decided he would watch this man incase it was the former.

'Well Sir John it was a pleasure to meet you. I will take the girl from you now so you can return to your duties.' Sir Cecil said.

'No,' said John, 'I insist that I see the fairy arrives safely to the king. She has after all escaped once already. It is only once isn't it?' he hadn't meant to openly oppose this man, a man who in fact out ranked him but he wanted to make sure he protected the fairy princess for as long as he could.

'Yes,' said Cecil tersely, 'she has only escaped once,' he then added, his tone now more friendly, 'I'd be happy for you to tag along, I'm sure the king would be happy to personally reward the man who found his little guest,' and with that Cecil mounted his horse and rode back to his men. The mounted pixies rode ahead just fast enough to stop those who were walking from catching up to them.

'Why didn't you tell me who you were Your Highness?' asked John.

'You would have just returned me to your king anyway,' stated Amber.

'You're right, I probably would have,' admitted the knight, 'but if it's any consolation I wouldn't have been happy about it.'

'It's not,' said Amber, 'why didn't you just hand me over to Sir Cecil?' she asked.

'I'm not sure really. It could be because I don't trust him and it gives me time to think about what to do next,' answered the pixie knight.

'John, keep it down a bit,' suggested Arthur, 'you never know who's eavesdropping.'

John nodded then asked in a more hushed tone, 'Arthur what do you make of this Cecil chap.'

'Wouldn't trust him as far I could throw him. I don't blame him though, I think it's his parents fault. Who calls their child Cecil, I bet he was bullied all his life and that was the result,' he said pointing to the knight riding ahead of them.

Amber and John looked firstly at Arthur then at Cecil and then both burst into laughter in spite of their current situation.

Amber looked over at the two pixies that were unlike any other pixies she had met since she was first captured all those weeks ago. She wondered how many others like that there were, good men just trying to survive. She decided this was no longer about her, it was about an evil king, a king who had to be stopped, not for her sake or even her people's sake but for the brownies and every nation conquered by Rupert and his evil predecessors but most importantly it was for pixies like Sir John and Arthur. Rupert had to be stopped and by all that was holy she was going to play her part.

Within an hour of leaving the battlefield behind them Dougal and his friends arrived at the edge of the woods. An invisible Phil saw them emerge and flew over to join them. They told him of the battle he had missed and he offered to fly back and make sure none of the pixies had freed themselves. They decided against this, as they were so close to their goal they did not want any further delays. If they were forced to fight again they wanted Phil with them.

Phil explained that they were only half a day away from their destination but it was over a fairly well populated area and there was no way they could cross in daylight hours without being seen. On a brighter note he had found a deserted farm within an hour of the castle with a barn large enough to hide Dougal and Derry and which they could use as a base.

'Well, should we stay, or should we go now?' Neave asked her friends.

'Neave how many of us could you turn into pixies like you did with Liam back at the cave?' asked Dougal.

Neave looked at Dougal and smiled, she was impressed.

'I'm not sure, I've never done it to more than one person at a time but now is definitely the time to see if it's possible to change several people all at the same time,' she replied.

Dougal watched as Neave closed her eyes and started to chant that strange language she always used when casting a spell. Then right before his eyes, all his friends (with the exception of Neave) took on the appearance of a pixie. Neave then opened her eyes, looked over to Dougal, smiled and then fainted.

Minutes later, 'how long have I been out for?' Neave asked looking up at the concerned pixie faces.

'A couple of minutes,' answered a pixie that sounded just like Derry.

'Someone help me up,' Neave ordered, 'we have to hurry, I don't know how long the spell will last and we can't afford to get caught out in the open.'

'Let me carry you,' said Dougal, 'although I look like a pixie I still feel as large and as strong as ever.'

Neave reluctantly agreed and the 'pixies' headed for Phil's abandoned farmhouse.

The figure that watched from the shadows was strangely relieved when he saw the fairy wizard rise. He had to admit to himself he was more than a little in awe of her. In all his years as a spy he had never witnessed anything as impressive as what he had just seen. The power needed to transform four fairies and two giants was beyond his comprehension and had he not just seen it with his own two eyes he would never have believed it.

His first thought was to send a message to the king and William to warn them of the girl's power, explaining to them what he had just witnessed. He decided against it however because he never liked the wizard and was more than happy to see him meet his match. He knew that the confidant wizard would underestimate the young fairy and thought it would be far more interesting to watch their confrontation should one eventuate.

The Shadow followed as the 'pixies' headed across the open countryside in the direction of the capital. He trailed them from a safe distance making sure they never saw him. Just when he was starting to think they were going to attempt to enter the city in broad daylight they stopped at a deserted farm. He watched as they entered the old dilapidated barn. When he was sure that they were settling in, for the time being anyway, The Shadow headed off to find a place where he could watch them without being seen himself.

Arthur and John both noticed the change that had come over Amber. Hours earlier they had caught her fleeing from the king but now she seemed almost eager to return to him.

'What does the king want with you princess?' asked Arthur.

Amber thought about not answering the question but decided it made no difference whether the pixie knew or not.

'He wants to marry me,' she finally answered.

'What, why?' stammered Arthur.

'To take control of Sarasidhe without having to take it by force,' it was Sir John who answered, not Amber, 'he's clever, I'll say that for him,' he continued.

'If it means I don't have to put my life on the line, I think it's a good idea,' said Arthur.

'It will not be good for the princess and her people though,' thought John to himself.

About an hour before nightfall Amber and her escorts arrived back at the inn that she had escaped from almost forty eight hours before.

Rupert was waiting for them (Sir Cecil had sent a rider ahead to tell the king of the fairy's capture) and the look he gave Amber chilled Arthur to the bone.

The king walked towards Amber pausing in front of her. He looked at her in undisguised hatred but she looked back at him defiantly. No one had ever stood up to Rupert before and he was momentarily at a loss. Not sure what to do next, Rupert struck Amber squarely in the face knocking her to the ground.

'Gag her, bind her hands and feet and tie her to a tree!' he bellowed, 'if she gets away again you know what will happen to the man responsible,' he finished.

With the princess momentarily forgotten, the king then turned to the princess's escorts who all instantly fell to their knees.

'You must be Sir John,' the king said looking at John, 'what can I give you to reward you for returning the fairy to me?'

'To serve you my king is more reward than I deserve,' answered Sir John.

The king smiled at Sir John, nodded in agreement and then said, 'you must join my guard and travel with me to Caledonia.'

'I would be honoured your highness and if it pleases you, my men and I would like to take responsibility for making sure the fairy does not escape again,' replied John who was more than aware of how much he was standing on the toes of Sir Cecil and the rest of the king's bodyguard.

'Yes it pleases me. I will leave the princess in your care. You,' said Rupert pointing to Sir Cecil, 'get some horses for Sir John and his men. We leave at first light and I want everyone ready is that understood?'

'Yes my lord,' said Cecil nodding. He then turned to John and smiled.

John looked at the smiling man and knew he had just made an enemy. He then looked over to Arthur, winked at him and mouthed, 'don't worry, I have your back covered.'

CHAPTER 11

TOO LATE

Two hours after nightfall the five fairies and the fairy dragon left the barn and headed for the pixie capital. Dougal and Derry were both disappointed to be left behind but they understood why. Neave would not be able to cast the spell to change everyone into pixies again until the following day and even if she could, it would leave her too weak to cast any other spells. The pixie towns and cities were not made to accommodate fairy dragons like fairy towns were, so the twins would be too large to enter the city. The unhappy leprechauns watched their friends disappear into night before them.

The fairies crossed the open country quickly with Phil flying ahead searching farms in the surrounding area for anything they could use to disguise the fairies making it easier for them to enter the city.

Phil returned to the fairies explaining he had found a farm where there was a clothesline full of dry washing within fifteen minutes walk of their present location. They all agreed it was worth the slight detour. While the men changed outside Neave entered a large barn to change in private. Once she had slipped on her new clothing she decided to have a look around the barn. She quietly called for the others to join her and as the four males entered the barn she noticed that Finn was still wearing his own clothes.

When Finn saw her looking at him he said in frustration, 'nothing was large enough to fit me.'

Neave smiled to herself and nodded her understanding.

'Neave, come and look at what I've found,' cried Adam softly.

Neave and the others hurried over to Adam who was standing next to a covered wagon in relative darkness at the rear of the barn. From where the others had been standing no one had noticed the wagon.

'Look,' said Adam, 'it's loaded with hay bales. If we can get hold of a couple of horses we can pretend we are delivering these to the city stables.'

'If you can get the wagon outside I'll take care of the horses,' said Liam as he left the barn. Neave slowly pushed open the barn doors praying they would move quietly and not alert any of the pixies in their nearby farmhouse. Once the doors were open wide enough for the wagon to pass through, Neave called softly for Phil who was still invisible.

She nearly jumped out of her skin when Phil said, 'Neave, I'm right beside you.'

Neave breathed deeply to compose herself then said, 'Phil, do you think you can get that wagon out of here without making any noise?'

'Yes,' answered Phil unhappily, the thought of being used as a lowly pack animal deeply disturbed the proud dragon.

Once inside the barn Phil became visible long enough for Dylan and Adam to tie the wagon's harnesses to the dragon. Slowly and carefully Phil pulled the wagon out of the barn and down the path away from the farmhouse and towards the road that would take them to their destination.

Halfway between the farmhouse and the road they met Liam who was leading two large carthorses. Phil, relieved to be trading places with the two horses, disappeared from sight.

The olive skinned Liam who looked most like a pixie, took up the wagon's reins while a well covered Neave sat beside him. Adam, Dylan and Finn all hid in the back of the wagon with their weapons drawn incase there was any trouble ahead.

It was around midnight when the wagon approached the main entrance to the high walled pixie city. Liam and Neave were surprised to see the city gates open and only two visible guards present. Liam slowed the wagon down but the disinterested guards just waved him on. Liam nodded to the guards as he passed them but they simply ignored him.

'That was easy,' whispered Neave relieved.

'The hard part is still to come,' answered Liam.

Although it was late the streets of the pixie city were far from deserted. Liam and Neave watched the pixies with mild amusement. Some were stumbling home from a night on the town while others simply slept at the side of the road. Every tavern and inn they passed seemed alive with activity and celebration.

'Phil, try and find out why everyone is so happy?' ordered Neave.

'I'm on it,' came the answer from out of thin air beside her.

The wagon plodded on towards the castle in the centre of the city for another ten minutes before Phil returned.

'Neave, I don't know whether I've good news or bad. Rupert, his head wizard and most of his bodyguard have been on a hunting trip for at least four days. From what I overheard no one seems to know when he's going to return but everyone's making the most of his absence,' said the voice of Phil again from out of nowhere.

'Well that most likely explains why we've had no trouble this far, so let's call it good news,' said Neave.

'And let's hope the situation is the same in the castle as well,' added Liam.

They continued on towards the high walled castle and finally arrived at its gates a quarter of an hour later and were stopped by two guards at the gate.

'State your business?' snapped a surly pixie guard.

'We bring hay for the stables sir,' said Liam adding a slight slur to his voice.

'You're delivering hay to the stables after midnight?' questioned the suspicious guard.

In the back of the wagon Adam, Dylan and Finn's hands all went to the hilts of their swords as they heard the obvious suspicion in the pixie's voice.

'We stopped for a quick drink sir, but stayed for a long one,' explained Liam in a slurred giggle like a man who had had a little too much to drink.

The two gate guards looked at each other and then laughed. Shaking their heads they waved the wagon on.

The three fairies in the back of the wagon all breathed a quiet sigh of relief as the wagon started forward. Even Finn who still looked forward to further physical confrontation with the pixies knew this was not the time or place for a fight.

'Where do we go from here Neave?' asked Liam.

'That's a very good question and I wish I knew the answer. For now just get us out of sight from the gate guards,' she replied.

She then turned to where she thought Phil was and asked, 'Phil are you there?'

'No I'm up here,' said Phil from slightly above and just behind her.

'See if you can get any information about Amber and we'll wait for you down that alley,' Neave said pointing to an alley a hundred yards to the right.

The fairies waited patiently for the return of the dragon in the relative safety of the dimly lit alley. They had been there just under a quarter of an hour when a pair of noisy drunken pixie officers approached the wagon.

As they approached the wagon, the unsighted Finn whispered from the back, 'Neave, how many?'

'Just two and I think they're both pretty drunk,' she answered.

'Excellent,' said Finn, 'move the wagon forward slowly so they don't get suspicious and leave the rest to us,' he then signalled for Adam and Dylan to follow him to the back of the wagon.

The pixies barely spared the wagon a second glance as they stumbled passed. Neither pixie was in any state to fight off the three fairies that quickly subdued them and then dragged their unconscious bodies into the wagon.

'What did you do that for?' asked Neave stunned.

'Their uniforms,' answered Finn, 'it will be far easier for us to move around the castle if we look like pixie soldiers.'

Neave nodded in understanding as the three fairies in the wagon stripped the uniforms off the two pixies then bound and gagged them. Adam and Dylan then dressed themselves in the officers' uniforms. Yet again Finn was too large to fit any of the pixie clothing.

Moments later Phil returned and explained that there was a prisoner being held in the highest tower in the castle. Apparently no one but the king and his wizard had ever seen the prisoner but even during their absence the room has been guarded at all times. The fairies all agreed it had to be Amber and with mounting excitement they headed for the tower.

Just before they reached the tower Adam and Dylan slipped from the wagon and headed directly for the tower entrance while Liam bought the wagon to a stop.

The fairy brothers walked boldly up to the tower door and pushed it open. Four startled pixies turned towards the door as it burst open.

Adam, on seeing the pixies on the floor playing bones and who had obviously been drinking on duty snapped, 'what is the meaning of this.'

The four pixies jolted to attention when they saw what they thought was a pair of pixie officers standing just inside the room.

'I'm waiting. Why, when you are supposed be on guard duty, are you gambling and drinking!' yelled Adam in feigned rage.

'Sir, we are in the middle of a well protected castle, we are here just for show,' stammered one of the guards.

Dylan turned to his brother and said, 'I'm sure they meant no harm my friend, perhaps we could overlook their little indiscretion.'

'Would the king overlook them do you think?' asked Adam, who was really starting to enjoy himself.

'No,' answered Dylan, 'he would not.'

The four pixies paled visibly at Dylan's reply.

Dylan then added, 'but we are not the king are we and their actions have harmed no one.'

'You might be right, I'll have to think on this matter,' said Adam. He pulled a notebook from his pocket, took the names of the four pixies and wrote them into the book.

He then added, 'return to your quarters as none of you are in a fit state for duty. While we finish your watch, I'll decide what action, if any, I'm going to take. Now get out of my sight,' Adam said waving his hand and dismissing them.

The pixie guards saluted Adam and Dylan then left the two fairies alone. After a couple of minutes Dylan went outside and signalled his friends who were still waiting in the wagon. Liam, Neave and Finn joined them in the room at the base of the tower.

They then began the long climb up the spiralling staircase to the top of the tower. Along the way they passed a dozen or so empty rooms, some furnished, others completely empty but they had to check each one to make sure they weren't surprised from behind.

As they approached the summit of the tower Liam and Finn dropped backed so they wouldn't be seen by any guards guarding what they believed to be Amber's cell.

Finally Adam and Dylan came face to face with two guards who stood before a single door.

'Open the door,' ordered Adam who was thoroughly enjoying his role as a pixie officer.

'I cannot sir,' answered one of the guards.

'Why not?' demanded Adam.

'Because as everyone knows only the king has the key,' said the pixie drawing his sword.

'Put the sword down and you will not be harmed,' ordered Finn calmly from behind the brothers.

The pixie guards, now both with drawn swords, took a step forward but then seeing Liam and the huge Finn coming up to join them, decided that discretion was the better part of valour and placed their weapons on the ground before them.

'Very wise,' said Finn the disappointment obvious in his voice.

Finn's tone only convinced the pixie guards that they had done the right thing laying down their swords without putting up a fight.

'Tie them up,' ordered Neave, 'but don't gag them, I haven't finished with them yet.'

Once the pixies were safely bound she began her interrogation. She was disappointed to find they were telling the truth about the king being the only one to have a key to the door and that they had no idea who the prisoner inside the room was. She knew she would have no trouble opening the door magically but was deeply concerned about Amber's welfare fearing she had been without food or water for over four days.

Finished with the pixies Neave walked over to the door, placed her hand on the handle, chanted a few words of magic and then pushed the door open. She walked into the room followed closely by her friends. She looked around the room and to her despair found it empty except for a few items of furniture.

The shocked fairies all looked at each other none quite believing they had come all this way for nothing. Neave thought about requestioning the guards but dismissed the idea knowing it would achieve nothing. She had used magic when she'd interrogated them and they truly believed their prisoner was still locked up safely in the room.

'Neave, look at this,' called Dylan pointing to something on the table.

Neave walked over to see what Dylan had found and smiled when she saw the words 'Amber' and 'north' carved into the top of the table.

Neave decided it was time to have another quick word to the pixie guards and turned and left the room.

'Where does the king hunt?' she started.

'In an old lodge a couple of hours ride north of the city on the edge of the woods,' answered one of the frightened guards.

'How exactly do I find this lodge?' she questioned.

'I don't know,' snapped the pixie guard, 'I'm hardly on the king's invitation list, am I?'

'If you value your life,' warned Finn grabbing the pixie by his collar and lifting him off the ground, 'I'd drop the attitude and answer the lady's questions to the best of your ability,' he finished dropping the terrified pixie to the ground.

'You take the main highway to the north and you'll find the lodge nestled somewhere amongst the trees at the edge of the woods, exactly where, I honestly don't know,' answered the pixie as truthfully as it was possible for him to do.

Neave nodded to Finn and both pixies eyes widened in terror as the huge fairy prince drew his dagger from its sheath and headed towards them. It was not the blade the prince used however, it was the hilt he used to knock the struggling pixies unconscious.

Finn then cut the ropes that bound the pixies and Neave cast a spell that would make them forget everything that had happened. As Neave finished her spell, Liam who had gone downstairs earlier, returned carrying two of the wine bottles that had belonged the downstairs guards. He tipped one bottle over the tunics of the unconscious pixies and placed the now nearly empty bottle in the hand of one of them. Adam placed the other bottle beside the second pixie guard while Dylan closed the door to the room that had once been Amber's prison.

Within minutes they were back in the wagon and heading back to the abandoned farm and their leprechaun friends.

They passed through the gates of the castle and into the city proper without being stopped by the gate guards. They then carried on heading directly for the citys main exit.

Not far from the exit Adam asked Liam to slow the wagon enough for him and Dylan to slip out the back. Liam did as requested looking over to Neave who just shrugged to show she had no idea what the brothers were doing.

Dylan followed his brother out of the wagon but like Liam and Neave at first he had know idea why but as soon as Adam pointed to the two saddled horses tied to a post outside a tavern he knew why he was there. Smiling at each other the brothers boldly walked up to the horses and untied them. They then casually mounted the horses and headed for the city gates waving as they passed the wagon carrying their friends. The brothers rode through the city gates and waited for the others to join them.

Reunited again they only stopped one more time and that was to untie and dump the still very drunk, unconscious and semi naked pixie officers a mile from the pixie capital.

They arrived back at the abandoned farm only a couple of hours before dawn and found Dougal and Derry both still awake and eager for details of the mission. Neave gave them a brief description of events then promised to answer all of their questions after she had had some sleep.

Finn, who had slept most of the return journey in the back of the wagon, took the first watch while his friends all got some much needed sleep.

CHAPTER 12

A STUNNING DISPLAY

Amber woke well before dawn, her muscles aching from her efforts of the previous days. Her pain was added too because the ropes that bound her hands and feet had been tied so tightly they had cut her wrists and ankles. When she had woken still tied to the tree her first thought had been to cry for help but she was still gagged.

Amber looked over and saw Sir John and his men sleeping nearby and wondered why he had asked to be assigned to guard her. She didn't recognise the guard who was currently on watch and then realised the only pixies of the small patrol that had recaptured her that she had payed any attention too, were the knight and his friend Arthur. She reprimanded herself for this believing that if she was going to get out of this alive she needed to be totally aware of what was happening around her and why it was happening.

She was surprisingly relieved when the camp slowly started to come to life an hour or so before dawn. Preoccupied by the activity in the camp Amber didn't notice Sir John approach. He cut the ropes that bound her to the tree and then removed her gag. He then applied some cream and bandaged her raw, bleeding wrists and ankles.

'After you have eaten princess, I'm afraid I'm going to have to rebind your hands and feet.' Sir John said apologetically.

'Please just call me Amber, my people are not big on formalities,' she said, 'and if you bind my hands and feet how do you expect me to ride a horse?'

'You will not be riding (he started to say princess but realising what he was saying corrected himself) Amber. The king has commandeered the wagon the innkeeper uses to carry his supplies. You, Arthur and I will ride in the back of the covered wagon while one of my men will drive it and the other two will follow behind on horseback. The king is determined to keep you well guarded. I'm afraid any chance you had to escape is well and truly gone.'

'Why did you volunteer to guard me?' asked Amber as John led her towards Arthur who was cooking breakfast.

The pixie avoided the fairy's gaze and completely ignored her question, instead turning his attention to Arthur.

'What's for breakfast my friend?' he asked and then added, 'I'm starving'.

'Porridge. I thought since we're going to Caledonia we might as well eat like Caledonians,' answered Arthur cheerfully.

'What's porridge?' Amber inquired.

John and Arthur looked at each other shaking their heads surprised that the princess had never heard of this nourishing meal.

'Rolled oats, water and salt. I then add hot milk and brown sugar.' Arthur replied.

'You're going to feed me horse food?' stated Amber appalled.

'Just try it, if you don't like it he'll cook you something else,' said John.

Amber took the bowl that Arthur handed her and sat down to eat. She watched the two pixies for a couple of minutes happily eating their portions. Finally she forced herself to dip her spoon into the bowl and she placed the smallest amount of the gooey mixture into her mouth.

'You're right, it's delicious!' she exclaimed, pleasantly surprised.

By dawn all the pixie king's guards were ready to depart the inn and continue their journey as the king had ordered. It was however two hours after dawn before the king appeared and another hour after that before he was ready to leave.

Rupert sent for John and issued his instructions for the transportation of Amber and then dismissed the pixie knight. The whole time John listened to the king's orders he had the unpleasant feeling that he was being watched. He turned to rejoin his men and saw that it was Sir Cecil who had been watching him.

Cecil smiled and nodded to John who suppressed a shudder and said to himself, 'I don't like that man.'

He walked over to the two of his men who would be riding behind the wagon and gave them their orders for the day's journey.

Within minutes of John's discussion with Rupert finishing, the king signalled for the day's journey to begin so John hurried over and entered the wagon and ordered the driver forward.

As the wagon began to move forward John looked at Amber and said, 'you've really upset him you know.'

'Oh, I haven't even started yet,' stated the princess defiantly and Arthur laughed in spite of himself admiring the girl's spirit.

'Amber, you can't beat him, you would be far better off just doing what he wants. Those that don't always end up dead,' explained John sadly.

'For now he needs me alive, if he didn't, I'd already be dead,' Amber said matter of factly.

'You very nearly were,' said John

'If you or your king expects me to jump at his every command you're both very much mistaken. I'm going to fight him every step of the way. There is no way that I am going to give him my people to use, as he sees fit, not without a fight anyway. You two may be happy to be his slaves but I'll never be anybody's slave for as long as I live and you can tell him that for all I care,' finished Amber calmly.

'We are not slaves,' said John weakly, 'we are citizens of Tudorland.'

'I've seen your king in action and as far as he's concerned every man, woman and child is his to do what he wants with. As you've just said yourself your people obey him or they die. If that's not slavery I don't know what is,' argued the fairy princess.

The pixie knight wanted to argue with her but deep down he knew she was right so he simply said, 'what is discussed in this wagon stays in this wagon. Arthur and I are here to stop you escaping, nothing more.'

'I've no intention of escaping, not for the time being anyway,' she added.

'Arthur, since I believe her, let's untie her for now,' said John, 'it's going to be a long trip, so we might as well be as comfortable as possible.'

After a moments silence Amber again asked, 'why did you ask Rupert if you could be my guard?' and again John ignored the question

It was late morning before Dougal, Derry and their friends were ready to head off in search of the kings hunting lodge, the only clue to Amber's possible location that they had.

An invisible Phil flew at the forefront of the small party while Adam and Dylan, still dressed in the uniforms of the pixie officers, rode infront of the horse drawn wagon. Liam again drove the wagon with Neave in the seat beside him. Finn, still to find pixie clothing large enough to fit him, was again forced to hide in the back of the wagon. The twins this time however walked openly for all to see.

They had decided that now they had the brothers impersonating pixie officers (with Adam particularly impressive in his new role) they would try and pass them off as an escort for two giant diplomats. The fairies of Sarasidhe had believed this, so they could see no reason why the pixies wouldn't.

They stayed well to the west of the pixie capital as they returned to the woods which they had only just left behind. After an uneventful two and a half hour journey they reached the woods and the search for the hunting lodge began in earnest.

During the search for the lodge, Derry moved over to walk beside Neave who still travelled with Liam in the wagon while Adam, Dylan and Phil scouted ahead.

'Neave,' Derry said, 'according to leprechaun legend we used to be able make ourselves invisible just like Phil can. Apparently we used hide from the big people and other more frightening things but not many of the big people believe in us anymore, leprechauns that is, and those who do, make money from selling the shoes that we make and taking the credit for them. Most of the terrifying things that we used to hide from died out a very long time ago, so we've had no need use the skill of invisibility therefore making it lost to us for hundreds of years. Neave, do you think you can help me regain the skill?' Derry asked.

Neave could barely contain her delight. She had been looking for this opportunity for weeks. It was only the king's orders that had stopped her from approaching Derry about the dormant magic she had sensed within the leprechaun girl but not even he could object now that Derry had asked Neave for her help.

'Yes,' said Neave, 'I'm sure I can.'

Before she could continue she was interrupted by Adam running back shouting, 'I've found it, I've found it!'

Neave turned back to Derry and said, 'we'll continue this discussion later.'

When they arrived at the run down old lodge, Dylan looked at his brother and said, 'Adam you fool, this is not a kings hunting lodge. Look at it, it's a hovel. I doubt even a rat would be caught living in a place like this.'

Adam looked around the small group and could tell by the looks on their faces they agreed with his brother.

He then took a deep breath and said, 'have a look at the fields and path. There has obviously been a small army camped here in the last week or so. If not a king's guard who else, I'm open to your suggestions,' he finished slightly terse.

'You're right Adam, it's worth a look inside,' said Neave more to humour her friend than any real belief that they were doing anything other than wasting their time, 'take Dylan and Liam with you and check it out.'

Liam jumped off the wagon and jogged over to join the others as they headed towards the old building.

It was then, that Phil who had been absent for the last two hours, reappeared shouting, 'Stop! Don't take another step toward the lodge,' he yelled loudly as he flew toward Neave as fast as he could.

The brothers and Liam stopped dead in their tracks and seeing Phil flying over to Neave hurried over to join them.

'What's wrong Phil?' asked Liam when they arrived at the wagon.

'Phil has sensed a wall of magical energy around the lodge but he can't tell if it's dangerous to touch or not,' explained Neave.

'How do we find out?' asked Dougal.

'By touching it,' answered Neave, 'but don't worry we won't have to. Phil can fly through without being harmed because of his immunity to magic. Once inside he can look around for any signs of Amber.'

Everyone followed Phil towards the magical wall stopping when he told them to. They all turned toward Neave when they heard her chanting words of magic. The fairies and Derry watched in disbelief as she disappeared only to reappear almost instantly on the other side of the invisible barrier. Dougal just smiled.

Neave looked over to Dougal, winked at him and said, 'I've been practicing.'

With that she turned and headed towards the front door of the building beyond. Not far from her destination she saw a small piece of white material lying in the dirt beside her. She bent to pick it up and upon seeing the gold embossed initials in the corner of the cloth knew instantly that Amber had indeed been here. She turned and ran back to her friends.

'You're right Adam, Amber's definitely been here,' exclaimed Neave excitedly, 'now everyone move back, I'm going to try and bring down this barrier.'

With that she pushed out both her hands and slowly walked forward until she felt her hands enter the wall of magical energy. She closed her eyes, steadied her breathing and slowly sent magic against it.

Her friends, including Phil, watched in silent awe as the previously invisible wall flared a bright red colour then slowly began to fade until nothing remained.

'Right,' she said weakly, 'let's see what we can find inside.'

Neave

It was not just Neave's friends who were stunned by what they had just seen, Wilberforce Smyth, who was watching from the shadows, couldn't believe what he had just witnessed either. Although The Shadow possessed no magical ability himself he had learnt a lot from his previous assignments. Seeing wizards preform spells that no one else could do was one thing but watching a wizard dispel a spell set by another wizard just as powerful, was to William, mind blowing.

He hastily scribbled a note for the king explaining what he had just witnessed, then placed it in the pouch on the Raven's leg and whispered, 'find your master.'

Without looking back the bird took to the sky flying towards the northeast.

The Shadow briefly wondered how the raven always seemed to know were to find the pixie king. He then turned his attention back to the fairies, the wizard in particular. He wished he could be there to see William's face when the king told him what she had just done. He was now left in little doubt that he was watching one of the most powerful wizards in the world.

Dougal, Derry and Phil listened to their friends description of the inside of the lodge, all three disappointed they were too large to see it for themselves first hand.

They were all enjoying a hot meal made from food they had acquired from Rupert's well stocked larder which they then washed down with an exceptionally fine vintaged wine from his cellar. After their meal was finished they filled the wagon with supplies they had 'borrowed' from the pixie king.

While his friends were loading the wagon, Liam studied the many tracks that he believed had been left by Amber, the fairy king and his bodyguards. Happy with what he had found he walked over to join the others telling them how easy it would be to follow the tracks left by so many horses.

Once they were packed and ready to leave, all the fairies went to have one last look at the wonders contained within the pixie king's lodge. They all found it difficult to draw themselves away from such beauty but knew they must as they had far more important issues to deal with.

'How did all these fabulous treasures end up here?' asked Adam.

'I'm guessing it was the same way Amber did,' answered Neave grimly.

With nothing left to say, the fairies, all in silent contemplation, left the pixie king's treasure trove.

CHAPTER 13

A HOMECOMING

It was an uneventful day for the fairy princess. Since they had left the inn that morning the only pixies Amber had had any contact with were Sir John and Arthur. For the moment at least it seemed that Rupert was content to leave her to herself.

The morning turned into afternoon and well before darkness fell they stopped at a small castle for the night.

'Why are we stopping here?' asked Amber, 'with at least two hours of daylight left. I thought your king was now in a hurry to reach our destination so he can deal with the brownie rebel leaders?'

'He is,' said John, 'but this castle and others like it mark the old border between Tudorland and Caledonia. Even before we conquered the brownies the borderlands were a lawless place. The pixie monarchs have for years paid both pixie and brownie bandits to attack anyone on the brownie side of the border in an attempt to destabilise the brownie nation. Since the occupation the area has become even more dangerous and is often used as a base by the rebels because there are so many places to hide and never be found in the highlands, so I believe his highness would feel much safer sleeping behind solid castle walls than out in the open, even though the rebels are leaderless at present.'

'Not the bravest man in the world is he,' said Amber. It was a statement of fact not a question and as much as John and Arthur would have liked to agree with her neither of them did.

Almost as soon as the wagon halted Sir Cecil rode over and said, 'Sir John, the king asks if you would escort the prisoner to the castle dungeon and see to it that she has no contact with anyone other than you, that way he will have someone to hold responsible if she gets away again. And by the way,' he added almost as an afterthought, 'he wants her hands and feet chained and manacled. If it was up to me I'd chain her to the wall as well.'

With that Sir Cecil glared coldly at the fairy princess and then smiled at John before turning and leaving.

Amber shuddered in spite of herself not because of the way the pixie knight had looked at her but because of the coldness and obvious insincerity in the smile that he had given Sir John.

When Sir Cecil was out of hearing range Amber turned to John and said, 'it appears I'm not the only one to have made an enemy and I believe yours could be almost as dangerous as mine.'

'It would seem so,' replied John who then led Amber towards the castle dungeon.

'You seem to know your way around here,' Amber said.

For a moment Amber didn't think the pixie was going to answer. He looked at her and the sadness in his eyes tugged at her heart.

He then took a deep breath and said, 'this was my home. My family lived here for over four hundred years from the time my ancestor Sir Edward Huntingdon built the castle, until my father died and left it and all his lands to the crown.'

'Why did he leave it to the crown?' Amber asked fascinated.

'I don't think he really did,' answered John in a whisper, careful not to be overheard by anyone other than Amber and Arthur, 'four other lords died within three months of my father, all leaving their lands to the crown and there has been half a dozen more since. My father and the others all died when their sons and heirs were all off fighting in one of the king's many wars so there were no valid witnesses to contest the wills. My elder brother, who had waited his whole life to assume the mantle of lord and master, queried our father's decision and was conveniently killed in battle the following day. The funny thing is the same thing happened to two other heirs who questioned their fathers' wills also.'

'Don't you ever dream of reclaiming your heritage?'

'No. I was always happy to be the second son. I never wanted to be the lord of the manor and if this castle and lands were returned to my family I would be but I must admit, I never realised how much I missed it until I walked through those gates.'

'How can you ignore your responsibilities!' gasped Amber.

'What responsibilities?' asked John confused.

'To your tenants or whatever you call the people that live on and work this land for one,' replied Amber starting to lose her temper.

'I call them my friends,' snapped John, 'but what use am I to them dead. My brother died for questioning the king's ownership of our land and it would be no different for me and I will not be responsible for the deaths of anyone who choose to support me.'

'Some things are worth fighting for,' continued Amber adamantly.

'I'm no different than you fairies,' John said, now livid, 'for years you've sat back and watched Rupert, his father and his grandfather before, conquer and enslave half the world and apart from the odd protest, you've sat back and watched, so don't you tell me what I should be doing, you haven't earned that right,' he finished angrily.

As much as Amber wanted to argue with him, she found she couldn't. Sir John was right. The fairies had sat back and watched as the pixies destroyed anyone that stood against them. Sure, there were those like her cousin Finn and her friends Neave and Adam who wanted to stop the pixies before they turned their eyes towards the fairies but they were always in the minority so the fairies continued to bury their heads in the sand.

'I'm sorry,' was all Amber could say fighting back her tears.

Sir John just nodded and smiled sadly in reply.

'I want the castle guards doubled tonight Captain Ferrier,' ordered Rupert.

'It has already been done your highness,' answered the man in command of the castle's garrison.

'Good. Now what do you have to report on the rebel activity in the area?' asked the pixie king.

'It has been quiet for the last couple of months. We send at least three patrols a day out there and have not even seen a brownie in three weeks, apart from the work parties of course. There was an attack on Gateshead Castle a week ago. It took place sometime in the night, six guards were found dead in the morning all killed by a single arrow. No one saw the attack, no one even knew when it happened. Capitan Fairfax sent out a patrol at first light but couldn't even find a trail to follow. It appears to have been a one off attack, perhaps it was their way of letting us know they're still out there.'

'Or it was planned before we captured their leader and now they don't know what to do without her,' suggested William who had been silent up until this point.

'So the rumours are true,' stated Capitan Ferrier.

'Yes they are. I'm on my way to personally supervise her and her second in commands torture and execution but for now Capitan, keep that information to yourself.'

'As you please your highness,' said Ferrier who was then dismissed by the king.

Arthur, who was returning to the dungeon with a tray of food for Amber, stopped dead in his tracks when he saw the pixie walking in his direction.

'Ferrier,' he gasped louder than he had intended.

The pixie captain looked up when he heard his name spoken aloud. When he saw Arthur he smiled cruelly and said, 'that's Captain Ferrier to you solider. Well, well, Arthur Purcell, I didn't think I'd see you in these parts again. So what brings you back here then?' he asked smugly.

'I'm currently part of the king's guard,' answered Arthur.

'You, in the king's guard, I doubt that,' sneered Ferrier.

'I'm guarding his prisoner and if the prisoner dies from hunger I'm sure the king will not be happy, so if that is all Sir, I will return to my duties,' replied a more than slightly shaken Arthur.

Ferrier waited until Arthur was almost out of hearing range and then shouted, 'say hello to Sir John for me!'

He had not seen John but he knew if Arthur was here, John would not be far away.

'John, he knows you're here and you know that next to him, Cecil and George are harmless pussycats. What I don't understand is how he became a captain and commander of this castle.'

'As a reward perhaps,' John suggested.

'A reward for what?'

'Killing my brother and removing the king's only challenge to his rights to this castle and its land,' answered John.

'I wouldn't put it past him. So what do you think he's going to do?' asked Arthur.

'I have no idea but I'm sure we will find out soon enough,' said John who couldn't believe how complicated his life was becoming.

Half an hour later Sir John received a summons from King Rupert requesting an immediate audience.

The guards opened the doors to the castle's council chambers (when John's family owned the castle this room was were the lord would settle the disputes of his tenants) and John entered the room. Memories flooded John's mind when he looked around the room and it took a concerted effort to clear his head.

He saw the king sitting on 'his father's throne' with Ferrier standing at the king's side, not a good sign he thought. There was no sign of the wizard but John knew he would be close at hand.

At the base of the five step stairway that led to the king's throne he stopped, dropped to his knee and lowered his head and said, 'you requested my presence your highness.'

Rupert replied, 'have you,' he paused as if to think of the right words, 'made our prisoner comfortable?'

'I have followed Sir Cecil's instructions to the letter my lord,' John answered.

'Good, so you had no trouble finding the dungeon then?' asked the king.

Although John was looking directly at Rupert he knew that Ferrier was now grinning broadly.

'No my lord, I know this castle and its lands like the back of my hand. It belonged to my family until my father bequeathed it to the crown on his death.'

'Do you look upon it as your rightful home? Do you believe I'm sitting in a throne that belongs to you?' demanded the king.

'No your highness. It ceased to be my home the minute my father died. As for the throne, I am but a second son, it was never going to be mine and I never wanted it either.'

'According to Capitan Ferrier, even as a child you dreamed of being a lord, he even believes you may have been responsible for your brother's death,' stated the king.

'With all due respect my lord, Capitan Ferrier has misled you,' said John now fully aware that his life was at stake. He had expected Ferrier to attack him in his sleep and had to admit to himself that this was a far more inventive approach. If he couldn't prove Ferrier was lying he would be tried and executed as a traitor.

'Sir John speaks the truth my king,' said William who had been hiding behind gold trimmed, thick burgundy velvet curtains, which were hanging behind the throne.

'Are you sure?' the king questioned.

'Yes. I cast a truth spell on Sir John and if he had lied he would have died right where he stands.'

'It would appear that Capitan Ferrier has attempted to dishonour your name,' the king said, then added, 'I grant you leave to demand satisfaction if you desire.'

'I do my lord, I do,' said John knowing he had no real choice in the matter.

'Are you mad,' ranted Arthur, 'he is the finest swordsman in all of the North of Tudorland.'

'In case you haven't noticed, I'm pretty good myself,' answered John.

'Yes, you are but if he's improved half as much as you have you'll last about thirty seconds,' stated the knight's friend matter of factly. Arthur then said sarcastically, 'why didn't you just challenge him to a joust?'

'He's not a knight so I couldn't,' answered John.

'Couldn't you just have said it would be beneath you to duel with someone so far below your station?' asked Arthur.

'You weren't there Arthur, I wasn't given a choice. I don't think it went the way Ferrier intended it to but I was still left with the feeling that I'd been set up.'

'What I do know is that it seems every time I turn my back these days someone is ready to put a knife in it and everyone I meet is keen to help them. Arthur, one way or the other, it's time for me to make a stand. If I don't, I'm not going to live long anyway.'

'You've always got Oliver and me watching for you,' said Arthur trying to reassure his friend the best he could.

'It's not enough anymore Arthur, it's just not enough,' said John.

John woke well before sunrise the next day. At first he simply sat on the side of his cot in silent contemplation. He then rose and walked over to the basin were he washed and shaved off the motley beard he had grown over the last few weeks that he had spent on the road. Then on impulse he shaved off the mustache he had worn since he reached manhood. Almost not recognising the clean shaven, dark haired, blue eyed man staring back at him in the mirror, he decided though that he liked the man he saw.

Personal grooming finished, he turned his attention to his sword and fleetingly remembered the day his father had given it to him.

He spent the next half hour sharpening its blade with the whetstone he carried trying to remember the last occasion he had taken the time to do this.

John looked over to the dull, dirty chain mail the king had sent him and wondered if Rupert knew that it had once belonged to his father. John decided that Rupert did, knowing his king's love for such ironies.

The next hour he spent polishing the armour and helm until it shined brighter than the morning sun. For the first time since his father and brother's deaths, John felt and looked like a real knight and he also realised he 'had' lied to the king, this was his home and he did want it back.

When John and Arthur (who was acting as his second) arrived at the parade ground they found Ferrier already waiting for them. Both men were surprised to see Sir Cecil acting as Ferrier's second.

'I was not aware you and Capitan Ferrier were friends Sir Cecil,' said John.

'Until yesterday we had never met but I like what the man stands for and what better way to see Tudorland's finest swordsman in action.' replied the knight.

'Sir Cecil, you have chosen sides and made your intentions quite clear. If I were you I would pray that the good Captain here wins because if he doesn't you could very well be next in line for my full attention,' said John so coldly that it sent shivers up the other knights spine.

'Do not worry good knight, this may not be how I planned this but little Johnny here will die and we will both get what we want,' said Ferrier with absolute confidence.

They then waited in silence for the king's arrival and to everyone's amazement he arrived on time obviously eager to witness the upcoming entertainment.

'Sir John you look splendid, infact you almost like a real knight,' said the king in a slightly mocking tone.

John and Ferrier knelt before the king waiting for his order to commence. John used this time to pray for his God's blessing should he lose this fight and for his forgiveness should he emerge victorious. Although John was a soldier, taking a life was not something he ever did lightly, even if it was someone like Ferrier.

Ferrier looked over at John expecting to see fear in the other man's eyes and was slightly shaken when he saw none.

'We will begin as soon as our guest arrives gentlemen. Don't worry, it will not be long, the wizard is just getting her now.'

Amber, who was being carried by two pixie guards while she was still tied to a chair, looked at the two men kneeling before Rupert. There was something familiar about the man in the gleaming chain mail but she was not sure where she knew him from. It wasn't until she saw Arthur that she realised it was Sir John.

The two guards placed her down unceremoniously beside the king, who turned to her and said, 'now that you have finally arrived we can see if Sir John here has what it takes to defend his honour.'

Now that she was closer to him it was obvious that it was John even though he was now clean shaven and dressed in armour instead of his well worn uniform. She couldn't help think how much he looked like a prince out of a children's fable.

Amber wondered what had happened since she had last seen him (only hours before) that had led him to such a desperate destination. She closed her eyes and prayed he lived to see another dawn.

When Amber opened her eyes and looked up she heard the king say, 'begin.'

The two men walked to the centre of the sparring ring (normally used for training purposes) and took up their positions. At the last moment John decided not to wear the helm that Rupert had given to him instead throwing it to Arthur for safekeeping.

The two fighters locked eyes momentarily and Ferrier asked, 'will you beg for your life like your brother did?'

'Stay calm, he's just trying to make you mad,' John told himself. He knew that if he lost his temper and control he was dead. He completely ignored Ferrier instead turning to the king and nodding to indicate he was ready to begin.

He then turned back to face the other man drawing his sword and stated coldly, 'this ends here and now.'

Ferrier charged at John unleashing a flurry of thrusts and slashes trying to end the fight quickly. He had been unsettled by John's lack of fear and did not want to give the other man any time to gain control of the fight.

Amber watched the man she didn't know viciously attack the man she had come to respect and watched in amazement as Sir John turned the attacks aside with seeming ease. She thought she saw panic in the other man's eyes but if she did it was gone in seconds.

The fight settled into a routine of thrust and counter thrust, each man looking for a weakness in the other but neither seeming to find one. All those present looked on in awed silence transfixed by the skill of the men before them.

Both fighters were now bleeding freely from small nicks and cuts, the worst being a gash on John's cheek and after fifteen minutes neither man held any real advantage.

Amber gasped as John slipped and fell to one knee. Ferrier, seeing this as his chance to finish this once and for all, stepped on John's sword as the knight tried to raise it to defend himself. With hate in his eyes he looked down at the man he thought helpless and thrust his sword aiming to kill John.

Ferrier had reacted exactly as John had hoped. John released his grip on his sword, rolled to his left drawing his dagger from its hilt as Ferrier's sword sunk into the ground just inches from his exposed body. Before Ferrier could recover John thrust his dagger deep into the back of his opponent's thigh severing his hamstring.

Ferrier fell forward screaming in pain and terror knowing he would not be able to defend himself.

'Please don't kill me,' he begged.

He screamed as he watched Sir John swinging his sword in what Ferrier believed would be the blow that would end his life.

At the last second John changed the direction of his sword and instead of killing Ferrier where he grovelled, severed four fingers from his right hand.

While Ferrier withered in agony John turned to Cecil and asked, 'now, do you and I still have unresolved issues?'

'No,' answered Cecil obviously terrified.

'Kill him!' ordered the king.

'No,' said John, 'I will fight and kill for you in your wars but I will not kill for your entertainment. If Ferrier does not die from blood loss he will no longer be a threat to me or anyone else for that matter and I will not take the life of a helpless man for anyone.'

Rupert looked at the bleeding man lying on the ground momentarily enjoying the man's agony.

He then yelled, 'you two,' pointing to the guards who had carried Amber to the duel, 'take him to a doctor. As for you Sir John, I will spare you your little outburst because so far you are the only one seemingly capable of controlling the fairy but rest assured you will not be spared again.'

'Now get her ready, we leave here within the hour and I will not be kept waiting. Have I made my self clear?' the king finished.

'Crystal my king,' answered John bowing.

With that the king turned and walked away followed by William one step behind and by Cecil at a far safer distance, the latter constantly glancing over his shoulder.

John walked over to Amber who was still tied to her chair and he cut the ropes that bound her hands and feet. Amber's hand went to her pocket with the intention of retrieving her handkerchief so she could use it as a bandage for John's cheek. However as she did so, she remembered that she had left it at the hunting lodge days before hoping her friends would find it and she now she wondered if they had.

'Why did you spare that insolent peasant my lord?' asked William.

'He intrigues me. True, he wouldn't kill Ferrier for me but he dealt with him brilliantly, Ferrier is no longer a threat to him is he,' it was a statement not a question, 'we may still go to war with the fairies and if we do I need good soldiers. More importantly I'll need good commanders so I'm going to promote him. He may not want it but I'm going to make him Sheriff of Huntingdon.'

'Why?' the wizard asked confused. The king had not long since seized this land and was now giving it back, it just didn't make sense.

'Because my inept wizard, Sheriff is an appointed position not a birth right and I can take it away from him whenever I choose. If he starts enjoying his new role I'll just take it from him. In the mean time he will take command of this region's army and lead them against the fairies if needed. The people here loved his father and I'm sure they will love him too and will follow him anywhere. Then when I no longer need him we'll address the lack of respect he showed me at the duel.'

When he finished his explanation, the king looked over to the wizard who was simply nodding his approval.

CHAPTER 14

CALEDONIA

'It's going to scar,' said Amber as Arthur finished stitching John's damaged cheek.

Both pixies laughed and John said, 'it's not my first and I hope it's not my last'.

'Why?' asked Amber.

'Because,' said Arthur, 'if we have a new scar we're still alive,' he pulled up his vest revealing several scars, 'any of these could have killed me but they didn't. A scar is a small price to pay if it means you survive.'

The wagon jerked into action and as it did John said a silent goodbye to his home totally unaware of the king's plans for his return.

'You should have killed him,' Arthur said after a few minutes.

'No Arthur, the princess is right, it's time to stand up for what I believe in. I had to take care of Ferrier but killing him would have been too easy for him and too hard for me. He will have to live with the knowledge I beat him and he is now no longer able to fight back. I have one less death on my conscience and did you see the look on Cecil's face? I don't think he'll bother us in the future. All in all, a good result I believe.'

Rupert and William now rode in the middle of the column flanked by three guards on either side. This close to the highlands and the centre of the rebel activity Rupert was taking no chance with his safety even with two of the rebel leaders locked up tight in one of his many dungeons.

They had travelled for three uneventful hours when the large black bird flew directly to the king landing on the pommel of Rupert's saddle. Rupert brought the column to a halt, stroking the bird's head fondly. He then removed the missive from the pouch attached to the bird's leg and read it. As soon as he finished Rupert ordered his men to spread out and search the surrounding area enabling him time to speak with William in private.

'Can you still cast the spell that protects us from missile fire?' he asked William.

'For a short time my lord,' William replied.

'Do it now!' Rupert ordered, 'the giants and the fairies have not only made it into the capital but they made it out again. They then headed directly to the hunting lodge where the wizard proceeded to magically penetrate your supposedly impenetrable magic barrier,' Rupert continued sarcastically, 'by the way, didn't you tell me that you were the only wizard that can do that? The wizard then found a handkerchief that the princess left behind, but don't worry, it gets worse, the girl then walked up to your impenetrable magic barrier and blew it apart. The only reason you still live, futile wizard, is because you are the best of a useless bunch but if your performance doesn't improve that will not save you!' he finished blustering as he did so.

'She is a most gifted wizard but I assure you my king I am superior in the art and given the chance I will prove it,' said the shocked and frightened William (more afraid of Neave than Rupert at the present moment).

'Let us hope you don't have to prove that', said Rupert in a tone that left no doubt the conversation was over.

It took no more than ten minutes for the entire column to reform. When they had reassembled and were ready to move forward Rupert sent for Sir Cecil.

When the knight arrived the king said, 'Sir Cecil, I have a job for you. I want you to ride back to Huntingdon then take an attachment of at least twenty mounted troops and as many wizards as you can find. Five fairies, two giants and a fairy dragon are following us and I want you to dispose of them. Kill the female first because she is a powerful wizard.'

'As you wish your highness,' said the knight saluting the king.

'If you fail me I'll hand you over to Sir John and tell him you insulted his honour,' said the king coldly.

'Have no fear my lord I will not fail you,' said the knight who now had no intentions of ever crossing Sir John after witnessing what he had done to Ferrier.

The rescue party followed the trail left by the pixie king and his escorts. The pixies had stayed on a road that headed due north and ran parallel to the woods to the west. After almost two days following their prey they saw a small tavern on the highway ahead. The tavern was a small, wooden, two story building with a thatch roof and had a small stable to the side.

The leprechauns and fairy dragon entered the woods to bypass the tavern without being seen. Neave, Liam and Finn rode past without stopping, meeting up with the other three north of the tavern. The two 'pixie officers' Adam and Dylan entered the tavern to see if they could learn anything that would be helpful and were surprised by how busy it was inside. All the tables were occupied, so the brothers found a place at the bar, ordered some ale and listened intently to the locals who gossiped excitedly about everything that had happened while the king had stayed at the tavern.

It was an hour before the brothers rejoined their friends. When they did Neave asked impatiently, 'well what did you learn?'

'They're only a couple of days ahead of us,' Dylan said excitedly.

'How have we caught up so quickly?' asked Neave shocked but delighted.

'It would seem Amber has been misbehaving,' said Adam with a wry grin. 'They stopped here for the night a few days back and while everyone was asleep she made a run for it. The king was so mad he killed the pixie that was asleep on guard duty, where he slept.'

'Apparently, she nearly made it but unfortunately stumbled into one of the hunting parties the king had combing the woods. The king then ordered the knight that found her to keep watch over her saying that if she escaped again the man or men responsible would die painfully. She may not have got away but she well and truly helped us close the gap,' Adam paused then added dramatically, 'what's more, I know where they are taking her and why.'

After a moment, Neave asked, frustrated by Adam's silence, 'are you planning on sharing this information with us or are you going to keep it to yourself.'

'I was just pausing for effect,' said Adam again smiling but the look on Neave's face convinced him it was time to continue, for as the famous talking frog once said, "Never upset a wizard."

'They're taking Amber to Caledonia and when they get there Rupert plans to marry her.'

'What! Are you sure?' asked Neave and Phil in unison.

'Yes, of course I'm sure,' said Adam sharply, 'one of the serving girls was forced to wait on the wizard and king and she overheard everything they said. It didn't take much encouraging getting her to tell Dylan and me what she knew.'

'He's insane! Amber would never marry anyone under duress, especially an evil murdering pixie king!' blurted out Neave and everyone, with the exception of Dougal and Derry (who didn't actually know Amber), nodded in agreement.

With discussions on the matter over for the time being they carried on for another hour and then stopped to make camp on farmland not far from the road.

While the others prepared the campfires, Dougal and Derry headed off in search for food and to their absolute delight came across a field of mushrooms. To the twins they looked like small button mushrooms but to their friends they were some of the largest mushrooms they had ever seen. Phil on the other hand, flew off by himself and ate his fill of the farmer's finest animals.

It was a happy and content campsite that night. They now knew they were not on a wild goose chase but were in fact closer to Amber then they had been at anytime since their mission had begun and to top it all off, they all really enjoyed the savoury mushrooms cooked superbly by Liam.

Derry and Neave took the first watch while the others turned in for the night. They had decided earlier that day that they would always take the first watch together so they could work on Derry's invisibility matter in private.

While they had travelled between the hunting lodge and their current location Neave had spoken to Phil at every opportunity with regards to his innate invisibility. She wanted to get a better understanding of how the natural magic worked for Phil because she believed the same principles would work for Derry.

They waited until they were sure that all their friends were asleep before they began.

Neave then asked Derry, 'is there any history of leprechauns using any magic other than being able to make themselves invisible?'

'Leprechauns love to sing about their history and heroes but I've never sang about anyone who was magic so I doubt it,' Derry answered.

'Well I guess you'll be the first then, if you want to that is,' said Neave, who before Derry could say anything, continued on, 'the first time I met you Derry I sensed untapped magical ability. Wizards as powerful as I am can sense magical talent in others, it's how we pick our apprentices. It's there with Dougal as well but it's much stronger in you. If you want me to Derry I'll teach you as much I can in the time that we have but I think it would be best if we kept it to ourselves for now.'

'Why didn't you tell me this sooner? We've lost so much time,' asked Derry not sure whether she was ecstatic or annoyed.

'King Strahan ordered me not to,' said Neave, 'he was worried it might put you in danger when you return home. In some worlds, people with magical ability are persecuted or even murdered in the most horrible ways. We don't know if your world is one them or not but Strahan did not want to take the chance just in case.'

'I don't know what happens in my world,' said Derry, 'but with all due respect to your king the decision was mine to make, not his.'

'I agree with you completely Derry and I did say that to the king but at the end of the day I must obey his commands,' Neave said with a sigh.

'So why are you disobeying his orders now?' Derry questioned.

'I may be splitting hairs here but Strahan never told me I couldn't teach you if you asked me to. I believe when you asked about the invisibility thing you opened up a loophole,' said the fairy wizard fully understanding how Derry felt.

'Thank you for looking for a loophole,' said Derry now starting to appreciate what Neave was doing. She then added excitedly, 'so let's get started.'

It had taken Sir Cecil over two hours of hard riding to reach Huntingdon.

He went straight to the office of acting Capitan Cowdrey and demanded thirty mounted troops. He was furious when he discovered there were only ten mounted troops stationed at the castle at any one time. To make matters worse Cowdrey said he could only spare fifteen foot soldiers and no matter how much Sir Cecil tried to bully him he flatly refused to give him anymore.

Cecil then stormed out of Cowdrey's office and went in search of the castle's wizards.

When he found them he wished he hadn't. There were only two wizards and both were just apprentices who were only good for keeping the wizard's tower clean while he was away on some personal business.

Two hours before nightfall, Sir Cecil led ten knights riding two abreast and fifteen infantry in three columns of five, out the south gates of Huntingdon, their prey less than a day's ride to the south.

Amber, Arthur and John watched from the back of their wagon as Cecil galloped off in the direction of Huntingdon.

'Where do you think he's going in such a hurry?' asked Arthur.

'Back to Huntingdon. Maybe Rupert's decided to give him command of the castle,' John suggested.

'I think if Rupert gave him command of a tent right now he'd take it just to get as far away from you as possible,' said Arthur laughing.

John nodded but did not answer and for the next half hour or so the three occupants of the wagon sat in silence all lost in their own private thoughts.

It was John who finally broke the silence saying, 'welcome to Caledonia princess.'

As John spoke Amber looked out of the wagon and realised that they had begun to climb a pass into the highland and within minutes the steep road was surrounded by small heather covered hills, the further they travelled the higher and more barren the hills became.

She looked back to John when she realised he was still speaking.

'Between here and Tantallon we are at our most vulnerable. If the rebels are going to attack us, it will happen soon.'

'How long will it take us to reach Tantallon?' Amber asked.

'All of today and the best part of the next two,' answered John adding, 'I hope you are not planning on trying to disappear between here and there because that would be a very bad idea. People who don't know this area have wandered into these hills and have never been seen again. And just to let you know the rebels tend to shoot first and ask questions later. As you can imagine they don't get too many answers.'

'I've given you my word remember,' said Amber more than a little hurt at the pixie knight's lack of trust.

'I'm sorry princess I know you have, it's just that to a lot of pixies their word doesn't mean much. There is, after all, the small matter of my life depending on you reaching Tantallon. What you do after we get there doesn't worry me, infact between you and me I'd love to see the weasel's face if you do manage to escape.'

'Rest assured Sir Knight I will not put you or Arthur's life at risk,' said Amber gently in an attempt to reassure both men.

The band stopped that night at the summit of a large hill that had been chosen because it would be easy to defend in the unlikely event of a rebel attack.

However unlikely an attack was, Rupert was no taking chances with his own safety. He evicted Amber and her guards from the wagon and had it placed at the centre of the camp.

Six guards surrounded the wagon at all times and four others guarded the perimeter of the camp.

Not content with the camp security, Arthur and John took shifts watching over the fairy princess, not because they were afraid she was going to escape but because they were both worried about her safety.

A camp in near panic woke Amber just before dawn. Two guards had been found dead at the edge of the camp. No one had seen or heard anything, all anyone knew was that it had happened some time between 2am when the watch changed and 6am when the bodies had been found.

A single arrow through the throat had killed both men but the most disturbing thing was each man had a note reading, 'Welcome to Caledonia Pixie King' pinned to his chest.

'Did you see or hear anything John,' asked Arthur who had been sleeping when the attack had happened.

'Nothing. I didn't even hear the guards hit the ground. Who ever did this was good, very good indeed,' replied John who couldn't believe two men had been killed on his watch without him even noticing.

'Sir John, the king requests your presence,' said a pixie guard neither John nor Arthur recognised.

By the time John arrived at the wagon Rupert, William and Capitan Woodward were all gathered and obviously anxious for his arrival.

'Sorry for keeping you waiting my lord,' said John bowing his head.

'You have heard of what happened in the night Sir John?' asked the king.

'I have my lord,' John answered.

'You fought the pixies in the Caledonian, did you not?' Rupert questioned and John nodded in answer. The king then continued, 'you are the only one amongst us who has had actual combat experience against brownies. What do you make of this attack?'

'I was awake when it happened,' admitted John, 'and I had no idea. They made no noise and have left no tracks for us to follow. These brownies are far more skilled than any I fought during the war. On the brighter side, I think it must have been a small band, maybe even a single brownie.'

'It would have taken more than one brownie to take out two of my men, they're the best men in the kings army,' objected Woodward.

'With all due respect captain,' said John, 'I doubt whether any of your men are half as experienced as Arthur or myself and neither of us had any idea what was happening. If it had been a large force we would have either heard them coming or we would all be dead now.'

'I'm really going to enjoy making the two brownie rebels squeal,' said Rupert with such venom that John shivered in spite of himself.

Rupert then turned directly to John and said, 'Sir John, you know how brownies think and you know this country better than any among us, so I'm giving you command of this column. When you get us safely to Tantallon I'm going to appoint you Sheriff of Huntingdon as a reward for your efforts on this mission.'

John was dumbfounded and it took him several moments before he was able to reply.

When he did it was only to say, 'what do you want me to do with the fairy princess my lord?'

'Do you trust the man who has been guarding her with you?' asked Rupert.

'With my life, your highness,' answered John without the slightest hesitation, then adding, 'he's been at my side for a long time now.'

'Good, then he can take care of our guest while you get us safely to Tantallon and since he's your right hand man I'll knight him when we reach Tantallon too, so then he will be able take up the position of your second in command in Huntington,' said the king in an almost friendly tone. He was beginning to believe that John was one of the few people he could totally depend upon.

After John had departed the king turned to William and Woodward, raised his hand and said, 'before you question my actions regarding Sir John and his little friend, just remember that since we began our journey those men are the only two who have proven themselves worthy of my approval, whereas the rest of you have proven yourselves to be incompetent fools!' he bellowed angrily, 'now both of you, get out of my sight,' he ordered.

'You cannot be serious,' said Arthur stunned after John told him about his meeting with the king.

'What really scares me is Rupert almost seemed sincere,' said John, who then added, 'Arthur I believe him, I think he really intends to make me Sheriff and you a knight. I'm sure he has ulterior motives I just don't know what they are.'

'Maybe he is just rewarding you both for services rendered,' said Amber (who had been momentarily forgotten by the two pixie soldiers) bitterly.

'I never intended any personal gain from your unfortunate situation,' said John now more then a little annoyed with Amber's attitude, 'perhaps if you had told me who you were when we first met I could have found a way to avoid our current circumstance.'

'How?' she snapped.

'I don't know,' said John as calmly as he could. He then turned to Arthur and said, 'I leave her in your capable hands my friend. And by the way, as a knight who is second in command to a sheriff, you will out rank Sir George,' he smiled, 'I don't think he's going to take that very well do you?'

'No, I don't think he will,' said Arthur smiling back, who of course, still had no memory of 'his' earlier altercation with the unstable Sir George.

Arthur waited until John was out of earshot before turning to Amber. Shaking his head at her like a parent disappointed with their child's behaviour he simply said, 'you had no right to talk to him like that.'

'I know,' sighed the princess unhappily, her head lowered in shame.

CHAPTER 15

ARRIVAL IN TANTALLON

'He must plan to take over Sarasidhe by marrying Amber,' said Neave to Finn, the pair were sitting in the back of the wagon as it headed for Caledonia.

'If he is, he hasn't done his homework,' said Finn.

'What do you mean?' asked Neave.

'If he was a fairy,' Finn answered, whose knowledge of fairy history, traditions and legends always amazed his friends, 'and he married Amber and then she died, by fairy law he would rule until the oldest child from the married couple turned eighteen and assumed the throne. If there were no children from the marriage, in theory, he would be king. This has only happened a couple of times in our history and on both occasions the new monarch abdicated immediately in favour of the rightful heir.'

'However, what Rupert obviously doesn't realise is, that if for any reason a member of the royal family marries a non fairy they immediately relinquish any right or claim to the throne.'

'Why?' asked Neave, trying to understand.

'There are two reasons, firstly it is very rare for such a union to produce children and secondly to make sure we fairies do not lose control of our own kingdom.'

'Who else knows of this law?' Neave said.

'The king certainly, the head of your order (wizards order) and most importantly Bishop O'Kelly and Cardinal Ormond because there is no way a coronation would go ahead without the blessing of the church.'

Neave felt the blood drain from her face as the implications of Finn's words hit her. If they didn't reach Amber before Rupert learned of his misinterpretation of fairy law her friend was as good as dead.

Any of the momentary joy she had felt at the tavern when they realised how close they were to their friend was forgotten.

'We've got to get to Amber fast,' she said, 'because there is no telling what that lunatic Rupert will do when he finds out that by marrying Amber he gains nothing but a wife.'

'Can't you just use your new spell to transport us to Amber?' asked Finn.

'No. I need to be able to visualise the exact location for it to work otherwise I could end up inside a tree or a stonewall or something far worse. The spell is still in its development stage and I don't even know if I could transport all of us at once,' answered the wizard.

Neave was about to go back to her seat beside Liam and tell him to speed up when she heard Phil yell, 'Stop!'

Neave hurried forward to see what Phil wanted. Once back beside Liam she looked for Phil but could not see him.

'Phil, you're still invisible, where are you?' she said.

'Sorry,' said the dragon regaining his composure.

'Right, tell us what has you so worked up,' Neave said to Phil.

'There's a column of twenty six pixies of which eleven are mounted and I think they're looking for us. We have to hide in the woods if we have a hope of avoiding them and we'll have to hurry, they're only about fifteen minutes away.'

'Are you sure they're looking for us?' Neave asked.

'No, but we can't take the risk that I'm wrong. We can't take on that many highly trained pixies without great personal risk,' Phil pointed out.

'You're right,' said Neave agreeing, 'but we need to find out for sure whether they are looking for us or not. We can hardly hide the wagon so one of us should stay with it and continue travelling along the road and see what information they can gather from these pixies.'

'That will have to be me,' said Liam.

'Are you sure Liam?' Neave said.

'Yes, it has to be me,' he replied, 'we're not running around some castle at night now or in some dimly lit tavern. Up close in broad daylight I'm the only one of us who can pass for a pixie, the rest of you are very obviously fairies.'

'I could cast a spell on any one of us to make us look like a pixie,' said Neave.

'Why waste your magic when you don't have to?' Liam said.

Before Neave could reply Phil cut in, saying pointedly, 'we're running out of time here, we have to take cover now.'

Liam watched his friends head for and eventually disappear into the nearby woods. Once they had vanished, Liam started forward again keeping the horses moving at a slow walk so his companions could keep him in their sight just incase he needed their help in the near future.

Liam was approaching the summit of one of the many small hills that he and his friends had encountered on their journey that day when he heard the sound of horses' hooves hitting the ground. As he crested the hill, he saw the pixie knight and his twenty five men less than a hundred yards away. Liam pulled his wagon to the side of the road as if to make room for the column to pass.

The leader of pixies raised his right arm to bring his men to a halt and then rode over to Liam and demanded, 'who are you and what is your business here?'

'My name is John sir,' said Liam saying the first pixie name that came into his head, 'and I am travelling to the borderlands to purchase Caledonian single malt for my master's tavern.'

'How far have you travelled this day peasant?' asked the pixie knight condescendingly.

'From just north of the last tavern my lord,' answered Liam bowing his head in respect.

'Why didn't you stay at the tavern?' Cecil asked for no other reason than sheer curiosity.

'My master will not let me enter any tavern other than his,' said Liam.

'Have you seen anything unusual in your travels?' Cecil asked.

'I don't think so my lord but I'm not sure what you mean,' said Liam hoping to draw out a little more information from the tight lipped pixie.

An exasperated Cecil yelled, 'have you seen any giants or fairies, man?!'

'I haven't seen any fairies and there's no such thing as giants,' said Liam shaking his head in mock disbelief.

Cecil looked at Liam as if he was the village idiot, then dismissed him with a wave of his hand and signalled his men forward.

Liam watched as the column disappeared to the south then continued forward to the north, waiting for his friends to rejoin him.

The others watched Liam from the distance and wondered what was happening. They were all relieved when the pixie troops headed south leaving their friend alone and heading safely north.

'I'll follow them and make sure they aren't planning on returning in a hurry,' said Phil.

'Good idea Phil,' said Neave, 'we'll keep to the woods until you return so we don't get caught in the open unawares.'

'On the way I'll let Liam know what's happening,' Phil said as he flew off.

Phil returned an hour later happy that the pixies had no plans to return in the near future. He found the twins, the brothers and Neave, who had fallen some distance behind Liam because of the difficulty they were having leading their horses through the woods.

Once clear of the woods however, the friends had no trouble catching up to Liam. Dylan and Adam rode their horses at a gallop, Derry and Dougal (being so much bigger than the others) only had to jog to keep up while Phil carried Neave on his back.

It was the most thrilling experience Neave had ever felt and it took all her considerable control not to scream in delight as Phil flew far higher than he needed too and then dove directly towards the ground. Neave watched as the ground sped towards her and just for an instant she feared Phil would not be able to pull up in time. At what seemed like the last second Phil levelled his descent mere feet from the ground and landed a few feet infront of Liam.

'Wow! What a thrill!' cried Neave as she jumped off Phil's back, 'we have to do that again and soon,' she finished enthusiastically.

'You're mad,' said Liam who had seen Phil's dive, 'there's no way you'd ever catch me on his back again.'

'I just hope our pixie friends didn't see the pair of you,' said Adam in a serious tone as he and his brother and the two leprechauns arrived.

'I'd better go back and get Finn,' said Phil a little sheepishly, 'and don't worry Adam I'll fly nice and low this time so no one will see me.'

'Just see that you do,' said Adam, a wry smile on his face.

Within minutes a low flying Phil returned carrying the last of the companions.

'I'm never doing that again no matter what the situation,' said a very pale and rather sick looking Finn.

'You big ninny,' said Neave laughing.

Finn, deciding now would be a good time to change the subject, ignored Neave's comment completely, turned to Liam and asked, 'is it us they are looking for or someone else?'

'Us,' said Liam bluntly.

'How is that possible?' asked Dylan.

'I wish I knew,' said Neave, 'it seems they have been one step ahead of us all the way. We get to Rupert's castle to find Amber and Rupert had been gone for days. Those hunting parties combing the woods must have been searching for us as well even if they didn't know it. And now this, it's as if they're watching our every,' she stopped mid sentence and chanted a few of the strange words her friends knew were magical and they all wondered what she was doing.

When she finished chanting, she shook her head in frustration and simply said, 'nothing.'

She turned to Phil and asked, 'can you sense any magic?'

'Only yours and,' he paused for a split second forcing himself not to look at Derry, then continued, 'and if anyone had been spying on us magically I would have sensed it immediately.'

'Could there be a spy in Sarasidhe?' asked Liam who was always slightly suspicious of what he called 'city folk', the ones he didn't know personally anyway.

'Not unless they are still following us,' said Neave.

'No one could have followed us all that way without us knowing,' said Adam.

'Phil, search the surrounding area, if you find anyone I want them bought here alive,' ordered Neave.

'On my way and rest assured if someone is following us I will find them,' said Phil confidently.

'I know you will Phil, we'll carry on and you catch us up when you can,' Neave finished.

The Shadow watched the group from a safe distance, relieved he had left his horse back where the fairy, which was driving the wagon, had separated from the others. He made this decision as he knew he would never have been able to hide the horse and would never be able to out run the fairy dragon.

He knew his present situation was dire but he had lived through worse and was sure he would live through worse again in the years to come. Calmly he covered himself in leaves and other foliage allowing a gap just large enough for him to breathe through.

Once covered, The Shadow settled down and waited, and waited, and then waited some more.

Finally an hour or so after dark he crept out from under his cover and headed back to retrieve his horse.

Phil began his search the moment his friends departed circling the camp in ever widening circles. After hours of searching the only thing he found out of the ordinary was a horse miles from the group. The strange thing about the horse however was that it was saddled but there was no sign of a rider anywhere. Phil thoroughly searched the area near the horse but found nothing and finally decided that the animal probably belonged to a nearby farmer and had somehow become free. He dismissed the matter and headed back to his friends noting happily that the pixie soldiers were still heading in the opposite direction and for now posed no threat to him or the group.

Phil found them waiting for him just south of a small castle.

'Well, were there any signs of anyone following us?' asked Neave.

'No, but I did find a saddled horse but no sign of a rider. My guess is that the rider was thrown from the horse and it galloped off for some peace and quiet,' answered Phil.

'What about the pixie soldiers?' asked Dylan.

'Still heading merrily south, they must be hours away by now,' the dragon answered. He then looked over at the castle and asked, 'so where are we now?'

'I don't know for certain,' said Finn, 'but I believe there are a number of small pixie castles like this one dotted all the way along the old pixie, brownie border. I believe this is one of them. So to answer your question as to where we are, I think it's just to the south of the Caledonian highlands,' he finished.

'So we're almost there then,' stated Phil.

'No.' said Neave. 'Finn thinks we're still at least three days away from Tantallon.'

'We'll have to keep well clear of that castle,' said Adam.

'Yes,' said Finn, 'but it's not just the castle we'll have to be weary of, there will most likely be pixies everywhere.'

'Right, careful it is then,' Dylan said.

They left the road and travelled over farmland until the terrain became too uneven. They thought about heading back to the road but decided it would be a better idea to stop for the night a safe distance from the road.

The Shadow reached the road hoping the dragon was gone. He almost wished the sky wasn't so clear and the moon light not so bright.

He did however admit to himself half an hour later that the fine night was a good thing allowing him to reach his horse far more quickly than he would have on a moonless night.

Finally reunited with his horse The Shadow slept for a short time to regain some energy and then set out in search of the pixie troops who were looking for the fairies.

He rode through the rest of the night and finally found Cecil and his men just as they were breaking camp and preparing to continue their hunt for the fairies.

The Shadow entered the camp demanding, 'who is your commander?'

The spy watched as a particularly pompous looking knight walked towards him. It was all he could do to stop himself from laughing in the knight's face. The man's long, waxed, pointy mustache was one of the most ridiculous things The Shadow had ever seen. This is the problem with the whole pixie army he thought to himself. The man before him had obviously reached his rank through an accident of birth rather than any military talent.

Just for the briefest second Wilberforce Smyth thought about turning his back on this entire mission. He no longer had any respect for anything pixie and as much as he hated to admit it to himself, he found himself admiring his quarry. He took a deep breath and reminded himself he was a professional and he had never failed to complete a mission.

'I'm in command here,' said the pompous pixie with the ridiculous moustache, 'what do you want and who do think you are coming into my camp and demanding an audience,' said Cecil in a superior, almost condescending tone.

'I'm Wilberforce Smyth, perhaps you've heard of me?' but when the spy saw no sign of recognition on the knight's face he added, 'I'm also called 'The Shadow' by some people.'

He smiled to himself as he watched the knight pale visibly when he realised who it was that stood before him.

'As to why I'm here, I was just wondering why, when your supposed to be searching for a small group of fairies and giants, you stop one of them, have a wee chat, then leave him to carry on his merry way while you head off in the opposite direction blissfully unaware.'

Cecil nearly snapped, 'what are you talking about,' but remembered who it was who was standing before him and instead said calmly and almost respectfully, 'I'm not sure what you mean sir.'

'That wagon you stopped,' said Smyth.

'Do you mean the tavern owner's servant?' asked Cecil bewildered.

'That was no pixie peasant you fool,' barked Smyth, 'it was a fairy forester, one of the party sent to rescue the fairy princess.'

'If you knew this then why has it taken you so long to tell me?' asked Cecil trying to stay calm.

As frightened of The Shadow as Cecil was, he was far more scared of his king, a king he may have just failed and he knew what happened to those who failed the king.

'Because Sir Knight,' said Smyth, 'there were four fairies, two giants and a fairy dragon between us. I would have been dead before you even knew I was there.'

'All right, I accept you couldn't have warned me immediately but I see no reason for it taking a mounted man this long to find us,' said Cecil now close to panic almost unable to think of anything other than what the king would do to him if the fairies got to their princess before he stopped them.

'Calm down you fool,' said the spy with undisguised contempt. Shaking his head he said, 'you can be rest assured I got to you as soon as possible but I have no intention of explaining myself to the likes of you.'

Cecil was about to interrupt but the deadly look on The Shadow's face convinced him now was not the right time to upset the man.

'As for the fairies,' Smyth continued, 'we will catch them well before they reach Tantallon. I know this area well, the highlands in particular and every shortcut between here and Tantallon. The fairies on the other hand will have to keep to the main highway or close to it anyway. We will have them within forty eight hours, if you and your men can keep up with me that is.'

'Well, what are we waiting for then,' said Cecil.

'It's happened again,' Cecil said to himself as he watched the spy riding infront of him. First Sir John had stolen his precious limelight and now this terrifying upstart had taken control of his men.

'I bet he won't take responsibility if we fail,' he muttered sulkily again to himself.

Smyth, whose hearing was remarkable, turned and looked at the knight and said, 'you truly are a pathetic little man, aren't you?'

Cecil couldn't believe the spy had heard his mutterings and made a mental note never to talk to himself again no matter how quietly he did it.

Smyth set a pace that the horseman had little trouble sustaining but at the same time pushed the footman to their limits. The experienced spy knew exactly how hard he could push 'his' men.

He finally brought the men to a halt half an hour after sunset. He did so only because he was almost exhausted, the spy had had only a couple of hours sleep over the last two days and he had driven himself far harder than he had intended.

He looked over to Cecil and said, 'see to your men,' then found a comfortable spot on the ground and was asleep in minutes.

'We'll take first watch,' said Neave as she and Derry walked towards the edge of the campsite.

In the day and a half since their close encounter with the pixie troops they had abandoned the small wagon and acquired three more horses. Liam had been upset at leaving the faithful draft horses behind but was realistic enough to realise they could never be ridden.

It was not just the wagon they had left behind they no longer travelled the well worn highway but instead now rode through the deserted highlands. This did slow their progress but they believed that it was a sacrifice worth making if it meant they reached their destination without running into more pixie troops. As long as they kept heading due north they believed at most they would only lose half a day.

Adam and Dylan watched the wizard and leprechaun take their position at the edge of the camp.

'Those two are almost inseparable these days,' said Dylan.

Adam nodded in reply and then stated, 'I think they're up to something. Yesterday when Phil checked the camp for magic did you see the way he looked at Derry?'

'No,' said Dylan.

'Maybe I just imagined it but between you and me little brother, I'm going to keep a close on those girls because you know how much I hate surprises,' Adam said.

'Hate not being 'in the know' you mean,' said Dylan laughing at his older brother's almost famous curiosity, 'one day your 'need to know everything' is going to land you in serious trouble.'

Adam looked at his brother and smiled, 'we had better get some sleep, you and Dougal are next on watch and no doubt it will be another big day tomorrow.'

'You have served me well again Sir John,' said the king relieved as they finally approached Tantallon.

'Thank you your highness. In ten minutes we will be safely behind the city's walls,' said the knight who was also relieved to reach the old brownie capital but for totally different reasons to his king.

For two full days John had led the king, fairy princess and their guards over passes and along roads that not even many brownies knew about. Some he had discovered during the war, others while camping in the region when he was a child.

The more time John spent in the highlands, the more he missed his past and the more time he spent with the king, the more he hated the man.

John decided that if the Rupert kept his word and made him the sheriff he would use his position to fight the king even though he would have to do it very carefully.

They rode through the main gates of Tantallon and were directed to General Broomfield who was not happy about having his evening meal interrupted, however when he saw who it was that interrupted him he decided it would be better not to complain and just send one of his men to gather food for his new guests.

While they waited for their food to arrive the king sent for Arthur while he and John listened closely to General Broomfield as he explained the current situation in Caledonia and the lack of rebel activity in Tantallon and its surrounding area since the capture of the two brownie rebel leaders.

Arthur arrived shortly after the food was delivered and was stunned when the king personally invited him to stay but it was what came next that really surprised him.

Rupert knighted him on the spot and ordered both he and John return to Huntingdon first thing the following morning to take up their new posts. The king also informed John that he would dispatch a runner in the morning with new orders for Sir Oliver and his men to report to Huntington immediately to assist him in raising a northern army to occupy Sarasidhe.

The cloaked figure slipped quietly through the castle keeping to the shadows. When he arrived at the dungeons he entered with absolute caution and silently crept up behind the sole guard who was sitting at a small table eating his evening meal.

The silent man drew his dagger from its sheath and slammed the hilt into the back of unsuspecting guard's head.

With the guard taken care of the cloaked man retrieved the cell keys from their hook on the wall and then wrapped them in a large piece of paper he had taken from his pocket. He then picked up a lantern from the table going from cell to cell until he found the one he was looking for.

Next he hung the lantern from a hook in the ceiling so it lit the cell before him. Finally he threw the paper containing the keys into the small cell and then disappeared into the night.

CHAPTER 16

THREE FUGITIVES

Izzy sprung from her straw bed at the sound of the keys hitting the cell wall and was immediately blinded by the light from the lantern illuminating the cell. It was not that the light was overly bright but to the brownie that had been locked in the cell for over a week, it was like looking directly into the sun.

When her eyes finally adjusted to the light Izzy looked around the cell to see what had made the noise. It did not take her long to find the object lying against the cell wall. She walked over to it and picked it up.

'What is it Izzy?' asked Cameron who had also been woken by the keys but decided to let the more excitable Izzy see what was happening.

Izzy who had just pealed back the paper to reveal its contents said simply, 'the keys.'

'Very funny, 'said Cameron adding, 'why is it so bright in here?'

'Cameron, I'm not kidding, 'said Izzy rattling the keys to get her friend's attention, 'what's more, there's a note with them.'

'What does it say?' asked Cameron now more excited and sitting up.

'That there is a fairy in the dungeons and if we don't take the fairy with us we will not get out of here alive and there's more, it says the spy is someone,' Izzy paused, 'called Murray.'

'Your cousin?' asked Cameron aghast.

'He's the only Murray I know,' stated Izzy, 'but we'll deal with that situation when we get back to the camp. The first thing we have to do is get out of here.'

'What if it's a trap?' asked Cameron.

'We've got nothing to lose, we're dead if we stay here so we might as well die trying to get away,' Izzy replied.

'You have a point but what about this fairy does the note say who it is?' asked Cameron.

'Nope, but we're about to find out. We've wasted far too much time discussing this, it's time to get out of here,' said Izzy as she walked over to the door, tried each key until she found the right one and then unlocked the door of the cell.

Izzy was about to start looking for the fairy when she saw the unconscious guard.

'We have to lock him in the cell,' she whispered to Cameron who nodded in reply and followed her friend over to the fallen guard.

They removed the pixie's weapons, grabbed an arm each and dragged him into their now vacant cell.

Once inside Izzy gagged him with material from his own tunic then tied his hands with some rope she had found outside the cell. They left the cell locking the door behind them and began a cell by cell search for the fairy.

It was Cameron who a short time later found who they were looking for.

'Izzy, over here,' she called as loud as she dared.

Izzy who was now carrying the lantern hurried over to her and shone the light into the cell.

'It's a girl,' gasped Cameron seeing into the small cell clearly for the first time thanks to Izzy's light.

Izzy hurriedly tried the keys until one finally opened the door. Before she had taken two steps into the fairy's cell the fairy girl was on her feet and ready to pounce.

'You're not pixies,' said the fairy. She then demanded, 'who are you and what are you doing here?'

'I'd like to ask you the same question,' said Izzy, 'but now is not the right time and most certainly not the right place. If we are going to get out of here we have to leave right now. Come with us and I will answer your questions later, if you answer mine that is.'

Amber followed the brownie women only because the alternative was staying as Rupert's prisoner. She didn't know where this new twist of fate would lead her but she believed she had to take what might be her last chance to escape the mad pixie king's grasp.

Izzy led the way through the castle and into Tantallon proper. The small brownie knew the castle and town as well as anyone having lived in the castle from the time of her birth until Caledonia had fallen to the pixies. When she had been a young child she had found an old book that dated back to just after the castle had been completed. The book detailed secret passages into and out of the castle.

Once she had explored the passages in the book she searched the castle from top to bottom until she was satisfied she knew every inch of it. After she had finished with the castle she moved into the town and to her delight had found a series of underground tunnels and catacombs. Izzy had spent years mapping the tunnels. In the beginning it had been a big adventure for her playing explorer hoping to find lost treasures but it eventually became on obsession.

It was to one of these tunnels she was now leading Cameron and the fairy.

'Izzy, this way leads to a dead end,' said Cameron with an anxious tone in her voice. Cameron had also lived her whole life in the brownie capital but although she knew the city well above ground she was still learning about the tunnels below.

Amber watched the blond brownie stop at a dead end and lean on the wall to her right side. The fairy watched the ground open up revealing a stairway leading into the ground beneath the wall.

'Come on, we should be safe down here,' said Izzy signalling for the others to follow her into the tunnel.

When Amber was half way down the stairs she heard Izzy shout, 'damn!'

'What is it Izzy?' asked Cameron concerned.

'I forgot, we need some oil and flint for the torches,' said the brownie annoyed by her lack of forethought, 'you two stay here I'll be back soon.'

Before the other women could argue Izzy had disappeared up the stairs leaving them in total darkness.

'I hate it when she does things like this,' said Cameron more to herself than to the fairy, frustrated that she couldn't see in the absolute darkness which surrounded them.

'Who are you?' asked Amber.

'My name is Cameron, unfortunately that is all I can tell you until my friend returns,' answered the brownie.

Then, like a bolt of lightening, it hit Amber and she knew without doubt who the two brownies were.

'You're the rebels Rupert was so keen to get his hands on,' it was a statement not a question.

As much as Cameron wanted to find out everything the fairy knew, she knew she would have to wait for Izzy's return, so she simply said, 'you now know my name, is there any chance of me learning yours?'

'Amber.'

The two women waited in silence for the missing brownie to return.

Amber briefly considered sneaking off into the darkness worried that she had escaped one prison for another. She decided against this only because she feared she would either get lost in the tunnels that could go on forever or fall and hurt herself in the darkness.

After what seemed like an eternity to the two women they saw a light approaching directly before them.

'Stay very quiet,' whispered Cameron, 'and hopefully they'll turn off before they reach us.'

Amber didn't reply she just slowly backed back until she had nowhere else to go.

They watched as the light grew nearer and nearer and just when they thought they would have to fight or be recaptured they heard a familiar voice call, 'you're not going to make me walk all the way over there are you?'

'Izzy!! You scared me half to death,' exclaimed Cameron, 'why didn't you tell us you wouldn't be coming back the way you left?'

'I didn't know it at the time,' said Izzy dismissively shrugging her shoulders.

'Right, now you're both here you can tell me what is going on,' demanded Amber.

'All right,' said Izzy, 'and I'll even go first but let's do it over dinner.'

With that Izzy put down her newly acquired lantern and then removed a pack from her shoulder.

The three women sat in a small circle and Izzy passed around the contents of the pack.

Cameron looked at the food delighted, the fine cheeses, fresh bread, exotic fruits, dried meats and fine wine were a far cry from the mouldy bread and stale water she had lived on while in her prison cell.

'Where did you get all this from Izzy?' Cameron asked, helping herself to the food.

'A certain pixie general's quarters. He's not going to be very happy when he wakes up and finds his breakfast gone,' laughed the small brownie.

'You broke into a pixie generals private quarters,' said Amber stunned.

'Not just his quarters, I left a note under his pillow while he slept explaining just what I'm going to do to him when our paths next cross,' replied Izzy still laughing.

Amber was speechless and Cameron just looked at her friend with disapproval written all over her face.

'Anyway,' said Izzy ignoring the looks on the other woman's faces, 'I said I'll tell you about Cameron and myself and now seems as good a time as any. My name is Isabella Wallace and my friend here is Cameron MacTaggart. We have been leading attacks on the pixie troops and generally making a nuisance of ourselves.'

'We were being held in the dungeon until Rupert arrived to deal with us but tonight someone unknown to us took care of the guard and threw the keys into our cell. The keys were wrapped in a note telling us that if we didn't take you with us we wouldn't get out of here alive, that's our story. Oh and by the way, if you call me Isabella you won't leave this tunnel alive,' she finished with a wry smile on her face.

'Wallace,' said Amber reconsigning the name, 'so you're a member of the brownie royal family, a princess perhaps?'

'Only just,' said Izzy, 'only a distant cousin to the queen. At the last count, I was twenty third in line for the throne but enough about me. Cameron and I are both very keen to know something about you, aren't we Cameron?'

'Yes we are,' answered the dark haired brownie, 'and Amber, call her Izzy, she really does hate being called Isabella.'

Amber started out by telling the brownies who she was, then she relayed the events since her capture. She hadn't intended to tell them everything but before she knew it she had.

'Great story Amber,' Izzy said impressed, 'I would have loved to have seen the 'Weasel's' face when he discovered you escaped from that tavern and I wish I'd known that Rupert, the Weasel, had arrived in Tantallon already. If I had I would have left him a little note as well. Perhaps I should go and visit him now.'

'No!' shouted both Amber and Cameron almost simultaneously.

'Settle down girls,' said Izzy, 'gee it's just as well these walls are sound proof otherwise you two would have the pixie army on us yelling like that.'

'Is she always like this Cameron?' asked Amber.

'No, I think she's on her best behaviour with you being a crown princess and all,' laughed Cameron.

Amber laughed in spite of herself and briefly wondered whether she would have been safer back in the small cell.

'Right,' said Izzy, 'since you two will not let me pay our 'friend' Rupert a visit, we should be on our way.'

Izzy stood up, hurled the backpack at Cameron who caught it and slung it over her shoulder asking, 'how long will it take to clear the tunnels Izzy?'

'Three hours give or take a few minutes but it will be light by then and the whole area will no doubt be crawling with pixies. So I'm going to take us to the closest exit to our camp. Once we get there we can get some sleep and then head out as soon as night falls,' explained Izzy who had already picked up the lantern and started forward.

'Where are we going Izzy?' asked Amber as they walked.

'We're going to see a man about a betrayal,' answered Izzy matter a factly.

'We're what?' stammered Amber.

'Cameron and I were betrayed by one of our own,' explained Izzy, 'and the note telling us about you has given us an avenue to explore.'

'Look Isabella,' said Amber, 'I haven't got time for this, I have to get back to Sarasidhe and warn my father.'

'No one is forcing you to do anything Amber,' said Izzy staying calm only because she understood the other woman's urgency, 'however if you return with us to our camp we will give you both a horse and armed guard and you will be back home before you know it,' she smiled at Amber and added, 'I'm sure I warned you about the whole Isabella thing.'

'I'm sorry Izzy,' said Amber, 'I'm just worried about my home and its people.'

'We know,' this time it was Cameron who spoke, 'we feel the same about ours, that's the reason that Izzy and I still fight on even though the war is officially over. We will continue to do so until we are either dead or victorious.'

Amber felt a strange sense of kinship towards the two women whom she had only known for a few short hours. The three of them continued to walk through the tunnels in a comfortable silence.

'Arrgghh nooo,' said Dylan who woke to a sword tapping him on the cheek.

'Don't move or you're a dead man,' ordered the man holding the sword.

Dylan looked around the camp and saw a dozen figures moving through. He opened his mouth to yell a warning to his sleeping friends but everything went black before he had a chance.

Minutes later Dylan was jolted back to consciousness after one of the camp's attackers tipped a bucket of cold water directly in his face.

It took Dylan a moment to realise where he was and what was happening. When he had regained full use of his senses he looked around the camp and saw his friends all with their hands bound behind their backs, even Dougal and Derry and Neave had even been gagged.

'If you disobey me again it will be last thing you ever do,' said his capture coldly.

The man helped Dylan to his feet and led him to his friends and then pushed him to the ground beside Finn.

'Finn, how did this happen and who are these people?' asked Dylan.

'I think they are brownie rebels who at first glance thought we were pixies. This is my fault, I was on watch when they attacked the camp and I never even saw them coming.'

'You two keep quiet,' demanded one of the brownies.

Then another brownie turned to speak, 'who is your leader?' he asked.

'The woman you have gagged,' said Liam.

'Wizard, I will remove the gag if you will give me your word you will not cast any spells,' said the brownie that seemed to be in charge.

'She can hardy do that while she's gagged can she,' said Finn who took a kick to the kidney for his trouble. The force of the blow caused Finn to cry out in pain.

'Angus, there was no need for that, the man had a point,' snapped the brownie who asked for Neave's word.

He then removed the gag, 'do I have your word?' he asked again.

'Yes, you have my word,' said Neave assessing the situation.

'Good, now who are you and what are you going here?' demanded the brownie.

'My name is Neave. I am the first wizard of the royal fairy infantry. Your man Angus just assaulted Prince Finn of the Royal House of Tralee. The brothers are Adam and Dylan the princess's bodyguards and the last fairy is Liam, I believe you would call him a ranger. The giants are Dougal and Derry O'Shea, their people are new allies to the fairy nation. As to why we are here, that's not something I can tell you not until you give us some reason to trust you. You can start by telling me who you are,' Neave finished.

'You are in no position to make demands Neave but out of politeness I will give you my name. It's Archie MacLeod. Now please tell me what you are doing in Caledonia.'

'Archie, you would be wise not to underestimate us. We have no dispute with any brownie, if we did you and your men would no longer be standing.'

'Do not threaten me fairy,' snapped Archie.

'Then untie us so we can be on our way,' said Neave firmly.

Before Archie had a chance to reply Dougal and Derry rose to their feet and moved over to stand beside Neave, the leprechauns towering over the brownies.

'Don't make us hurt you,' said Archie.

'Don't make me rip you to pieces,' said Phil appearing out of nowhere above Archie's head, 'tell your men to lay down their weapons or I'll eat every one of you.'

For a split second there was a stalemate, both sides knowing that if it came to a fight individuals from both sides would perish.

'Let him go Phil, I'm sure we can solve this peacefully, don't you Archie?' said Neave.

'Lay down your weapons men I believe the time for diplomacy has arrived,' admitted Archie.

He then drew his small hunting knife and personally cut the ropes that had bound the hands of Neave and her companions.

As a gesture of good will Neave spoke first telling Archie and the other brownies all about Amber's kidnapping and their mission to free her.

'The pixie king is an evil man,' agreed Archie, 'you are not far behind him though, he travelled these hills only a couple of days ago, Angus stumbled across their camp while on patrol. He killed the men on guard just to let Rupert know that although he has won the war our fight continues.'

'We have been fighting a gorilla campaign against the pixies since the fall of Tantallon but recently suffered a major setback when our leaders were captured by pixies. They are being held in Tantallon's dungeons.'

'When we saw you were a wizard being escorted by two pixie officers,' he pointed to Adam and Dylan who still wore their pixie uniforms, 'we thought you may have been important enough for us to trade for our leaders. To be honest it is not wise to roam the highlands dressed like a pixie soldier, infact it is quite often fatal.'

'How far from Tantallon are we?' asked Finn.

'A day,' answered Archie, 'but with the king present you'll never get to your princess without our help. Come back to our camp, it's between here and Tantallon. Meet my superiors, I'm sure if we join forces we can rescue your princess and my friends,' suggested Archie.

'We will travel with you until we reach your camp,' said Neave, 'I would like to talk to your commanders. I agree we stand a far greater chance of rescuing Amber with your help.'

They waited until sunrise then Angus led the way followed by the unusual mix of brownies, fairies, two leprechauns and a dragon, the likes of which had never been seen in Connaught before.

It was about an hour before sunrise when the three women arrived at the end of the tunnel.

'We're here,' said Izzy, 'we made far better time than I expected but there is still not enough time to get to safety before the sun rises. You two might as well get some sleep. I'll take the first watch even though we don't really need one down here.'

The other women, both extremely tired, happily accepted Izzy's offer.

Izzy watched and waited until she was sure both women were asleep. She then quietly backtracked a few hundred yards leaving Cameron and Amber behind her.

She had believed for years that she could navigate these tunnels blindfolded and now she was putting that theory to the test having left the lantern behind for the other two women.

She stopped, knelt on the floor and searched for the small lever that opened the secret door that she was looking for. Izzy cringed as the door creaked open. Praying the sound hadn't woken the others she entered the new tunnel closing the door behind her.

The tunnel she had taken led directly to the city's main gates. Now that her friend and the fairy were no longer slowing her down, Izzy almost sprinted down the passageway. It was still dark when she exited the tunnel and slipped into the night.

She positioned herself where she could get a look at the city gates to see if she could see how many guards were on duty. She watched as two pixie men rode out of the gates and briefly wondered who they were and what they were doing leaving the city so early but quickly forgot them when she realised there was not long until sunrise and if she was going to kill Rupert and escape she would have to hurry.

She crept through the city and entered the castle using a rarely used trade entrance. She then slipped into a secret door that led to passages that in turn led to all rooms in the palace that stood at the centre of the castle.

From the secret passage she could see into every room in the palace through a series of peepholes. By the time she found the room that Rupert was using he was gone. She knew it was his because the king had left behind a sword that bore the royal pixie crest in its hilt. He may have escaped her grasp for now but she was sure their paths would cross in the future and what could be better than killing the evil pixie with his own sword. She left Rupert a note explaining just how she was going to do that and then returned to the secret passage.

The castle was alive with activity when she exited the passageway. She had been inside the palace far longer than she had realised and the sun now shone brightly in the sky above. Although it was obvious to Izzy that the pixies were now aware of Cameron, the fairy princess's and her escape, she was confident that as long as she was careful she would have no problem avoiding capture.

Keeping to the shadows she made for the nearest tunnel and had to admit to herself she was relieved when she entered a tunnel that would lead her to her fellow escapees and to safety.

She arrived to find the other women still sleeping, laughed to herself and decided to join them.

The two riders left Tantallon before dawn keen not only to reach their destination but also intent on being nowhere near the city when it was discovered that the prisoners had escaped.

'Do you think it worked,' asked Arthur when they were well clear of the city.

'I hope so,' said John. 'I'm sure the brownies would have made it and taken Amber with them, as long as they took her with them, that is.'

'Do you think they would have taken the risk of leaving her behind?' asked Arthur.

'No,' said John. 'I think the fact that you managed to get the keys into their cell would have convinced them we had the power to carry out our threat to kill them if they left her behind.'

'Maybe we should have stayed behind to make sure,' suggested Arthur.

'No, if we had done that, Rupert would have made us stay behind and search for the rebels and Amber. This was definitely our only option,' replied John.

'You don't think the king will suspect our involvement because of our early departure do you?' Arthur asked John.

'No, he ordered me to return to Huntington as soon as possible and begin raising a northern army just incase it is needed. He was very happy when I told him we would leave before dawn,' John replied to his friend.

'I almost wish I could be there to see his face when he finds he has not only lost his rebels but his future bride as well,' laughed Arthur.

John laughed and nodded in agreement as the two pixie knights galloped towards Huntingdon.

CHAPTER 17

FRIENDS REUNITED

Amber was the first of the women to wake and was shocked to find Izzy who was supposed to be keeping watch, sleeping on the floor next to the lantern.

'Izzy, wake up,' said Amber shaking the sleeping brownie as she spoke.

'What is it?' demanded the brownie as she leapt to her feet.

'You were supposed to be on watch,' scolded Amber, 'why didn't you just wake me or Cameron when you were too tired to carry on?'

'Settle down princess,' said Izzy (who was not used to being spoken to in such tones by anyone other than Cameron) in a slightly mocking tone.

'Izzy, Amber's right, you should have woken one of us to relieve you,' said Cameron.

'Cameron do you really think I would leave us without a sentry if I thought we were in any danger?' said Izzy now more than a little annoyed. 'Look around, we are in a tunnel that no one except us knows about.'

'If you didn't think we were in any danger why did you suggest you took the first watch then?' continued Amber.

'Because it was the only way I could pay Rupert a little visit without a major argument with Cameron,' explained Izzy.

Cameron and Amber just stared at Izzy in silence, both women stunned by Izzy's revelation.

'You're determined to get us all killed aren't you,' said Cameron shaking her head almost resigned to her fate, 'now we know where you've been, you might as well tell us what you saw on your travels.'

Izzy told her brownie friend and fairy princess everything she had done and seen while they had been sleeping. She explained how unhappy she had been to miss her chance at ridding the world of the evil king while he slept. She could barely contain her delight as she described the absolute chaos in the castle. The pixies knew that they had escaped and Rupert was not a happy man and there was not a single pixie soldier who did not fear for their life at the moment.

She then described the two pixies she had seen leaving the city well before dawn. Amber knew immediately from Izzy's description that they had to be John and Arthur and was pleased they were no longer in the same city as the unstable king.

Izzy finished the tale by saying, 'and if Rupert's unhappy now, imagine how he's going to feel when he returns to his room to find his sword missing replaced by a note telling him that I've stolen it and his days are numbered.'

Both women had admit it was a beautiful sword and agreed Rupert's face would be worth seeing.

'What time do you think it is?' asked Cameron who had lost all track of time in the eternal darkness of the tunnels.

Izzy walked over to the end of the tunnel and removed a panel one foot long and one foot high.

She then turned to her companions and said, 'it's still light and there are pixies everywhere.'

'How do you know that?' asked Amber.

'Come and have a look,' said Izzy waving the other two over.

Cameron and Amber went over and looked into the small portal Izzy had uncovered. They looked into the tiny hole in the wall and could not believe their eyes. Before them they could see an open field with several pixie units heading in different directions.

'Is it magic?' Amber said amazed at what she saw.

'No, it's all done with mirrors,' said Izzy.

'If we can see them, how do you know they can't see us as well?' Cameron asked.

'The mirrors only work one way, all they can see from the outside is a small hill with what looks like a rabbit hole at its base,' replied Izzy.

'How far outside the city walls are we Izzy?' asked Cameron, 'all I can tell from what I can see is that we are somewhere to the east of the main walls.'

'A couple of miles, that's why so many pixies are running around up there,' answered Izzy, 'how much food have we got left, I'm starving and since we're not going anywhere in a hurry we might as well use the time constructively by planning our next move over a meal.'

Dougal and his friends reached the brownie rebels main camp not long after midday. The arrival of a couple of giants accompanied by a dragon and five fairies caused quite a stir in the rebel camp.

'Archie, what is the meaning of this?' demanded a particularly tall, rosy cheeked brownie, 'why have you brought these strangers here?'

'Duncan, I assure you my reasons are sound. Call a council meeting and I will explain them to you and everyone else,' said Archie.

Half an hour later Archie and his guests were called before Duncan and the rest of the brownie council. With Izzy and Cameron both captured and other members of the brownies away with other patrols, only five of the council were present.

Duncan sat at the centre of the council flanked on the right by an overweight man with a mustache and a thin, strangely dressed woman with short white hair. On his left side sat two fairly non descript looking brownie men.

Archie explained who his guests were and what they were doing in Caledonia and how he believed it would benefit both parties if they worked together against the common foe.

Duncan agreed and sent a runner to call in all the rebel patrols in preparation for an attack on Tantallon.

As the council meeting broke up Dougal watched as two of its members made their excuses and left. He could not explain why the pair left him with a strange feeling of unease but they did.

'Who are they Archie?' Dougal asked pointing at the departing pixies.

'Murray and Liz,' said Archie, who then added,' whenever you see one, you know the other is never far away. Murray is Izzy's cousin and may even be the next in line to the throne. No one has seen any other members of the royal family since Tantallon fell.'

'Do you think the pixies killed the royal family,' asked Dougal shocked.

'We don't know. There are rumours that Rupert had them sent to work in his mines but nobody knows for certain if this is true or whether he simply had them executed,' answered Archie.

'The sooner we deal to this man the better,' said Dougal. He then asked, 'how long until the rest of your troops arrive so we can get on with this?'

'They should all be here by early afternoon tomorrow,' explained the brownie, 'that will give them time to rest before we make our attack on Tantallon.'

'Shouldn't we leave as soon as they arrive?' asked Dougal.

'No. Our men and women will need to rest before they fight. Anyway we would be like lambs to the slaughter if we attacked the city in the full light of day,' Archie explained.

'So all we can do is sit here and wait? Oh well, I guess one more day can't hurt can it,' said Dougal hopefully.

'Right, I think we should make a move,' said Izzy as she looked into the small portal and saw that night had fallen.

Izzy pushed the hidden switch that opened the secret door that allowed them access to the surface. She then drew the king's sword from its scabbard that was now firmly strapped to her waist and led the others out of the tunnels.

'How long will it take us to reach your camp?' asked Amber.

'In this light and with pixies search parties everywhere, at least five or six hours,' said Cameron.

'You two keep it down,' whispered Izzy, 'sound carries a long way on a still night like this and the last thing we need is to let every pixie in Tantallon know we are out here.'

'Sorry,' whispered Cameron who then added very quietly, 'let's go home.'

They travelled cross country avoiding all the roads and anywhere that may have them stumble across enemy units. Amber was impressed by how well the two brownies knew the area. Even in the almost total darkness of night they seemed to have little or no trouble finding their way. As well as she believed she knew the area around her own city she knew she could never travel its lands at night without a lantern.

When they reached the foothills of the highlands Cameron risked lighting the lantern that she carried with her.

'Is it safe to do that?' asked Amber.

'The alternative is to risk falling into a ravine or worse,' said Cameron.

'I doubt that we'll find too many pixies in the hills. They tend to avoid them because those who enter the hills very rarely leave, alive anyway, that is,' said Izzy, a slight smile on her face. They continued on for another half hour or so then stopped briefly to finish the last of the food Izzy had 'borrowed' from General Broomfield and then continued on towards the rebel camp.

As they finished their meal Amber asked, 'how long until we reach your camp?'

'An hour, two at most,' answered Izzy. She then added as she got to her feet, 'the sooner we leave, the sooner we arrive.'

'Look Norman, do you see that light?' said the brownie sentry pointing, 'it's heading directly towards us, wake the others.'

The sentry named Norman hurriedly woke the rest of the brownies who manned the small outpost which was only half an hour west of the main rebel camp.

'What is it Norman?' asked the brownie in command of the outpost.

'There is someone heading this way,' he replied.

The other brownie asked, 'is it a pixie?'

'I don't know, they are still too far away. All I saw was a single light heading in this direction, I don't even know how many of them there are,' said Norman.

'Go to the main camp and warn them,' ordered the brownie officer, 'the rest of us will join Gordon and deal with whoever it is.'

'On my way sir,' said Norman who turned and ran off in the direction of the main rebel camp.

The officer then turned to the rest of his men and said, 'right you lot, follow me.'

Moments later the brownies arrived at Gordon's sentry post.

'How far away are they now?' asked the brownie officer quietly.

'Down there Andrew,' whispered Gordon, 'they should pass directly below us within the next ten minutes.'

'Right then,' said Andrew who then ordered his men into a position from where they could ambush whoever it was that approached them.

The brownies waited silently preparing themselves for the battle that may lie ahead. Some of them were secretly hoping a pixie patrol was heading their way, while others just hoped they would live to see the dawn. They all lay in wait watching the light get closer and closer.

The silence was broken when Gordon cried loudly, 'it's Izzy and Cameron!'

Every brownie including Andrew left their positions and ran to greet the approaching women.

Amber watched startled as five figures appeared from out of nowhere from the ten feet above and fifteen feet ahead of her. Initially she believed that they were attacking all three of the women but she then heard them yelling Izzy and Cameron's names in obvious delight.

'I knew they wouldn't be able hold you two for long,' shouted Andrew triumphantly grinning from ear to ear.

'It took us far longer than we had hoped my friend,' said Izzy a broad smile on her face too.

'Gordon, take command while I escort our friends,' said Andrew who noticed Amber for the first time, 'and their guest to the main camp.'

As Andrew and the three women vanished from sight Gordon turned to the man beside him and said, 'I bet that's the fairy princess.'

The arrival of the brownies and fairy caused great excitement not only amongst the brownie rebels but also the small party that had journeyed for many days in search of their princess. Amber was delighted to see her friends and very pleased to meet the leprechauns. In between embraces and hugs they all exchanged tales of their recent adventures and how they came to be at the brownie rebel camp at the same time.

Liam was particularly pleased to hear that Sir John and Arthur were both alive and in good health (if it was of course the same two men he had encountered earlier whom he had come to admire).

'Do you think it was one of them who gave the brownies the cell keys?' asked Liam.

'It had to be, no one else knew I was there apart from the king, his pet wizard and his bodyguard. There's no way any of them would have helped me escape unless it was in a wooden box,' said Amber.

'I don't know many pixies,' said Liam, 'but of the ones I've met over the last couple of weeks, they're the only ones who would put themselves at risk to help someone else.'

Sometime later it was decided that they should retire for what was left of the night so they would be refreshed for the full council meeting that had been called for noon the following day by which time the full council should be present.

Before Izzy retired she called Andrew aside and asked him to watch Murray and Liz and to wake her if either of them made any attempt to leave the camp that night. She told him that she would explain everything to him in the morning. He accepted his assignment and she headed off for some much needed sleep.

Not everyone in the brownie camp however was happy about the safe return of the rebel heroes. Murray and Liz at first watched the celebrations from a distance. They both reluctantly joined in, Murray hugging his cousin and patting Cameron on the back praising them for their escape and the rescue of the fairy princess. They only did this as they knew that if they didn't join in with the celebrations their absence might cause suspicion.

After the brief but buoyant celebrations the now worried traitors headed away for a private conversation.

'Do you think she knows?' asked Murray, now close to panic, 'I'm sure I saw her glaring in our direction when she was talking to Andrew.'

'Snap out of it, you're just being paranoid as usual,' scolded Liz, 'there is no way she can know it was you who betrayed her,' she added with extra emphasis on the word 'you'.

'We are in this together,' snapped Murray.

'Of course we are,' said Liz not altogether convincingly.

'What are we going to do now?' asked Murray.

'Nothing,' said Liz with indifference.

'Shouldn't we contact General Broomfield and tell him that my cousin and the fairy princess are here?' persisted Murray.

'You really are a fool aren't you Murray,' said Liz, 'for one thing, if Izzy is on to you, I mean us,' she quickly corrected herself, 'don't you think she'll be expecting us to make a run for it tonight? We wouldn't make it to the first outpost and are you forgetting that there is going to be a council meeting tomorrow. Not your normal run of the mill council meeting but one with two members of the fairy royal family, not to mention a high ranking fairy wizard and two giants. Don't you think that the good General and more importantly the pixie king would like to know what matters are discussed at such a meeting?'

'As always you are right and you will be well rewarded when the pixie king makes me Governor of Caledonia,' said Murray, his confidence returning.

CHAPTER 18

IZZY'S PLAN

Dougal woke to the smell of sizzling bacon and frying eggs, he stretched and looked around the campsite. Already the rebel camp numbers had grown to over two hundred with another fifty expected to arrive by early afternoon.

He watched as brownies carried whole deer and other animals which had already been prepared for cooking to the campfires in preparation for the evening banquet which would follow the council meeting.

'They're a busy lot aren't they,' said Derry who had woken and seen her brother studying the camp.

'They certainly are and it looks like we could be in for another late night,' said Dougal.

'There must be two hundred brownies here now, I wonder how many more are coming,' said Adam joining his friends.

'I thought I heard one of them say last night that they numbered just over two hundred and fifty in total,' said Dougal, 'and they have all been recalled for the council meeting.'

'I thought they might have cancelled it now that their leaders have arrived home safely,' Adam said.

'Apparently the one called Izzy insisted upon it,' said Derry, 'I think she has something special planned.'

'I guess we'll find out all in good time,' replied Adam, 'let's eat, I'm famished.'

And with that the three friends went off in search of breakfast.

'It could work Izzy but it's risky even for you,' said Cameron.

'But you'll back me up tonight, right?' asked Izzy.

'Don't I always Isabella,' said Cameron, a mischievous smile on her face, 'but we are going to have a hard job convincing everyone else that it is a risk worth taking.'

'They always see our side in the long run Cammy,' said Izzy deliberately using the nickname that Cameron hated as much as she hated being called Isabella.

Cameron was about to ask Izzy how she intended to put forward her proposal when she saw Andrew approach.

'Good morning Andrew,' she called to warn Izzy of his approach and to make sure Izzy didn't say anything they weren't ready for him to hear.

Izzy turned to face the approaching brownie and said, 'good morning my friend, any news from that little task I assigned to you last night?'

'Nothing out of the ordinary,' said Andrew, 'they talked for a while then retired. Liz surfaced half an hour ago and Murray was last up as always, he has only just left his tent.'

'Are you sure they were both there all night?' asked Cameron.

'Positive,' was his simple reply, 'I don't suppose you're ready to let me know what this is all about are you?'

'All in good time my friend, all in good time. You have been up all night. I think you should get some sleep before tonights meeting.'

Andrew, who was used to not knowing what was going on, just shook his head and smiled at the two women then headed for bed.

'So our chubby little friend held his nerve last night, that does surprise me, good for him,' said Izzy who always enjoyed a challenge.

Dougal looked around at the unusual mix of races gathered together. The council was made up of ten brownies, three fairies and one leprechaun.

The brownies were made up of the five members present the day before, along with Izzy and Cameron and three others who had arrived over the last twelve hours. Some of the brownies like Duncan were lairds (the brownie equivalent of a pixie lord), others were officers from the brownie army. Izzy and Murray were minor royalty and the rest were those who had proven to be highly skilful in the art of guerrilla warfare or displayed sound leadership. Amber, Finn and Neave represented the fairies and Dougal the leprechauns.

Dougal had not wanted an active part in the council but Derry had insisted saying only he could represent the leprechauns because he was a direct descendant of Seamus O'Farrell and was to be a future councillor of Caer Gorias.

With the exception of a few sentries all two hundred and fifty brownie rebels had gathered to watch the meeting. All eyes turned towards the small blonde brownie and silence fell as she rose to address the council.

Instead of calling the meeting to order Izzy looked at each member of the council and then simply said, 'I have a plan.'

'Izzy we are not here to listen to one of your hair brained schemes,' said Murray, 'we're here to share knowledge with our new friends and discuss the possibility of an alliance against the pixies.'

'Yes Murray we are,' said Izzy keeping her tone light and friendly, 'and with the help of our fairy and giant friends here, we can take the fight to the pixies together. Now, as I said, I have a plan on how we can do that.'

Before she had a chance to continue Murray again interrupted her saying, 'Izzy we cannot force our new friends into helping us in our war against the pixies.'

'What are you talking about Murray?' asked Izzy beginning to lose patience with the brownie traitor but she was not ready to expose him yet.

'Let's just say you have a way of manipulating people without them knowing it cousin,' explained Murray.

'Rest assured Murray, it is Murray isn't it?' said Amber who carried on before he could answer, 'neither my friends nor I will be manipulated into doing anything we do not want to do. As for your war with the pixies, I think it became our war as well the day Rupert kidnapped me. Now don't you think we should let Izzy tell us what she has in mind then we will be able to decided whether it is worth doing or not because I've always believed you have to hear a question before you can answer it.'

'Thank you your highness,' said Izzy politely, 'now if there are no further objections,' she looked directly at Liz when she spoke, then after a small pause continued, 'I think now is the time to send the pixies a message. Before Cameron and I were captured we managed to do a full recognisance of Tantallon. The pixies only have about five hundred troops stationed there at the moment and they have grown complacent. So far our raids have all been hit and run against small forts and border towns, or against their supply columns and patrols. The last thing they will expect is an attack on Tantallon particularly this soon after our escape.'

'Izzy,' this time it was Duncan who interrupted her, 'we don't have enough men to attack a well defended farmhouse let alone a highly fortified city like Tantallon. If there are five hundred troops behind its barricades it would take at least a thousand of us to liberate it. Even if by some miracle we managed to take the city we'd never be able hold it so what's the point?'

Izzy waited patiently for Duncan to finish and when it was obvious that he had she then continued, 'I'm not saying we should stage a frontal attack on the city walls, I'm suggesting we take the city from the inside,' she saw Murray start to rise to protest so she quickly added, 'if everyone could just let me finish I'll explain how we can do this.'

Murray shook his head and mumbled something indecipherable but returned to his seat and Izzy continued.

'There is a series of tunnels running under Tantallon and as far as I know I'm the only one who knows where they are. The only reason I haven't mentioned them before is I believed it was best to keep them secret until we needed them. Cameron, Amber and I used these very tunnels to escape our captors.'

'Now, my plan is to enter the tunnels after dark and then split into two forces. One will secure the city while the other will take the castle and the palace. I propose that I lead a smaller force in the attack on the palace and Duncan you take command of the larger force that will take the city.'

'We'll have to attack after dawn unfortunately because it will take most of the night to get into position so we will lose the advantage of the dark. I don't think it will matter too much however as they should be thrown into disarray by the unsuspected attack from within the city walls.'

'You're right Duncan, we won't be able to hold Tantallon but imagine what it will do to pixie moral when we take the city but I have to admit that it is not my main reason for attacking the city.'

What I really want to do is kill Rupert and this may be the only chance I ever get.'

Amber, Finn and Neave looked at each other and nodded.

Amber stood and then said, 'we are with you.'

'So are we,' said Dougal, 'although I don't think we will fit in your tunnels,' he said with obvious disappointment.

Izzy looked up at Dougal and smiled saying, 'you, your sister and the dragon are vital if my plan is going to succeed.'

'How?' asked Dougal getting excited.

'Do you see that rock over there?' asked Izzy pointing to her right.

Dougal looked over and saw what was to him, a large stone. He walked over to it and picked it up.

'Do you mean this stone?' he asked surprised and confused.

'Yes, I do,' she answered, then asked, 'how far do you think you can throw it?'

'Only one way to find out,' he said as he turned and threw the stone with all his might.

Izzy smiled as she watched the rock disappear into the distance.

'Right,' said Izzy, 'we have our diversion. Dougal and Derry can be our 'catapults' and they can lob rocks at the outer wall. The pixies will most probably reinforce the city wall incase we stage a full frontal attack. When we attack them from within the castle they won't know what's hit them. The castle will be ours in minutes, we can't fail.'

'I like it,' said Duncan, 'and I think it will work as long as your tunnels are large enough to hold our entire force and as long as we can move through the tunnels quietly.'

'The tunnels are large enough to hold five times our number and were built to be soundproof,' Izzy said reassuringly.

'Then you have my support Izzy,' said Duncan.

One by one the brownies stood and offered their support of Izzy's plan until only Liz and Murray remained uncommitted.

Before Murray could protest, Liz stood and said, 'as always you have my unconditional support Izzy.'

'Yes, yes,' said Murray, 'I agree now is the best time to cut the pixies deeply. When do we attack Izzy?'

'Tomorrow we rest, many of us have travelled through the night and haven't slept properly in days. I want us at our best for this attack and we need some time to work out the details of the attack,' said Izzy.

'It's settled then,' stated Duncan, 'we make our preparations tomorrow and break camp early afternoon the following day.'

'Bring on the food and entertainment!' shouted Izzy.

It was not the late night that Dougal and Derry had expected. Everyone was far too preoccupied with the task ahead of them and within a couple of hours the leprechauns and their fairy friends sat alone around the fire at the camps centre.

'Has anyone seen Phil?' asked Liam who had just realised he hadn't seen the dragon all day.

'He's off helping Izzy with something,' said Amber.

'Doing what?' asked Adam.

'I don't know, it's top secret,' laughed Amber.

'You spent some time with her Amber, what's she like and can we trust her?' Neave asked.

'Yes we can trust her, she rescued me when she didn't have to.'

'Didn't the note with the keys tell her she was dead if she tried to leave without you?' Dylan asked.

'Yes it did,' replied Amber, 'but the way Izzy knows Tantallon, once out of her cell she and Cameron could have easily disappeared without being seen. The only problem with Izzy is that she takes far too many risks. While Cameron and I were sleeping she went back into the castle and into the palace trying to find Rupert. She wanted to kill him were he slept. She has no regard for her personal safety and that could be a danger to all of us.'

'So what are we going to do about her?' asked Neave.

'Nothing.' said Amber. 'This plan of hers is going to work, Tantallon will fall. You and I just have to make sure she doesn't get herself killed in the process. As for the rest of you, I want you with Dougal and Derry outside the castle.'

'No!' said Finn standing and almost shouting, 'I must be part of the attack. Since we left Sarasidhe we have been avoiding pixie soldiers. Now that I finally have a chance to fight them you're not ordering me to sit outside and watch the others fight, I just won't stand for it,' he finished adamantly.

'Finn, you're not thinking,' said Neave gently, 'we can't leave Dougal and Derry unprotected. The pixies aren't going to sit back while 'catapults' bombard their walls. They're going to send troops out to deal with the danger and that's where we need you. You are most likely going to be heavily out numbered and the fighting will be fierce. It will take a commander of considerable skill to complete the mission successfully.'

Finn thought about what Neave said.

'All right I'll do it but it is with reluctance. I still think I'd be much more use in the thick of the fighting.'

Not long after that the friends decided it was time to call it a night and all but Dougal headed off to get some sleep. Left by himself the leprechaun looked into the embers of the dying fire, took out his little tin whistle and played a quiet tune.

'What are we going to do?' asked Murray.

'I'm not going to do anything,' said Liz, 'I think you should leave immediately and warn your friends of the impending attacks and try to return before dawn so hopefully no one notices your absence.'

'Why do I have to warn the pixies?' he asked.

'Because if Izzy succeeds and kills Rupert the pixies will return in larger numbers and wipe us off the face of Connaught. If she fails what do you think Rupert will do to you if you don't warn him?'

Murray thought about what Liz said and then asked, 'what if I'm late back?'

'I will cover for you,' she lied.

'All right I'll go,' said Murray but only because he could see no other alternative.

Murray made his way to the horses, looked around to make sure no one was there to see him and then untied one. He led it away from the camp avoiding all the camps outposts and then left in the opposite direction to Tantallon. He had an uncomfortable feeling he was being watched but he was certain no one was following him. When he was satisfied he was safely clear of the camp he mounted the horse and galloped towards the city. The only thing that gave the brownie traitor any joy was that three of the four moons were full and shining brightly in the night sky so at least he would have no trouble seeing where he was going.

The more the distance grew between Murray and the rebel camp the greater his feeling of being watched became. He stopped his horse, looked all around him but still saw nothing, so he continued on. As he rode on he briefly considered turning south and hiding in the highlands but dismissed the idea as he sighted Tantallon in the distance.

Murray sighed in relief as he neared the city. He would soon deliver his message to the pixie general or perhaps even the king himself and then he could return to the camp. He was making exceptional time and he knew that if he continued on at the same rate he would be back well before dawn.

Then suddenly from out of nowhere, he felt himself being torn from his saddle by what felt like a giant bird. He struggled to break free then froze in terror when he realised he was being held by something he couldn't see. Within seconds he was hundreds of feet above the ground, panic set in.

'Why are you going to Tantallon?' asked a booming voice, 'if you lie to me I will know and I will drop you like a hot stone.'

Murray took one look at the ground way below him and told his unseen captor everything, fully convinced he was going to die if he didn't co-operate.

When Phil heard the explanation he turned and headed back to the rebel camp. It took all his self control not to drop the traitorous man and let him fall to his death, a death Phil believed he richly deserved.

Murray, terrified, had a thousand thoughts going through his head. Who or what had him, where was it taking him, and what was his fate. He begged to be released but knew it was futile.

Phil made the flight back as uncomfortable as possible for Murray. From time to time he would fly so high that the brownie found it hard to breathe as well as it being unbearably cold. He would then dive thousands of feet towards the ground pulling up only yards from the surface. His final means of torturing the terrified brownie was to occasionally let go of him, letting him fall a hundred feet or so before catching him again. Yes, it was fair to say Phil was enjoying the return journey back to the rebel camp.

CHAPTER 19

THE ATTACK ON TANTALLON

'Why?' shouted Izzy.

Murray who was tied to a tree just looked at her saying nothing but all those gathered could see the fear in his eyes.

'When this gets out it's going to badly affect morale,' said Duncan.

'If we kill him now and hide the body, we can say he's gone ahead on a scouting mission,' suggested Cameron the only other brownie present.

Izzy looked over at her friend in surprise. She'd known Cameron her whole life and had never heard her talk like this before.

Cameron seeing Izzy's expression said, 'it's one thing betraying you and me but he was prepared to sacrifice two hundred and fifty lives,' she turned to Murray, 'what was in it for you, you worm!' she demanded poking him in the chest as she spoke each word.

When Murray still remained silent Neave (who was also present along with Amber, Finn, Phil, Dougal and Derry) said, 'I have a spell that will make him talk.'

'Is it painful?' asked Cameron.

'No,' answered Neave shaking her head.

'Pity,' stated Cameron bluntly.

'Do it,' said Izzy.

· Murray watched as Neave walked towards him and before she had a chance to cast her spell he blurted out, 'they promised to make me Governor of Caledonia.'

'You fool,' spat Izzy, 'as far as we know you're now the next in line for the throne. When we win and drive the pixies from Caledonia you would have most probably been our king!'

'We can't win,' snapped Murray, 'even if you take Tantallon and you kill Rupert do you think that will stop the pixies. They'll just return in greater numbers and wipe us off the face of Connaught.'

'Even if you're right and we can't beat them at least we will die free. What makes you believe that the pixies would ever make you governor?' asked Izzy.

'The pixie general gave me his word,' said Murray.

'You are a fool, only Rupert could grant you governorship and he gives those he conquers nothing,' stated Izzy.

'Who is in this with you?' asked Duncan.

'No one,' answered Murray a little too quickly.

'He's all yours Neave,' said Izzy.

'Liz, it was all Liz's idea,' sputtered Murray terrified of Neave and her magic.

'Well that's no surprise is it,' said Cameron, 'now what are we going to do with this worm?'

'I just don't know,' admitted Izzy honestly.

'I have an idea,' said Neave.

'If it's using him for target practice I'm right there with you,' said Cameron.

'No that's far too easy for him,' said Neave, 'I have a spell that will force him to do what we want him to. We can make him go to Liz and tell her he has warned the pixies. Then we can make him fight in the attack on Tantallon so there is no need to expose him and affect your troops morale. He will be a puppet and you can pull his strings Izzy and the whole time he will know what is happening but he will be powerless to do anything about it.'

'What do you think Rupert and Bloomfield will do to him if they get hold of him for 'betraying' them?' Izzy asked to no one in particular.

'I've seen what he does to those who let him down and let's just say it's not pretty,' answered Amber.

They all watched in fascination as Neave walked over to Murray, placed her hand on his head and chanted strange words of magic. Phil felt the power of Neave's magic and was stunned. Every day she seemed to grow more powerful. He was very glad that they were on the same side and he almost felt sorry for the pixie wizard who was heading for a show down with his friend.

As they headed back towards the rebel camp Dougal turned toward Phil and said, 'Phil, when you were telling Derry and me about your world before we came here, you told us that most pixies lived in trees but from what I can see most of them live in cities, towns or on farms.'

'I had only ever seen a couple of pixies before we started this mission and had never actually spoken to any of them. So when my father told me that, I believed him, I had no reason not to,' answered the dragon.

Cameron who had heard the conversation came to Phil's father's defence saying, 'four or five hundred years ago your father would have been right. Back then, there were only a few pixie towns, most of them were villages really, although pixie kings have always lived in castles as far as I know. Even today a lot of the pixies that live in the southeastern counties still live in villages built in tree tops.'

'I knew I was right,' said Phil indignantly.

When Murray returned to his tent he found Liz waiting for him. Before he had a chance to say anything she snapped, 'what did they say?'

Murray tried to tell Liz his version of what had happened but Neave's spell instead forced him to say, 'they were pleased. They intend to let the rebels believe that they have succeeded in catching them by surprise before they spring their own trap. Broomfield wouldn't tell me what he had in mind, I don't think he trusts me completely.'

'Did you see the king?' asked Liz.

'No, I think Broomfield wants to take all the credit for himself. Now if you'd excuse me I'd like to get a couple of hours sleep before dawn.'

'Fair enough, I will see you in the morning,' said Liz happily.

She had been worried that Murray was losing his nerve but was now content that everything was back under her control.

The day dawned fine and warm and although tired from the lack of sleep due to her interrogation of Murray, Izzy was determined to personally supervise the preparation for the upcoming attack on Tantallon.

There was a lot that needed to be done. She looked all around the camp and saw warriors, sharpened weapons and mended armour as well as fletchers making hundreds of arrows while other men and women prepared healing potions that would be needed the next day.

She saw Murray running around the camp giving orders to some and even stopping to help others. Izzy couldn't help but laugh knowing that no matter how hard the man tried to do otherwise Neave's spell forced him to help and prepare for the upcoming assault on Tantallon.

'This has to be killing him,' said Cameron pointing at Murray as she walked over to join her friend.

'Yes it would be horrible to have control of your mind but not be able to control your actions and speech,' Izzy said.

'Izzy I'm glad Neave is on our side.'

'So am I,' agreed Izzy, 'we've fought plenty of wizards over the last couple of years but I've never seen anything like what she did to Murray.'

'I was talking to the giants and the dragon on the way back to the camp last night and according to Phil we haven't seen anything yet,' Cameron explained.

'Two giants, a wizard and a dragon, yes we certainly did the right thing rescuing Amber didn't we?' said Izzy. She then added mischievously, 'come on let's go torment Murray a bit.'

'You have a truly nasty sense of humour my friend,' said Cameron, a big smile on her face.

Izzy just smiled back at her friend and winked.

'Have you seen Neave or Derry?' Adam asked Liam and Dylan.

'No,' answered both fairies.

'I still think they're up to something,' said Adam almost ranting, 'if you can't find one, you know you won't find the other.'

'Adam let it go,' said Dylan.

'Aren't either of you the least bit interested in what they're always talking about?' Adam went on.

'Whatever it is Adam they'll tell us when they're good and ready,' said Liam.

Adam tried to continue the conversation but his brother and friend ignored him.

'Well done, you're picking this up much faster than I thought you would,' said Neave.

Derry smiled at the compliment, she had mastered invisibility days ago. It had been easy really. Neave had explained to her how Phil made himself invisible and it worked exactly the same way for her. Neave had explained that innate magic's normally worked the same way and lost ones were normally easily regained.

From there Neave had started to teach Derry simple spells like lighting fires by creating small flames out of thin air and small balls of light that worked better than any lantern. The leprechaun had mastered these and other simple spells in no time. Today they had moved onto a more complicated and aggressive spell but so far Derry had only studied the theory of the spell.

'Right,' said Neave, 'we had better head back.'

'So soon?' Derry sighed.

'If we stay out here much longer Adam might find us,' said Neave.

'He's like a dog looking for a lost bone isn't he?' laughed Derry, 'is he always like this when he doesn't know what's going on?'

'No, he's not as bad as he used to be,' joked Neave.

Unlike many in the camp that night, Izzy had little trouble sleeping. It had been sheer strength of will that she had made it through the day but as soon as she was sure that the brownie rebels were fully equipped and tactically prepared for the upcoming battle, she had taken her leave and returned to her tent for some private contemplation and much needed sleep.

Adam and Finn, who had waited for years to have a 'crack' at the pixies, talked well into the night in their excitement. Both fairies were still deeply disappointed about not being involved in the main assault but were determined to get involved even if it meant they had to storm the main gates to do so.

Neave spent half the night memorising the spell she would need in the upcoming battle and wishing she had had more time to teach Derry. She was nervous about facing William and would have liked to know for sure if there were any other pixie wizards in the city.

That night Amber found herself thinking of John and Arthur and hoping that it had been them that Izzy had seen leaving Tantallon on the morning of her escape from the city. She did not want to fight or see either man harmed in an attack on the former brownie capital. Her last thoughts were of the pixie knight as she drifted off to sleep.

Murray spent the entire night plotting his revenge on Izzy and her new friends. In particular the annoying wizard, oh how he was going to make her pay. Unfortunately for the brownie, he could plan all he liked but as long as Neave lived, her spell would hold firm, preventing him from carrying out his well thought out plans.

Phil, who didn't need to sleep anywhere near as much as his friends, flew into the highlands in search of mountain goats or some other equally tasty morsels.

Of the remaining members of the little company from Sarasidhe, Dylan, who like his father could sleep anywhere, anytime, slept soundly as did Liam after he had sharpened his sword in preparation for the upcoming battle.

Derry chose this night to show Dougal everything she had learnt from Neave. At first Dougal had been surprised that his sister had not told him about this earlier. He had to agree though that the whole thing had a much greater impact with her telling him while she was invisible while at the same time holding a magical ball of light.

She then explained that her invisibility wasn't so much a spell but the rediscovery of the innate leprechaun ability. She then spent several hours teaching Dougal how it was done. Although it took him far longer to master it than it had taken her, master it he did.

'This is where we part ways,' said Izzy. 'Archie and his men will lead you to your positions outside the city walls. Good luck.'

After brief goodbyes they all went their separate ways.

Archie and his men had been chosen to accompany the twins, dragon and fairies, not just because they were Tantallon locals but more for the fact they were all highly skilled archers.

Within two hours of leaving the main body of the rebel force they arrived at their destination (only a stones throw for Dougal and Derry) at the main gates of Tantallon.

While the twins gathered 'stones' to throw, Phil had a look inside the city. The others found the best locations to ambush any pixies that left the city in search of the catapults.

Once everyone was satisfied they were ready for the dawn attack, Phil kept watch while the others had a couple of hours sleep.

'We're here,' said Izzy opening the door to the secret tunnel that would take them to the very heart of Tantallon.

'Andrew, take fifteen men and cover us just in case there are any pixies running around out there, follow us once we're all inside.'

Andrew nodded and signalled for his men to follow him. They circled the rebels and studied the surrounding area finally joining the others in the tunnels below.

After about a quarter of an hour they came to an intersection and Izzy turned to Duncan and asked, 'do you have your map?'

'Yes,' he answered pulling the parchment from his tunic pocket.

'Neave, can you bring your ball of light a little closer please?' asked Izzy.

'Sure,' answered the fairy wizard.

When she had enough light Izzy held the map against the wall.

'We're right here,' she said pointing at the map, 'you need to follow this tunnel to here and then take the right passage until you come to a dead end. There is a small lever on the right hand wall that will open a door that leads into the cellar of 'The Rose and Thistle'. Don't stop to drink the cellar dry and be careful leaving the tavern, we have to take them by surprise if this is going to work.'

'The only brownie I know who would stop to have a drink is leading the attack on the palace,' he said smiling.

'Don't forget, wait for Dougal and Derry to start throwing their rocks before you attack,' Izzy reminded Duncan who needed no reminding.

'Good luck Izzy,' he said, then led his troops away.

'Right you lot, let's go,' Izzy ordered.

She led the rebels through the maze of tunnels. Liz had tried to memorize their passage but found herself lost in minutes. She was even starting to think they may even be going around in circles until Izzy signalled for everyone to stop.

'Right, we're leaving the tunnels for a short time,' said Izzy, 'I want absolute silence while we're on the surface, our lives may depend on it,' she looked over to Neave who nodded back to her.

Izzy then led them into the streets of Tantallon again thankful that the fairy wizard (who had just cast a silencing spell on Liz) was on her side. Within two blocks they were back in the tunnels below the city streets and heading directly towards the palace.

Liz couldn't understand what had just happened. While on the surface, she had tried several times to make enough noise to alert any nearby pixies of their presence but to no avail. In desperation she tried to scream when she saw those infront returning to the tunnels but not even the slightest whisper left her lips. She looked over to Izzy who was watching her with a mocking smile spread across her face and Liz felt a chill run down her spine. Her first thought was to flee right there and then but she knew she wouldn't get ten feet before she was cut down, knowing Izzy and the others were obviously watching her, so she decided to carry on for now as if nothing had happened and try and slip away in the darkness of the tunnels.

Izzy and Cameron were the last to enter the tunnel. They had waited a few minutes to make sure they hadn't been followed.

'Did you see the look on Liz's face?' asked Izzy in a whisper as they hurried to join those waiting in the tunnel below, 'she was terrified.'

'Wouldn't you be?' said Cameron, 'how long did Neave say that spell would last?'

Izzy answered happily, 'at least two hours.'

Twenty five minutes later they reached the point from where they were going to launch their attack.

'Cameron, Neave and I are just going to have a quick look around, you're in command until we return, we won't be long,' said Izzy.

'Neave, try and keep her out of trouble,' said Cameron smiling.

The wizard and brownie returned in less than half an hour.

'That was quick,' said Cameron.

'He's gone or at least moved rooms,' said Izzy, disappointment obvious in her voice.

'Stealing his sword from out of his private chambers might have unsettled him,' Cameron replied.

'You think,' laughed Izzy adding, 'if he is here I'm going to find him.'

'I'm sure you will,' Cameron said.

Izzy then turned and addressed her troops.

'Everyone, ready yourselves, dawn is close and the attack will begin within the hour.'

'Dougal, Derry it's time,' said Finn.

Dougal took a deep breath and threw his first rock.

'What the hell was that?' shouted a pixie guard from the city walls.

'I don't know,' yelled another guard who looked up just in time to see a large rock heading towards him.

'Catapult fire, take cover!' he screamed as he dove behind the cover of the wall. The force of the impact just below him nearly knocked him from the catwalk, 'sound the alarm, we're under attack!' he yelled.

Within seconds the sound of bells pierced the air and the city burst to life as soldiers everywhere ran to their posts.

'Where's the attack coming from?' bellowed the captain of the guard (from the safety of the stone gatehouse) as two more rocks hit the other walls.

'Directly south of the main gates sir!' yelled a guard from the catwalk.

'Runner,' cried the officer and a pixie ran to his side, 'first, tell Flinders to take his men out to take care of the catapults and find out how many rebels are out there. Then inform the king and General Bloomfield that we are under attack.'

The pixie sprinted away as soon as the last word left the officers mouth.

Within minutes twenty mounted soldiers rode out of the main gates in search of the rebel catapults.

The pixies didn't stand a chance. The fairy and brownie archers heard the pounding of horses' hooves on the hard ground long before the horseman came into view. The skilful bowman cut them down to the man well before the pixies drew close enough to fight back. The whole time Dougal and Derry continued to pound the city walls with their well placed rocks.

'You fool,' snapped Broomfield, 'you sent twenty mounted men against an unknown enemy. It would have only taken a dozen semi decent bowmen in well defended positions to slaughter them. Join your men on the wall and on the way tell Captain Gillow I request his presence forth with.'

A short time later Capitan Gillow arrived and before he had a chance to say anything Broomfield said, 'Gillow you're in command of the city. I'm going to take forty men and deal with whoever it is that is out there. We're going to be on foot so we could be gone for a while. Send fifty men back to the palace to keep the king safe and don't open the gates unless it is safe to do so, even if it means I die. Do you understand?'

'Yes sir,' said Gillow.

'Excellent,' said Broomfield who turned and disappeared from the catwalk.

'It's time,' said Duncan more to himself than his followers, 'Taran begin.'

The brownie put his lips to the mouthpiece of his bagpipes and began to play as Duncan opened the secret door that lead to the city above and the rebels charged into the city crying for freedom.

'There's a large party of pixie infantry heading our way,' said Phil materializing infront of Finn.

'We'll meet them here,' said Finn, 'this is as good a place as any to make a stand.'

'No Finn there's too many of them,' said Phil matter of factly.

'I'm not running from this fight,' said Finn defiantly.

'Don't be a fool Finn. Listen, can't you hear the pipes, the attack has began, our job here is done,' insisted Phil.

'We'll take care of these men just like we did the cavalry,' said Finn adamantly.

'Finn they're not going to attack us blindly like the over confident horsemen did. They'll just pin us down and pick us off one at a time,' explained Phil.

'So we're just going to run like cowards?' said Finn appalled by the idea.

'No, we'll draw these men away from the city which will even the odds inside,' said Phil, 'but if you insist on fighting, I'll drop you inside the city, while the rest of us let Archie lead us a game of cat and mouse against these pixies.'

'Take me to the city now then,' said Finn more an order than a request.

Disappointed, Phil lifted his friend (a little more roughly than he needed) and flew towards the city.

'Your highness, they have attacked from within the city itself,' said Captain Woodward, 'it is a well organised attack my lord, the city may fall, we have to get you out of here.'

'Don't worry about me captain, William and I have our own way out of here,' said Rupert, 'go back and join the fight but if it does look like Tantallon will fall, you and your men get out and meet me in Huntingdon,' the pixie king finished.

'As you wish my lord,' said Woodward who saluted his king and then left the room.

Captain Gillow's command of Tantallon was short lived. He turned as he heard the sound of bagpipes behind him and was struck in the chest by an arrow. He fell from the catwalk, dead before he hit the ground, the first casualty inside Tantallon itself.

All around the catwalk pixies fell, a few managed to fire a salvo or two at the rebels below.

'To the towers!' yelled a pixie running for the safety of one of the turret topped towers, a safety he almost made.

Duncan was momentarily distracted by what looked like a fairy flying towards the battlefield and seconds later Finn stood beside him (after Finn had picked himself off the ground where Phil had unceremoniously dumped him).

They were forced to fall back behind cover as the last of the pixies made their way to the safety of the towers. The battle had raged for less than twenty minutes and already at least fifty pixies had fallen with others wounded.

'We have to take the towers,' said Duncan, 'Finn you take half the men and take the right tower and the rest of us will attack the left.'

Finn nodded in understanding and signalled for the rebels to follow him as he headed towards his target.

Izzy and her followers emerged from the tunnels directly into the palace's courtyard. Izzy was surprised to see the palace walls empty and its gates wide open.

'Where are they?' asked Cameron.

'Our diversion must have worked better than we expected,' answered Izzy, 'they must have sent all their available troops to the main walls.'

'Andrew, find Duncan and tell him we have secured the palace walls and we are now starting a room by room search for Rupert.'

Cameron watched as the last of the rebels exited the tunnels and joined their companions, it was then she realised that Liz was missing. 'Izzy,' she called, 'Liz is gone.'

'The fool,' said Izzy, 'she must have slipped away in the tunnels. It doesn't really matter, she can't do us any damage now and it's highly unlikely she'll ever escape from the tunnels.'

Izzy then ordered the majority of her followers to close the gates to the city and man the walls. Once the rebels were in place

Izzy, Cameron, Amber, Neave and a reluctant Murray began their search for the pixie king.

Andrew found Duncan, who along with his troops was pinned down and unable to get close enough to launch his attack of the tower which was being held by the still larger pixie force.

Finn and his men faced the same problem at the other side of the city. The battle for Tantallon had reached a stalemate, neither side in a position to strike at the other.

'They are close my lord,' said William looking into the glass ball he held in his left hand, 'I believe now would be a good time to depart.'

'Ready your spell wizard but don't cast it until the last possible moment, I want to look this rebel in the eye and see her disappointment when we slip from her grasp,' said the king smugly.

Minutes later William dropped the glass globe and began to chant.

The door to the room flew open and the king watched three brownies and two fairies enter the room.

'So you're the troublesome rebel,' he said calmly. He looked over at Amber and added, 'I must say, I don't think much of the company you keep.'

'You're mine,' said Izzy venomously as she charged the king, blade held high.

'No, I don't think so,' said the king arrogantly as he and the wizard shimmered and then vanished from within Izzy's grasp.

'Nooooo!' screamed Izzy as she threw herself at the empty air before her. She hit the ground with such force that all of the air was knocked from her lungs.

Cameron hurried to her friend's side.

'Izzy, it's alright, you'll get another chance.'

It took Izzy several minutes to regain her composure enough for her to speak. When she did all she said was, 'let's get out of here and see what's happening in the city.'

While Rupert had held the attention of Amber and the brownies, Neave had watched the wizard. The second they had entered the room Neave had known they could not stop the king and his wizard from escaping but in the little time she had, she studied the wizard and he had met her gaze. Neave saw intense hatred in the man's eyes and although he did his best to hide it she also saw fear. She could feel his obvious power and in return, he hers, although there was no way of knowing which of them was stronger in the art of magic until it was put to the test. Neave believed the man's fear would give her the advantage when their inevitable confrontation eventuated.

'Neave are you coming or not?' called Amber.

Striking the wizard from her private thoughts she mumbled, 'sorry,' and ran to catch up to her friends.

'It's no good Izzy,' said Duncan, 'we could take the towers but it's simply not worth the cost.'

'I agree,' said Izzy, 'we've given them a hell of a fright and done some serious damage already but I not going to risk anymore lives to take a city we can't hold. Taran, signal a withdrawal to the tunnels.'

The piper did as he was ordered and within the hour the brownie rebels had returned to the tunnels leaving Tantallon behind them. The pixies had repelled the rebel attack but had payed an extremely high price for their victory.

For over four hours Dougal, Derry and their companions led General Broomfield and his men on a merry goose chase, just leaving enough of a trail to force the pixies to maintain their pursuit keeping them out of the battle being fought in the city behind them.

Finally fearing they were being led into an ambush the pixie general ended the hunt and returned to the city.

'They're definitely gone,' said Liam, 'their tracks are heading back to the city.'

'What do we do now?' Adam asked.

'Head for the meeting point and wait for the others to arrive I guess. It appears our work here is done,' said Dougal.

'I'll fly to the city and see what's happening there. I'll catch up to you as soon as I can,' said Phil.

The dragon flew off leaving the small band to carry on without him.

They reached their prearranged camp not long before nightfall and found Izzy and the rest of the rebels waiting for them. The meeting point was a hidden cave complex that had been chosen because it was large enough to house both the leprechauns and fairy dragon. It was about two miles into the foothills and could only be approached by following a small stock trail.

The dragon returned a short time later relieved to find his friends already there. He had almost panicked when he had arrived at Tantallon and found it completely empty of brownies and still safely in pixie hands.

Around the campfire and over dinner the companions swapped tales of what had happened during the attack and all agreed that even though they had failed to take the city or kill the pixie king, their attack on the city must have severely shaken their enemy.

CHAPTER 20

THE JOURNEY HOME

'Come with us Izzy?' said Amber who sat by a small fire along with Izzy, Cameron and Neave.

A full day had passed since the attack on Tantallon and the rebels had retreated into the ragged highlands. Phil had flown back to investigate the results of their actions the pervious day. Although the attack on Tantallon had failed in both of its objectives, the rebels had at least left the cities pixie occupiers in total disarray and feeling vulnerable.

'I can't leave my people Amber, they need me,' Izzy said finally.

'Bring them with you,' said Neave.

'What! You want us to give up, hand Caledonia over to the pixies and forget about the brownies who are being forced to work as Rupert's slaves in his mines and work camps?' Izzy asked appalled at the mere thought.

'No not at all,' said Neave. 'What I'm suggesting is you fight on a different front. Rupert is going to send more troops to reinforce Tantallon and you simply don't have the numbers to hold out for too much longer. It's not going to be long before he invades Sarasidhe. Fight with us there and when we defeat him we'll help you drive him from Caledonia.'

'How large is your army?' asked Cameron.

'If Strahan has had time to fully mobilise our army, we'll have four thousand infantry, one thousand horse and one hundred wizards, give or take a few men,' said Neave.

'How many of them are regulars?' Cameron asked.

'The horseman, wizards and five hundred infantry,' explained Neave who then added, 'the rest are militia made up mainly of farmers, labourers and retired soldiers.'

'It won't be enough,' Izzy said bluntly.

'The militia are well trained,' replied Amber defensively.

'I'm sure they are,' said Cameron before Izzy could tactlessly continue, she then explained, 'it's not the training of your troops that's the problem, it's the number.'

'How large can the pixie army be?' said Neave, 'I've practically covered every inch of land between here and the pixie capital and I haven't exactly seen thousands of pixie soldiers running around.'

'Rupert's standing army,' explained Cameron, 'numbers about ten thousand pixie soldiers of which at least two thousand are stationed in various parts of Caledonia and I'm picking there will soon be an extra thousand on the way to Tantallon. He has at least another thousand men guarding the mines and work camps.'

'That makes the odds about even,' interrupted Amber.

'She hasn't finished,' said Izzy who then took over from Cameron. 'Yes Rupert may only have five or six thousand pixie soldiers available for an invasion of your kingdom but he does however also have three thousand mercenaries made up of mainly troll infantry and esprit follet cavalry. That is at least eight thousand highly trained, very experienced troops up against sixteen hundred regular soldiers, most of which have never actually seen action and three and a half thousand 'well trained' farmers.'

'Well, what would you suggest then, that we just give up perhaps?' asked Amber slightly sarcastically while raising her hands.

'Of course not,' said Izzy, 'I'm just telling you what you,' she stopped, changed the 'you to 'we' and said, 'we're up against.'

'You're going aren't you Izzy,' said Cameron.

'It may be my last shot at Rupert,' she said a smile on her face.

'Do you think the others will follow us?' Cameron asked.

'That's up to them,' said Izzy. 'I'll talk to Duncan and the others but either way I think we should leave at dawn tomorrow. We have to get you home as soon as possible because we won't have much time to prepare for Rupert's invasion.'

'How does she do it?' Amber asked no one in particular as she watched the brownie rebels prepare for the long march.

'I have no idea,' laughed Neave, 'I'm just surprised she didn't just talk Rupert into leaving Caledonia and taking his troops with him.'

'I think she only talks to those who are on her side,' said Adam smiling.

'If anyone did to Sarasidhe what the pixies have done to their home I'd do my talking with the point of my sword as well,' said Finn pointedly.

'Well it looks like you're going to get your chance doesn't it?' said Liam who was growing somewhat disturbed by Finn's growing bloodlust.

'We're ready whenever you are,' called Izzy cheerfully and minutes later almost two hundred and fifty brownies, two leprechauns, a dragon and the six fairies began their journey towards Sarasidhe.

Following Izzy's suggestion they travelled directly west heading for the coast. Izzy didn't think they would come across any pixie troops while they were in the highlands. She also hoped to round up a few brownies that may have been hiding in the ragged hills.

'What are you going to do with your cousin?' Finn asked Izzy as they marched towards the coast.

Izzy looked over at Murray and watched the man for a couple of minutes. There were still no outward signs of the inner turmoil that he must be experiencing.

'As long as Neave's spell lasts, nothing,' she answered.

'I admire your self restraint,' said Finn. 'I don't think I could calmly sit back and watch a fairy traitor marching along side a loyal soldier even if he was magically muzzled.'

'You have to look at the big picture Finn,' explained Izzy, 'yes I could expose Murray but what would it achieve? At the moment Murray is still considered to be a hero among our people and a member of our royal family. There are rebels marching beside us only because Murray is with us. During the war Murray was a great leader who fought bravely and led his troops well.'

'If Murray is such a hero why did he betray you and his people?' Finn questioned.

'I wish I knew for sure,' said Izzy with a sigh, 'all I know is that Liz is somehow behind it. With her lost in the tunnels of Tantallon I'll probably never find out for sure. What I do know however is that if we expose Murray it could shatter the morale of these fine and noble warriors.'

Finn simply nodded in understanding for the first time realising how intelligent the small brownie was.

For the rest of the day Finn thought about how he would have dealt with Murray and he had to admit to himself that before listening to Izzy he would have handled the situation badly.

The first day of the journey passed uneventfully and they spent that night camped on the summit of a high hill which they had chosen because it would be easy to defend.

By mid morning of the third day from Tantallon, the small rebel army approached a seaside town called Kyle. Kyle was only an hour's ride north of the pixie brownie border and had been the first brownie town to fall to the pixies. Before the war Kyle was a fast growing community that had started out as a small fishing village but had grown rapidly since the discovery of iron ore in the nearby hills.

Since their occupation the pixies had turned Kyle into a giant work camp forcing every brownie over the age of ten to work the mines like slaves. All the children under the age of ten had been taken from the town and had never been seen again.

Rupert however was unhappy with the progress being made in the mines, so from Gwyllion, a small country that the pixies had conquered hundreds of years before, he bought in two hundred Ellyllon slaves. The Ellyllon were expert miners and once in Kyle had increased the production three fold.

From Kyle, the ore was shipped to Lorne in the north of Caledonia, where it was used to make weapons of many various types. The finished weapons were then shipped to the pixie port of Thames and from there they were sent overland to wherever they were needed. The weapons travelled by sea to lessen the chances of them falling into rebel hands.

Although the slaves outnumbered the guards five to one they no longer tried to escape their captors because not long after the brownies had been put to work in the mines they had tried to overthrow their overlords but they had failed dismally. After the revolt was over and unsuccessful, Rupert had come to the town to personally oversee the brownies punishment. His first command had been to round up a selection of some of the youngest slaves and then have them executed infront of their families. He then personally executed the surviving leaders of the revolt so never again did the brownies of Kyle revolt against their overlords.

Izzy, Neave, Cameron and Finn looked down from the small hill on the edge of the town.

'I think we can take them,' said Izzy with her usual confidence, a plan already forming in her mind.

'What's the point?' asked Neave.

'We can stop the iron ore reaching Rupert's weapon smiths for a start,' said Izzy, 'added to that, there must be close to a thousand brownie miners working those mines and I'm sure many will join our fight against Rupert.'

'Not to mention two hundred Ellyllon's as well,' added Cameron, 'and they're the best longbow men in all of Connaught,' she finished.

'Will the Ellyllon fight for or against us?' Neave asked.

'To be honest, I've no idea,' said Izzy. 'Most hate the pixies but some are fiercely loyal to them almost considering themselves to be pixies.'

'Even without the Ellyllon, the gains from taking Kyle are too good to pass up,' said Finn who had remained silent up until this point.

'I agree,' said Neave, 'let's hope we can get the others to see our point of view.'

It was just after sunset when Neave, Finn and the two brownies, along with the rest of the ragtag rebel army, returned to the small hill overlooking Kyle.

'Right,' said Izzy turning to Phil and the leprechaun twins, 'it's up to the three of you to check out what is happening inside that town.'

Before she had even finished her sentence Dougal and Derry had both vanished from sight very eager and excited to put their newly rediscovered innate skill to the test.

It was over an hour before the leprechauns and fairies returned.

'There's only a couple of dozen pixie guards on duty,' said Dougal.

Izzy nearly jumped out of her skin taken completely by surprise by the still invisible Dougal.

Before he could stop himself Dougal said, 'I can see why Phil loves doing that,' but he then saw the look on Izzy's face and added sheepishly, 'sorry, did I say that out loud.'

'Behave yourself Dougal,' scolded Derry appearing beside her brother followed closely by Phil.

Izzy regained her composure then asked, 'if there are only two dozen guards on duty in the town what are the others doing and how are they keeping the miners under control?'

'The miners are all locked up in large barracks that have been magically sealed,' said Phil.

'It's not a strong spell. Neave and I will have no trouble getting the doors open,' Derry said confidently.

'As for the guards,' said Dougal, 'most of them are in the taverns drinking themselves stupid. There are others in barracks playing bones, sleeping or generally killing time. The last thing they are expecting is a visit from us.'

'Normally I'd say let's charge on in,' said Izzy, 'but with all those miners locked up and defenceless I think we need to be a little more subtle.'

She turned to Phil and Dougal and asked, 'do you two think you can take care of the guards?'

Dougal said 'yes' and Phil simply nodded in reply.

'Good,' said Izzy taking charge. 'I want Dougal and Phil to leave immediately and clear out all the guards. We'll give them an hour, then Neave, I want you to magically seal all the doors to the taverns and barracks. I'll go with you and cover your back and while we are trapping the pixies, Derry and Cameron can free the miners if Derry's magic is strong enough to break the pixie magic. Don't free the ellyllon until Neave and I arrive, I want to find out who's side they are on before we let them out.'

'What if I can't break the seals?' asked Derry hesitantly.

'Then as soon as Neave and I have locked up the pixie guards we'll start freeing the captives. It will just mean we spend a few more hours in the town,' Izzy said reassuringly.

'Don't worry Derry,' said Neave, 'you have far more power than you realise, you'll have no problems breaking a few weak pixie spells. I like this whole plan Izzy, we should be able to take the town with little or no bloodshed.'

'Exactly!' said Izzy who then added, 'you boys had better be on your way.'

'How are we going to do this?' said Dougal to his friend he couldn't see.

'Simple,' answered Phil, 'we walk up to them, you bang their heads together knocking them out and I carry them back to Adam, Dylan and Liam who will then tie them up. You wait for me exactly where I left you and then we'll move on to the next guards.'

'You make it sound so simple,' said Dougal.

'It will be. Just make sure you don't hit them too hard, we are only going to take a life if it means saving our own,' said Phil in a determined tone.

Dougal didn't reply but he had to admit to himself he was happy that Phil felt that way.

'It's time,' said Izzy who turned first to Cameron and then to Derry, 'good luck and remember don't free any ellyllon until we find out who's side they're on.'

With that the four women headed off in different directions, Cameron and an invisible Derry to the edge of Kyle where the brownies were being held and Neave and Izzy (who were quickly becoming good friends) towards the town centre.

Without the aid of invisibility and heading directly towards the main body of pixie troops, Neave and Izzy had by far the most dangerous mission.

They kept to the shadows, moving silently towards their goal, both hoping that Dougal and Phil had removed any guards that may have stood in their way. Time almost stood still for the two women as they slipped through the town, building by building, until they finally heard the sound of drunken singing coming from a tavern no more than a hundred yards ahead of them.

Neave took a deep breath to calm her nerves and looked over at Izzy who just smiled back at her, her excitement clearly visible on her face. Neave almost laughed inspite of herself and try as she might, she couldn't understand the brownie's love of danger.

With Izzy covering her back, Neave crawled towards the open main doors of the tavern, now the only exit she hadn't already magically sealed. As she stood and placed a hand on each side of the doorframe so she could cast her spell, she heard a voice cry, 'Fairy!'

Izzy ran towards the open doors, weapon in hand and called as loudly as she dared, 'hurry!'

Neave almost panicked and it took all her self control (as four of the more sober pixies charged towards her) for her to finish the spell she was casting. She had only just finished as the four pixies threw themselves at her only to hit what felt like a brick wall and fall to the ground dazed.

Izzy looked down at the stunned pixies and taunted them mercilessly for a few moments.

'Come on Izzy, we've got plenty of work to do,' said Neave impatiently, already on her way to the next inn.

While Izzy and Neave were busy with the dangerous job of magically locking up the pixie soldiers of Kyle, Derry and Cameron (who was finding it hard enough following her invisible companion) were finding it surprisingly difficult convincing the brownies they had freed to leave their prison cells behind them.

It wasn't until they had opened the magical locks that bound the third prison barracks, that they found a brownie willing to follow them.

Artair McCall was the eldest son of one of the town elders and was respected by most of the locals of Kyle and when he immediately joined Cameron, the rest of his barracks quickly followed him.

Artair insisted they went back to the already open barracks before continuing on. After a short but scathing speech about how he could not believe the cowardness and lack of fight amongst those he had always thought of as a proud, brave and noble people, he finished by saying that they could stay here and die as slaves to the pixies if they wanted to but he would not die with them.

When Artair, Cameron and a now visible Derry walked towards the next prison barracks, they were followed by every brownie they had released.

'How long will your spells last Neave?' Izzy asked.

'At least two days unless they have a powerful wizard in their ranks,' answered the fairy wizard.

'Judging by the ease in which I broke through their spells, I doubt they have any wizards of any great skill,' said Derry.

'Don't sell yourself short Derry, you have far more skill than you realise,' Neave said to her pupil.

'She is right however,' said Phil, 'because if there was a powerful wizard nearby, I would sense their presence.'

'Good,' said Izzy, 'in two days we'll be well gone.'

She then turned her attention to Artair.

'So Artair, can we trust the ellyllon?'

'Yes. Llewellyn and his men hate the pixies more than we do,' answered Artair with great conviction.

'Right then, we better let them out. Would you and Artair like to do the honours Neave?' asked Izzy, 'tell Llewellyn we'll talk to him in the morning after we've all had some sleep.'

A single rider rode out of the southern gates of Huntington. He looked at the sun still rising to signal the beginning of a new day and thought back to his conversation he had had with Rupert the night before.

The Shadow had never seen the pixie king so shaken. Not only had he apparently been lucky to escape Tantallon alive but had also lost his chance to personally torture the rebel leader as well as losing his princess just to top things off. It was fair to say the last week had been the worst week of the king's life.

The only way Rupert was going to take over the fairy kingdom now was with force. The volatile king had already made up his mind that his sole mission in life was to now wipe the fairy people off the face of Connaught. The king already had Sir John raising a northern army to deal with the brownie rebels once and for all, while Rupert and William organised the southern army and of course his ever growing mercenary force.

Right now, at this present moment in time, the pixie king thought The Shadow was heading directly to Sarasidhe and for a few fleeting seconds The Shadow had actually considered doing exactly as the king had ordered.

'No,' he said to himself, 'that would not be a good idea at all.'

And with that he stopped his horse, blew three long piercing whistles then waited.

It was not long before a black speck appeared in the distance and within minutes the large black raven landed on the pommel of his saddle.

'Hello my friend,' he said to the raven, 'I believe it is time for us to return to our master.'

The raven cocked his head and looked at the man.

'Yes you're right, I'm sure the master would like to know the outcome of this little war but I don't want to find myself dead in the middle of it. No matter who wins, both sides will take years to recover, giving our master plenty of time to decide her next move. Anyway, I believe she will want to know about the powerful fairy wizard and her new apprentice. Now settle down my friend, we have a long journey before us.'

The raven rubbed its head against the man's hand and The Shadow wasn't sure whether he was patting the bird or the bird was patting him. He laughed out loud, spurred his horse and galloped off to the south.

Izzy had left Tantallon with approximately two hundred brownie rebels. Now as she looked around the busy campsite, she saw nearly eight hundred adult brownies along with three hundred others under the age of sixteen. Added to that there were also just over two hundred ellyllon men who had promised to follower her until 'their debt to her' was repaid. As to when they considered this debt paid she had no idea.

For the first time in her life the little brownie doubted herself. It was one thing to lead a small band in hit and run raids against an enemy who did not know the territory they defended but it was totally another thing to command an army of over one thousand and she suddenly felt totally out of her depth.

'You're not on your own,' she reminded herself looking over to Cameron, her new friends and the remaining members of the rebel council who were at present trying to ready 'her' army for the march ahead.

She shook her head to clear it and started to think about the problems she might encounter on their journey to Sarasidhe. She decided their only real concern was feeding so many people. They had taken what they could from Kyle and Liam and some of the best brownie hunters searched for game in the surrounding hills while Artair and others from Kyle slaughtered the few remaining farm animals left on the town's nearby farms and loaded the meat onto wagons in preparation for their impending departure.

At this moment she was probably most relieved to have Finn and the fairy brothers on her side. The three professional soldiers had spent the entire morning organising 'Izzy's' army into units of two hundred, each under the command of one of them or a member of the brownie rebel council or a town elder from Kyle. Each of the larger units was then divided into smaller ones of twenty five soldiers.

When they had the brownies sorted, Finn and the brothers then moved on to the ellyllon miners only to find their help was not required. Llewellyn's well disciplined miners were already organised and ready to begin the journey to Sarasidhe.

Before her very eyes, Izzy watched this mix of farmers, miners and even shopkeepers become an army.

By noon, less than twelve hours after the miners had been released from their captivity, the now not so small army was marching towards the fairy capital.

If any pixies saw the army marching through their country, they stayed well clear of it, as Izzy and her followers arrived at the Corrib River unopposed.

Neave turned from the river and towards her friends and said, 'well, we're almost there.'

'I just can't wait to get to the other side,' said Amber excitedly, 'it will feel so good to sleep in the forest of my home land tonight.'

While the army crossed the river, Dougal (who had helped Llewellyn and his men build the bridge by carrying all the timber required to the river) watched as the ellyllon gathered wood.

He turned to Llewellyn who was standing next to him and asked, 'what are they doing?'

'Those saplings are perfect for making longbows,' explained Llewellyn, 'and my men are all master archers.'

Llewellyn went on to give Dougal a full history of the longbow and how there was no armour its arrows could not penetrate.

Four days later, cheering fairies lined the streets, ten deep in some places, as Amber and her comrades rode into the fairy capital on horses which they had borrowed from farmers not far from the city. Dougal and Derry walked beside their friends followed by the brownie and ellyllon army.

Strahan looked down from the city walls with mixed feelings, obvious relief for the fact that his daughter had been returned safely to him but also apprehension for what lay ahead for him and his people. Strahan had now known for days that the army was on its way as Phil had flown ahead to tell the king that his daughter and her friends were all safe and on their way home, with a few extra heads in tow. The King had had plenty of time to assess the situation and mull it over, not sure what the 'few extra heads' would mean.

However, upon hearing the news that Amber was coming home, the fairy king had immediately started preparations for a public celebration in his daughter's honour and at this very moment in time, this was his main concern.

CHAPTER 21

PREPARATION FOR WAR

Dougal woke well after noon the following day, the celebrations the night before had gone well into the early hours of the morning but Dougal like most of his friends had slipped away relatively early, the lure of a real bed far too great to turn down.

He was tempted to stay in his comfortable bed (the same one he had had in his last stay in the city) but the smell of fresh bread finally grew too much to ignore. He walked out to the little dining room he shared with his sister and saw half a dozen bread rolls (large loaves to the fairies) along with a selection of jams, cheeses and butter.

He buttered a roll and covered it with jam and went to wake his sister only to find that she had already left so he sat down, finished all six rolls and then went off in search of Derry.

It was not long before he came across Adam and Dylan who were heading in the opposite direction.

'So you've finally risen,' laughed Adam.

'I've been up for hours,' said Dougal sheepishly, 'have either of you seen Derry?' he asked deciding quickly to change the subject.

'She's off somewhere with Phil and Neave doing magic stuff,' said Dylan.

'We were coming to get you to see if you wanted to get something to eat before this afternoon's council of war,' said Adam.

'That sounds like a good idea,' said Dougal, 'I haven't eaten since breakfast and that was just a little bit of bread and cheese and about now I'm more than ready for something more solid.'

'One of the advantages of being in the city is not always being hungry not like when you're on the road,' said Dylan happily.

'Enjoy it while you can little brother, if we're put under siege the first thing the king will do is ration food and water,' said Adam.

'Well then we had better hurry hadn't we,' Dylan said only half joking.

The council was held in a special chamber that in the past had been used as a meeting room for the fairies and their dragon allies so there was plenty of room for the twins and Phil. It was attended by the highest ranking wizards and the commanders of the fairy army as well as Strahan, Finn, Amber, Liam, Adam, Dylan, Phil, Dougal, Derry, Cameron, Izzy and Llewellyn.

The main reason for the gathering was to discuss the defence of the city and to assign areas of responsibility to all present.

Cameron and Izzy explained the tactics the pixies had used in conquering Caledonia and what they believed the brownies could have done to at least slow them down if they had had wizards to help them defeat the pixies (the brownies had only had a handful of wizards in their entire history and none in the last hundred years).

The council continued well into the night with each of the captains been given orders for their troops ready to be deployed. The wizards were to make sure all the lesser wizards were taught as many battle spells as possible in whatever time they had left.

Just before the meeting broke up Liam was given his orders. He was to take two dozen foresters to the border and watch for the enemy army, count its numbers and then report back to the city so they were as ready as possible for the pixies arrival.

Dougal was woken at dawn the next morning by Adam who had been given command of four hundred fairies assigned to assist the ellyllon in their post outside the city walls.

Within the hour the leprechaun and fairy stood beside Llewellyn in a field outside the cities main gates. Llewellyn and his men had camped outside of the city by choice wanting to be close to their worksite and after being locked up in cramped pixie prison barracks, the ellyllon all wanted the freedom of sleeping under the stars.

Dougal knelt down so he could see the plans Llewellyn had spread out on the small table before them and was amazed by what he saw.

'You drew this since last night?' he gasped genuinely impressed.

'Yes but don't worry it's only a rough copy and if we have time I'll add extra fortifications but we have to start somewhere don't we?' said Llewellyn misunderstanding Dougal's comment.

Adam and Dougal just looked at each other and shook their heads thinking that it would take years to dig all the trenches and tunnels drawn on the map not to mention build the fortifications.

'We'll never finish all of this,' said Adam.

'You and your men take care of the fortifications,' said the miner handing Adam a copy of his plans, 'and leave the rest to Dougal and my men.'

Adam took the plans, said his goodbyes and left to join his men to begin the construction of the defensive fortifications.

'What do you want me to do?' asked Dougal.

The miner pulled back a large piece of canvas revealing a large spade.

'My men made this for you last night,' he said, 'I think a man of your size will move more soil in a day than dozens of my men would in a week.'

Dougal picked up the spade and simply said, 'show me where you want me to dig.'

In the week that followed Dougal, Adam and his men also camped outside the city. No one wanted to waste any time moving to and from the city.

The defences were already starting to take shape. Everywhere Strahan and Amber (who were standing on the city walls studying the plans below) looked was alive with activity. What only days before had been flat open land was now changed beyond recognition.

Adam's men had been busy burying hundreds of large logs deep into the ground and then sharpening the exposed ends. Llewellyn believed these barricades would stop or at least slow down Rupert's mounted troops.

New hills had begun to appear made from the soil taken from the ground by Dougal and the miners as they dug their pits, trenches and tunnels. With the help of the wizards, the city's gardeners had compacted the soil changing the cities landscape forever.

'It's hard to believe they have done all that in a week isn't it,' said Amber to her father.

'If I had not watched them do it with my own eyes I wouldn't have believed it possible,' replied the king looking at his daughter.

He was about to say something else when Amber grabbed his arm. 'Father, a rider,' she said pointing in the direction of a mounted fairy galloping towards the city.

'It's one of Liam's foresters, we had better go to the gates to meet him,' said the king already heading for city gates.

When the forester saw the king and princess waiting for him at the gates of the city he stopped and dismounted from his horse.

He looked at Strahan and said, 'there's three hundred pixie knights heading this way, they'll be here in an hour or two, three hours at most.'

'Three hundred knights, do you think they are scouts?' asked the king.

'It is a strange thing King Strahan, they ride under a white flag. Liam recognized several of them and told me, to tell you Princess Amber, that they are led by a knight called Sir John and his friend Arthur. He said you knew both these pixies and would want to know they were coming.'

'Thank you for this information. Rest now, have something to eat, then return to your post,' said the king.

Once the scout had departed the king turned to his daughter asking, 'is this the pixie that you believe helped you to escape?'

For a moment the king wondered if Amber had heard his question and was just about to ask it again when she finally nodded her head in reply.

Strahan studied his daughter for a moment but could not read her thoughts so he said, 'I will go and make the preparations for the arrival of this pixie knight and his men.'

Left alone overlooking the plans Amber was left wondering what all this meant.

An hour and a half later Strahan, Amber, Finn, Izzy, Neave and Dylan, with five hundred troops and ten wizards, rode out of the city's main gates. The king had decided to intercept the approaching pixies well before they reached the city not wanting them to see the defences that were currently under construction.

'I find even the idea that I may owe my life to a pixie quite disconcerting,' said Izzy to Amber.

'It had to be him,' said Amber, 'if it had been a brownie we would know by now and anyway a brownie wouldn't have insisted you freed me because you would have been their only concern.'

'What I can't understand,' said Neave joining in, 'is why a pixie would risk his life saving a fairy and a couple of brownies. If caught the best he could hope for is a quick death but from what you two have told me Rupert is not exactly a forgiving king.'

'I think a lot of what Sir John does he does to keep his friends alive,' said Amber.

'I'll have to take your word on that,' said Neave, 'having never met the man. However, the fact that Liam likes and respects him does not hurt your argument, he is after all an excellent judge of character.'

'Yes, he is,' said Amber lapsing into a guilty silence thinking about how mean and nasty she had been to the pixie last time they had spoken. Even after that, she believed John had risked his life to save her but the thing that she understood even less than that, was, what was he doing now heading directly towards them.

She was shaken from her thoughts when she heard her father call the fairies to a halt. He ordered the soldiers to fan out and wait for the arrival of the pixie knights.

They did not have to wait long. Less than quarter of an hour had passed before the pixies appeared on the road before them.

Strahan turned to Neave as two pixies broke out of the pack and headed towards the fairies.

The king said, 'cast a spell to tell us if they are lying to us or not.'

Neave nodded and then whispered a few magical words and then said, 'it is done.'

Amber watched as Sir John and Arthur rode forward surprised to see both men wearing chain mail and riding heavy warhorses. The two pixies stopped their horses and dismounted well short of the fairies and again Amber wondered what they were doing. None of this was making any sense to her and she asked herself not for the first time, 'why are they here?'

As John walked forward he studied the faces before him. Even from this distance he could see the puzzled look on Amber's face. He was more than a little surprised to see a brownie sitting on a horse beside Amber. He, like Rupert, had expected the brownies to remain in Caledonia. The next fairy to catch his eye was a small redheaded woman dressed in a green robe and he knew without a doubt that this was the wizard that William was so afraid of. He continued to walk forward until he and Arthur stood ten feet away but directly in front of the fairy king.

Strahan, Amber, Neave and Izzy dismounted and walked forward to meet the two pixies.

'Why are you here Sir John?' asked Strahan a little more coldly than intended.

'My friend Sir Arthur and I are looking for King Strahan of the Fairies,' said John who paused before adding, 'have I found him?'

'Yes you have found my father,' said Amber.

Sir John looked over at Amber and smiled saying, 'I'm glad you and your friends have arrived home safely princess. You'll be happy to know that King Rupert was most unhappy about you and your brownie friend's disappearance.'

'Sir John,' said Strahan, 'you still have not answered my question. Why are you here?'

'To make a stand for what we believe in,' replied the pixie knight. After a moment he continued, 'princess, you may remember me telling you about pixie lords who had their land stolen from them by the king.'

'Yes,' said Amber softly.

'This is some of them, the ones that think like me anyway,' said John.

'Your king stole all these pixies' land?' said Strahan stunned by the thought of any monarch stealing land from his subjects.

'No,' said Arthur speaking for the first time. 'Some like myself don't like what the king has done to our friends or to innocent people like the brownies.'

'Why now?' asked Izzy.

'Better late than never,' said John, guilt evident in his voice. 'Let's just say that Princess Amber helped both Arthur and myself see things more clearly and we found there were others who felt the same as we do.'

'Are you saying you want to fight beside us?' asked Izzy amazed.

John replied softly, 'yes.'

'You would fight and kill your own people?' asked the fairy king also shocked.

'No, that is one thing we won't do,' said John.

'Then you are not here to fight beside us,' snapped Izzy.

'Yes we are,' said John calmly, 'no, we won't fight our own but we will fight against the troll and esprit follet mercenaries. Arthur and I have fought campaigns alongside both General Bergen of the trolls and General Reims of the follet. We know how these men think and how they will fight in the battle ahead.'

The king turned to Neave and said, 'well?'

'He speaks the truth,' she said confidently.

'My daughter and others who have crossed your path speak highly of you Sir John,' said Strahan, 'added to that you have passed Neave's magical lie spell. Yes, I trust you and Sir Arthur but how do we know all those who follow you do so honourably?'

'Many of these men I have known most of my life and others I have trusted with my life. Those I cannot personally vouch for, my friends can,' said John adamantly.

'Why now?' asked Izzy again almost angrily, 'why not when you invaded my people?'

'Because,' said Arthur, 'until now we have never had a man brave enough to lead us.'

'I will grant you and your followers entrance to my city,' said the pixie king, 'there we can discuss this further. Return to your men and tell them what is happening and then follow us to the city.'

'Thank you your highness,' said Sir John who bowed firstly to the king and then to all those before him. He and Arthur then turned and walked briskly back to their horses, mounted them and galloped back to their men.

As they rode back Arthur turned to John and asked, 'apart from Amber who else has crossed our path?'

'I've have no idea,' answered John.

'Can we trust them?' asked Strahan more to himself than those beside him, concern creeping in.

'I would entrust my life to John and Arthur, in fact I still think Izzy and I owe them our lives,' said Amber who wished she had asked John if it had been him who had helped her escape.

'It's not them I'm worried about, it's the other three hundred pixies we have no reason to trust,' said Strahan.

'You could lock them in your dungeons until after the battle,' suggested Izzy.

'We don't have dungeons,' said Neave.

'Right then', said Izzy, 'that's me out of ideas then.'

'I'll have to interview each of them individually,' said Neave, 'it will take me a couple of days but I'm sure I'll be able to expose anyone who would betray us.'

'I can't afford to release any other wizards to help you,' said Strahan.

'I won't need any,' said Neave reassuringly, 'Derry and I will work far more effectively by ourselves. To be honest I'll be much happier assessing the pixies personally.'

'How is Derry's training coming along?' asked the fairy king, his disapproval obvious.

'Better than I could have ever hoped,' said Neave, 'and you know the only reason I'm teaching her is because she asked me to.'

'A technicality you were quick to latch on to,' replied the king.

'Her people have innate magically ability,' argued Neave, 'and as a wizard I had no right to turn down her request.'

'I just hope that Derry does not regret her curiosity and your eagerness for a willing pupil in the future,' said Strahan. 'Anyway how much power does she possess?'

'It's hard to say at this early stage. She's a quick learner, she mastered invisibility far quicker than her brother but apart from that innate ability I don't think Dougal has a magical bone in his body. As for how powerful Derry could become, I just can't say. I don't know if she has any limitations because she is a leprechaun but I can say this much, she will be more than useful in the days to come.'

'Maybe I was wrong,' said Strahan, 'but I was only thinking of Derry.'

'I know you were,' said Neave softly.

'How many to come?' asked Derry.

'Another dozen or so,' replied Neave who along with Derry had spent the best part of the last two days screening the newly arrived pixie soldiers. So far only four had been taken away and locked in a storage room. King Rupert had not sent them but all believed they would be well rewarded for betraying both Sir John, his followers and most importantly the fairy defences.

It was not a job that either woman had enjoyed but now that there was light at the end of the tunnel both felt their enthusiasm lift.

Neave was delighted when it was Derry, without her help, that had detected the lie told by the last pixie.

'What will happen to the spies that we have uncovered?' asked Derry.

'I don't know, that is up to the king to decide,' said Neave, 'he may just hand them over to Sir John and let him deal with them.'

'These pixies are a strange people aren't they?' Derry commented.

Neave merely nodded in reply and then called out loudly, 'next!'

Both women intently studied the pixie as he entered the room and walked towards them.

Later that night Derry, Neave, King Strahan, Sir John, Sir Arthur, Izzy, Cameron, Amber and Finn all met in the king's private study.

'Only seven spies?' queried Strahan.

'That's right but the real question is what are we going to do with them now?' it was Neave who replied.

'I believe that is not our decision to make Neave. It was Sir John and not us they were going to betray,' said the fairy king who then turned to John and asked, 'what would you like us to do with them Sir John?'

The pixie knight was silent for a moment, deeply disappointed by the fact that seven of his followers were disloyal. His first instinct was to make them pay but after a quick reflection he said, 'can you hold them somewhere secure until after this war ends?'

'Yes,' said Strahan, 'but what will you do with them after that?'

'Release them,' the knight answered. 'When we win this fight they will no longer be a threat to us and as they will no longer be a threat I can see no reason to harm them.'

Strahan smiled and nodded his approval at the pixies decision. He had not known the pixie long but was already beginning to understand why his daughter and Liam held him in such high regard.

'Finn, see that Sir John's prisoners are made comfortable for the duration of their stay,' ordered Strahan.

'At once uncle,' said Finn who turned to leave the room.

'Also Finn, have the cooks send some food up and return here as soon as you've finished making your arrangements,' ordered the king.

The fairy prince merely nodded his head in agreement as he hurried out of the room to fulfil to his duties.

At the same time as Finn was seeing to the pixie prisoners, Adam and Dougal sat at the foot of a newly formed hill outside the city walls.

'Arrgghh,' said Dougal grimacing in pain, 'every muscle in my body aches.'

'Don't be so soft,' laughed Adam.

'It's all right for you,' said Dougal, 'you just wander around shouting the occasional order or two while I've more soil to dig and move then all your fairies and Llewellyn's miners put together.'

'You shouldn't be so good at it then should you,' said Adam still laughing.

'I'm just glad we've almost finished,' said Dougal.

'So Llewellyn still thinks we'll be finished in a couple of days then?'

'No,' said Dougal, 'he thinks we'll be finished tomorrow afternoon.'

'I wish he'd keep me informed, after all, I'm supposed to be in command out here,' replied Adam more than a little annoyed with the ellyllon miner.

Llewellyn, Dougal, Adam and their followers had changed the landscape of the city forever. The guards who manned the city walls could not believe their eyes as they watched the plains transform right in front of them.

It was however the changes they couldn't see that would pose the greatest threat to the pixie invaders. There were covered pits filled with sharpened poles. The covers were undetectable to the eye and could take the weight of a pixie or fairy but were rigged to collapse under the weight of mounted troops. Some of the larger hills were hollow and made to accommodate ellyllon longbow men. These 'hills' were built with hidden arrow slits that would allow the archers to fire their arrows at the unsuspecting enemy. There were also escape tunnels that led to the safety of the city. These tunnels were rigged to collapse after the archers had retreated.

Just before dusk the following night, Llewellyn gave Strahan and his officers a guided tour of the city's outer defences. It was fair to say they were all stunned by what they saw. They had all watched the landscape changing from within the city walls in what little spare time they had to observe but none had guessed what lay hidden from the naked eye.

All that was left to do now was to assign troops to their positions and while the troops waited the commanders of the newly formed alliance revisited their strategies for the upcoming battle.

Most of the fairy battle plans had been developed with the help of Izzy, Cameron and their followers using the knowledge of pixie battle plans they had gained in their defeat by Rupert's men.

The arrival of Sir John and his supporters had changed everything. The pixie knight, his friend Arthur and many of the other knights were seasoned veterans of the pixie army. This gave the city's defenders inside knowledge of pixie tactics and that could be invaluable in the upcoming battle.

Two weeks after the completion of the city's defences tension was running high in the defenders ranks.

There had been no sign of the invading pixie army and as always the waiting was the hardest part. While not on duty the soldiers tried to keep themselves occupied by playing games of cards or bones but this did little to calm their nerves and in some cases even led to the occasional fight breaking out.

Strahan spent as much time as he could with the troops on the front lines, the popular monarch trying to lift the morale of his people.

Few among the fairies wanted this fight but now that it was inevitable they just wanted to get it over with.

So it was almost with an element of relief when soldiers of the alliance greeted the two fairy woodsmen who rode into the fairy capital with the news that the vast pixie army was, at most, only three days from the city.

CHAPTER 22

AN ATTACK IN THE NIGHT

It had been two days since the first fairy scouts had returned to the city with the news of the approaching pixie army. Dougal and Derry who were walking around the cities fortifications could see the glow from the hundreds of enemy campfires only a few miles away. It was obvious to both of them that tomorrow would see the pixie assault begin.

The twins had seen little of each other in the weeks since their return to the city and had spent most of the day catching up. Derry told Dougal all about everything that Neave had taught her and he told her all about the defences he had helped build. Neither leprechaun was overly concerned about the upcoming battle thinking their size meant they were in little, if any personal danger. They were determined however to keep their friends as safe as possible.

An old soldier passing by saw the twins looking at the last moments of a beautiful sunset and said, 'tis a wonderful sight is it not?'

'Yes,' said Derry, 'it truly is. I love the sunsets of my homeland but yours are the most stunning I have ever seen.'

Then the old man said, 'don't know if I will see another one,' and then he began to sing a song.

Dougal and Derry listened to the first verse of the sad and haunting ballad and then took out their tin whistles and joined in.

After the song was finished the old man said, 'you both play well.'

The twins thanked him and Dougal asked the old soldier about the song. The fairy told him it was an old song that dated back to a time before the fairy people united to become one nation. It was a song about a king of one of the ancient tribes who fled into the woods thinking his wife and family had been killed and his people destroyed by raiding trolls. The king had lost hope and was never seen again, his body never found. The sad thing was his people won the battle and his family were all safe. 'While we still draw breath,' the old man explained, 'there is still hope'.

He then told the twins it was not himself he was worried about, for he had lived a long and happy life, he worried for the young men and woman of both armies who would not live to see the next sunset.

As they left Dougal made a private vow to himself to return and spend some time with the old fairy as soon as he could.

Dougal and Derry joined their friends just before dawn the following morning. The pixie campfires stilled burned brightly in the distance as the friends gathered to eat what may well be their last meal together for sometime.

The mood around the table was solemn, even Finn who looked forward to 'teaching Rupert a lesson he would never forget' was unusually quiet.

Dougal, who could not stop thinking about his meeting with the old man the night before, was for the first time starting to realise that this was not a game he was playing. Although he had travelled deep into pixie territory and had fought in the attack on Tantallon he had only encountered pixie soldiers on a couple of occasions and had never been in any real danger. He still did not believe he, his sister or Phil was in any serious danger but he now held real concern for all his fairy friends.

The last to arrive to the small gathering was a tired looking Liam who had only arrived back in the city in the early hours of the morning. The fairy forester had only had a couple of hours sleep and looked a little worse for wear. It was the first time any of the friends had seen Liam since he left the city weeks ago and all were happy to see he had returned safely. They all had lots of questions for him and they even asked him the odd one but for the most part all picked at their food in relative silence.

After breakfast was over (if not eaten) the friends wished each other good luck and good fortune and after hugs all round headed for their posts.

The pixie army did not appear until just after midday and the entire city's defenders were stunned by its sheer enormity.

The invaders stopped well outside the range of the fairy archers and the newly erected fortifications.

Dougal and Derry stood together behind the newly built outer wooden walls of the fairy capital watching the massive army form and then do nothing.

'What are they waiting for?' asked Derry.

'I don't know, maybe they're just trying to unsettle us,' suggested Dougal.

'Neave has taught me a spell that lets me see invisible and hidden objects. So if we make ourselves invisible I can follow you and we can find out what they are playing at.'

'Well, as long as one of us knows where the other one is, what are we waiting for,' said Dougal as he vanished from sight.

Derry mumbled a couple of words and then, like her brother disappeared saying to Dougal, 'after you.'

The invisible twins slipped over the wall and headed towards the enemy army, Dougal hoping his sister was close behind him. It did not take the leprechauns long to reach the enemy lines where they had their first look at the troll mercenaries.

Both were surprised by the appearance of the trolls. The races they had encountered so far in Connaught had all been of similar height and build and apart from subtle differences looked very similar. The trolls however looked like nothing Dougal had ever seen before, they were on average a head taller than any one he had encountered in this world. They wore what looked like boiled leather armour that was dyed jet black as was all the clothing they wore. They were not just taller than the other races but far more muscular as well. Finn, who was by far the largest fairy Dougal had seen, paled in comparison to the fierce looking trolls. Dougal could see why the pixie king hired these mercenaries and used them as his shock troops.

'Dougal,' whispered Derry, 'we have to keep moving.'

Dougal nodded, taking one last look at the trolls who were digging in. All around them the pixie army was digging in as if they had no intention of attacking the city anytime soon.

Dougal decided it was time to see if he could find King Rupert and see if he could end this all here and now, once and for all but he found no sign of the pixie king.

After an hour or so behind enemy lines Derry whispered, 'Dougal, we had better head back.'

'Okay,' he whispered back to Derry, disappointed they had achieved nothing on their impromptu mission.

As they headed back Dougal saw a pixie officer lying on the ground halfway between the pixie army and the outer walls of the fairy city. The man appeared to be looking through some sort of tube and studying the city.

On a sudden impulse Dougal ran forward, picked the pixie up and sprinted towards the city. The startled pixie tried to scream in protest but found he couldn't due to the fact his face was covered with a giant hand that he couldn't see.

'Stay still and I might let you live,' said Dougal as fiercely as he could.

It was obviously all too much for the pixie who fainted in the leprechaun's arms.

The pixie woke to the shock of having a bucket of cold water thrown over him. He found himself tied to a chair in a very large room. He saw two fairies, a giant and a brownie looking at him intently. The pixie tried to look behind him but found he couldn't because he was tied too tightly.

'Who are you?' asked one of the fairies firmly.

The pixie said nothing.

'I'll make him talk,' said the giant happily, 'I'll start by slowly pulling his arms and legs off, that's something I've always wanted to do, as you all know'.

'My name is Sir Cecil,' blurted out the terrified pixie.

'Can I pull his legs off anyway your highness?' asked the giant.

'Only if he doesn't answer my questions to my full satisfaction,' said Strahan who despite the situation was enjoying Dougal's little act.

'I'll tell you everything I know, just keep him away from me,' pleaded the pixie.

'Why is your army digging in, what are they waiting for?' asked Strahan.

'We are waiting for our artillery to arrive,' answered the prisoner.

'How long will it take to get here and what do you have?' asked Finn who was standing beside his uncle.

'It should start arriving before nightfall,' said the pixie that looked over to Dougal (who was smiling at the pixie and pretending to pull something unseen apart) nervously.

'How many?' repeated the fairy prince.

'I don't know for sure but most probably a hundred catapults of various sizes and at least a dozen heavy ballista,' replied Cecil.

'When will the assault begin?' asked Finn.

'I don't know. There will be the odd faint attack just to test the strength of your defences but we have had to re-evaluate our plans.'

The king waited for the pixie to elaborate but when he didn't asked, 'why?'

'Your defences are not as our spy led us to believe them to be.'

'Spy, what spy?' demanded the king who was now looking at Sir John (who was standing directly behind Cecil, unbeknown to Cecil) not at his prisoner.

Sir John just shrugged his shoulders and shook his head in reply indicating that he didn't know anything about a spy.

'The Shadow,' answered Cecil, still believing the king was talking to him.

'Where is this shadow now?' Strahan continued.

'I don't know, he could be in this room and I wouldn't know,' explained Cecil.

The king again looked over to Sir John who gestured for the king to join him outside of the room.

'Finn I'll be back in a few minutes,' said Strahan who then added sternly, 'Izzy we need him in one piece.'

Izzy smiled at the king innocently as she slid a dagger back into its sheath. The pixie prisoner, who did not miss the brownie's obvious action and now knowing who she was, decided that she was far more frightening than the giant.

'Actually Izzy,' said Strahan after a moment thought, 'I think you had better come with me.'

Everyone in the room found it quite amusing when Cecil let out an audible sigh of relief.

Once outside the room, John told the king and Izzy everything he knew about The Shadow, explaining all about the man's legendary ability to see all and yet not be seen himself. He went on to explain how not even Rupert knew what the man really looked like because he was a master of disguise and how it was also rumoured that he may have had a sister or apprentice working in Caledonia.

'How do you know they're not here now?' asked Strahan when Sir John had finished.

'If they were here, Rupert's men would have known about your new defences,' Sir John replied.

Izzy, who had been in quiet contemplation up until this moment added, 'if there was a pixie spy in our ranks, I believe she is now lost somewhere in the tunnels beneath Tantallon.'

The unusual trio spoke for a few minutes more before re-entering the room that held their prisoner and continued with his interrogation.

As twilight approached there was still no sign of an attack being made by the pixie army that night. The defenders watched as the cooking fires of the enemy began to light the slowly darkening sky.

Then suddenly, without warning, a rock sailed through the air and crashed harmlessly onto the ground halfway between the city's main wall and the newly erected outer wall.

Over the next hour an increasing number of rocks headed towards the fairy defences and unfortunately for a dozen or so of the city's defenders, not all of them fell as harmlessly as the first one did.

'Let me go out there and do something with those catapults uncle,' demanded Finn who was now getting restless, 'we can't just sit here helplessly watching as our people are being hurt and killed.'

'Finn, it's too dangerous, there are too many enemies between us and the catapults,' replied Strahan as calmly as he could.

'I think a small party could sneak through,' said Izzy, 'I'll go with you Finn,' she then turned to Cameron and asked, 'are you coming too?'

Cameron just nodded knowing it was pointless arguing with her determined friend.

'Count me in too,' said Neave, 'you'll need my help destroying the catapults.'

'No', said the king getting more and more agitated, 'I can't order anyone to do this.'

'You're not ordering anyone to do anything,' said Izzy, 'we are volunteering. Cameron and I have been doing this sort of thing for years and we will do it with or without your approval. You may be able to forbid your subjects from joining us but neither of us are your subjects and if we're going to do this we might as well have some help.'

'I want to help,' said Adam.

'So do I,' added Liam and Dylan as one.

'All right, all right,' said the king knowing he was defeated, 'but you are not going with them Amber,' he said adamantly looking at his daughter.

'I wouldn't let her uncle, she doesn't have enough experience,' said Finn not looking at his cousin but knowing she was glaring angrily at him.

The king dismissed Finn and his followers who left to make the necessary arrangements for the dangerous mission ahead.

Within the hour Finn, Adam, Dylan, Liam, Neave, the two brownies and five more fairy volunteers slipped over the city's outer wall and headed off in search of the pixie artillery. The mission nearly ended before it had begun as a huge rock from a catapult crashed to the ground a few inches from Finn, Cameron and Neave. The force of the impact knocked all but three members of the party off their feet.

Every member of the small force, including Neave, was dressed from head to toe in black clothing with their faces painted black as well. Each had a backpack filled with oil and carried a long sword, a longbow and a quiver full of arrows.

Liam fell into his usual role as scout and lead the party forward. Neave cast a new spell that she had been working on that would enable the warriors to communicate telepathically.

They decided to skirt around the enemy camp and avoid contact with the pixies for as long as possible.

'Down!' Liam's voice suddenly boomed in the minds of his companions and all threw themselves instantly to the ground. Seconds later a patrol of at least twenty trolls walked past them no more than ten feet from where they lay.

'Did anyone hear that?' grunted one of the trolls anxiously.

'No,' snapped three other trolls simultaneously.

Finn silently drew his long sword from its scabbard as the first troll said, 'I'm sure I heard something.'

'You're always hearing things that aren't there,' said an obviously annoyed troll who then turned to the soldier next to him and asked, 'why are we always stuck with him when we're out on patrol?'

'Because he's your brother and no one else will have him,' the third troll answered.

'Come on hurry up,' ordered an unseen troll from the front of the column.

The trolls started forward again and the last thing the fairies and brownies heard was a troll's whining voice saying, 'I know I heard something, I know I did.'

After a couple of minutes Liam signalled his companions forward again and after about an hour they found themselves at the rear of the enemy camp and looking at ten lightly guarded but gigantic catapults.

'They're the biggest catapults I've ever seen,' said Dylan amazed, 'we should have brought Dougal and Derry with us.'

'We don't need them,' said Neave confidently, 'you guys cover us and Izzy, Cameron and I will take care of the catapults.'

The three women took their companions backpacks and crawled towards the closest catapult while Finn, Adam, Dylan, Liam and the other fairies all positioned themselves in a location that would enable them to provide covering fire if it was needed.

Neave however was not quite as confident as she had led the others to believe. As she crawled forward she surveyed the area before her. Yes it was true the over confident trolls had left the catapults without guards but Neave and her friends were highly out numbered. Each catapult had a crew of over a dozen and most of those were trolls and large trolls at that.

As they approached the nearest catapult its arm sprung forward sending another potentially deadly missile towards the fairy city.

Neave watched as the crew sprung into action, several members pulling on leavers that lowered the catapults giant arm while others began rolling a huge bolder forward.

Neave realised that while the trolls were busy preparing their weapon for its next attack, they payed little or no attention to the weapon itself.

She raised her arm to stop the brownies that were following her and studied her prey and waited.

Ten minutes later the catapult fired again and Neave signalled for Izzy and Cameron to remain where they were. She then crawled forward as quickly as possible not stopping until she reached the base of the catapult.

She risked a quick look at the trolls to make sure she hadn't been seen then took out a vial of oil from her pack and emptied its entire contents over the pack and then tied it to the catapult.

Izzy, Cameron and Neave repeated the painstaking process until all ten catapults had packs with their highly flammable contents tied to them. They then crawled back to join the others.

When they returned Finn said, 'right, the easy part is done, now how are we going to light them?'

'Don't worry, I've got it all under control,' said Neave.

Neave then sent seven of the small party to the far side of the artillery camp and waited.

Arrows felled eight of the trolls before they even realised they were under attack. A large troll at the centre of the camp began to shout orders but was silenced almost immediately as he was struck simultaneously by two arrows ending his life instantly.

By the time the trolls had organised themselves, over a dozen of them already lay dead and a further score were injured. The remaining trolls charged toward the fairy archers who fired one last volley dropping another four trolls and then slipped into the night and headed back to the city.

As soon as the trolls left their camp in search of the archers that had attacked them, Neave, the brownies and the two fairies that had remained, placed rags into the top of the vials of oil from the two remaining packs. Neave then spoke a few words of magic and all the rags began to burn. The brownies and fairies ran forward throwing the burning oil vials onto the oil filled packs already tied to the catapults and within seconds the entire site was ablaze. Then, like their companions, Neave and the others headed back to the city.

It was only an hour before dawn when Neave and the remaining others entered the city, the blaze from the burning catapults lit the night sky like beacons.

Of the twelve who had left the city only nine returned. Two of the archers were unfortunate, they were caught by trolls before they could disappear into the night. One of the fairies with Neave had been hit in the back by a troll's arrow as he fled the burning catapults.

Almost none of those who retuned to city did so free of injury. Most had minor cuts and bruises but Finn had suffered the worst injuries with a gash that ran the length of his forearm as well as a stab wound to his side.

He had received his wounds when he had stumbled into a small pixie outpost. Finn had been lucky that the pixies were caught flatfooted and three had died before they had had a chance to draw their weapons. Two others had 'got in' what Finn later described as 'lucky shots' before they died.

While Finn went to have his wounds tended to the other members of the mission left to get some sleep.

Dougal and Derry woke two hours after their friends had returned from their attack on the pixie catapults to a grey overcast morning. Light rain had just started to fall but passed by within minutes.

As he walked towards his post Dougal bent down and picked up one of the boulders that had been fired into the city the previous night and tossed it from hand to hand testing its weight.

'It's too heavy for me to throw back,' he said to his sister.

'It doesn't matter Dougal, there are some smaller ones over there,' she said pointing to dozens of rocks that had been fired into the city over night.

'Why do you think the catapults have stopped?' asked Dougal, who like his sister did not yet know about the actions of their friends in the early hours of morning.

Derry just shook her head indicating she had no idea either. For the rest of day like the day before the twins watched and waited for an attack that still did not come.

CHAPTER 23

THE FIGHT FOR SARASIDHE

For the next two days the two armies watched each other from their defensive positions, neither side seeming prepared to launch an attack.

Neave and Izzy had led another night attack on the camp in the early hours of the morning following their assault on the catapult. The pixies were not going to be caught out again however and Izzy, Neave and their troops were forced to turn back before they reached enemy lines as the increased pixie and troll patrols made it impossible to proceed without risking major losses. This was the last attempt by either side to strike at the other.

Then just before midday the catapult barrage began again. The king sent Phil out to see where the catapults were positioned.

The fairy dragon returned in minutes and said, 'there's at least forty light catapults just behind their frontlines, most are still being set up but they won't do anywhere near as much damage as the heavy catapults that were destroyed the other day would have done.'

The king thanked the dragon and waited for the barrage to end wondering what the pixies planned to do next.

Dougal, seeing that the rocks that flew towards the city were far smaller than the ones from the earlier attack, decided to catch as many as he could and throw them back at the enemy army. It was not long before Derry joined him and although they only stopped a fraction of the missiles from reaching their destination their action had a remarkable effect on the defenders moral. Every time one of the twins caught and returned one of the missiles it was greeted by hearty cheers.

Then two hours after it had all begun the barrage ended. There was then a sudden cry from the troll ranks as they charged forward.

All along the defensive line fairy officers bellowed instructions telling their archers to hold their fire until ordered. Dougal picked up a rock from the ground beside him and threw it at the charging trolls knocking several to the ground.

The fairies watched as the trolls closed the gap to the temporary wooded wall.

'Fire at will!' screamed a fairy officer and the fairy archers fired volley after volley at the charging trolls.

The fairy defenders watched as the trolls stopped their charge and retreated leaving behind a couple of dozen of their comrades who had been killed by fairy arrows or Dougal's rocks.

'What are they doing?' asked Strahan as he watched the trolls withdraw.

'Testing the range of our archers,' said Sir John who then added, 'the attack will come at dawn.'

'They never did that when they attacked Tantallon,' said Izzy, who had watched the troll advance beside the fairy king and pixie knight.

'We knew that you only possessed brownie weapons,' explained John, 'they were trying to see if we had any ellyllon longbows. We were lucky they timed their attack when our ellyllon friends were resting.'

The king called a runner over and ordered him to instruct Llewellyn and his followers not to return to their posts on the outer wall until an hour before dawn.

'Well, at least they're in for one surprise tomorrow,' said John grimly.

As soon as the trolls withdrew the catapult barrage began in earnest. Rocks rained from the sky like giant hailstones only far more deadly. Fortunately for the defenders of the city, most either fell short of the city or harmlessly in the open spaces between the new outermost wall and walls of the city proper. This however was of little compensation for the twenty or so fairies that were unlucky not to avoid the falling rocks.

The assault began as the first ray of sunlight lit the morning sky. The trolls walked slowly forward, the front rank carrying shields so large that only their heads and feet were visible to the city's defenders.

The closer the trolls came to the city the quicker they moved, quickly closing the gap, content in the knowledge that they were still out of range of the fairy archers.

Llewellyn and his miners waited until the trolls were well within range of their powerful longbows (but still outside of the range of the bows used by their fairy allies) before they opened fire on the unsuspecting trolls.

The well disciplined trolls simply broke into a charge as scores of their comrades fell to the rain of ellyllon arrows.

As the trolls closed in on the city's outer wall, horns sounded from inside the city proper signalling for the soldiers on the outer wall to withdraw. The archers fired one last volley and then set fire to the oil soaked wall and fell back to the second line of defences.

The outer wall was never meant as a defensive position, it had simply been built as a diversion to slow the enemy down.

The wall had been burning for over an hour by the time the first soldiers from Rupert's army began tearing down its smouldering remains. The city's defenders had now all taken up their intended positions in which they would make their stand.

As soon as the wall was disposed of Rupert's army charged towards the fairy barricades.

All along the defensive line fairy troops lowered ramps from where the fairy cavalry (along with Sir John's knights who all wore fairy uniforms) entered the battle. The surprised trolls momentarily held their ground but then buckled in the fierce mounted assault. The trolls fell back as horns sounded behind them.

Sir John looked up at the sound of the horns and saw the esprit follet cavalry charging towards them. His first instinct was to ride out and meet this new threat head on but then decided this early in the battle discretion was the better part of valour. He turned to the knight beside him and ordered him to sound the retreat.

The fairy cavalry then turned and returned to the safety of the barricades and as the last rider crossed the ramps they were all pulled back.

The esprit follet cavalry having nowhere to go were forced to leave the battlefield.

Rupert's infantry made two further attacks on the barricades that day but both were beaten back and the day ended in a stalemate.

Strahan, Amber, Neave and Sir John watched from the battlements as the second assault finally faltered.

'Where are their wizards?' asked Neave.

'It's too early,' said John, 'they're just trying to soften us up a bit. I don't think we'll see them for a couple of days yet, they won't want to let you know were they are until they have to. By the same rule Neave, I think you should keep your wizards quiet for now as well. We don't want to make targets of them or give too much away.'

'So what are they going to do next Sir John?' asked the fairy king.

'They'll try and weaken the barricades tonight.'

'How,' interjected Strahan before the pixie could explain further.

'They'll send special engineers forward under the cover of darkness. Some will work on damaging the fortifications while others will dispatch unweary defenders,' explained the pixie knight.

'So how do we stop this from happening?' Neave asked.

The knight thought for a moment before he answered and then said, 'I don't know. The only thing I can think of is to fire flaming arrows into the air to light up the sky, that way at least we might see them coming. I don't know how successful that will be but I can't see any other option,' he John.

The defenders of the city slept in shifts that night as they had done every night since the appearance of the pixie army. Those on duty sent a steady stream of flaming arrows into the night sky to shed light on any activity.

On several occasions small groups of pixies were seen crawling towards the fairy barricades. On each occasion the pixies were forced to withdraw or they died trying to.

Liam, Finn, Izzy and Cameron decided that if the pixies intended to make covert raids on the fairy defences it was only fair that they returned the favour.

So without telling anyone what they planned doing they met after dark by the entrance to one of the tunnels that had been dug by the ellyllon miners. The commander of the garrison responsible was about to challenge the four conspirators but decided against it when he saw the fairy prince.

Finn looked at the man and said sternly, 'you have not seen us, is that understood.'

The fairy officer nodded his reply as the two fairies and two brownies disappeared into the tunnel that would lead them to just beyond where the temporary wooden wall had stood before its destruction.

When the four commandoes reached the end of the tunnel, Liam looked through the small periscope to ensure they would not unintentionally give away the location of the secret tunnel to any nearby enemies. Once they were safely back on the surface they headed off in search of their prey.

For the next two hours Finn's small band wiped out several sentry posts and on a couple of occasions narrowly avoided (in some cases more through good luck then good skill) large bodies of troll and pixie troops.

As they were returning to the tunnel that would take them back into the city, Liam heard a shout that made his blood run cold. He and his friend crawled off in the direction of the raised voice and saw a large gathering of pixie knights and footman. In the centre of the group stood Sir George berating a battered pixie soldier.

Liam's hand went to his short bow but Finn placed a restraining hand on his arm.

Liam looked at his friend and Finn mouthed, 'now is not the time, there's too many of them.'

Liam nodded reluctantly agreeing with him but silently vowed to himself that he would personally make the evil knight pay for his actions.

The four friends quietly withdrew from Sir George and his men and headed back to the tunnel that would take them back to the city.

Fourteen fairy soldiers were found dead at their posts the following morning. Despite the fairies best efforts to keep the pixie hunters away from their defences they had not been completely successful.

If the fairies were shaken by their losses it was fair to say the pixies were stunned by theirs. So far they had discovered twenty trolls, thirty four pixies and four esprit follet officers all dead. It had indeed been a very successful night for Finn and his friends and they intended to repeat the same dose that night.

By nightfall it was obvious to the commanders of the fairy army that they would not be able to hold the barricades for long the following morning. Although the defenders had fought with valour there were not enough of them to hold off Rupert's enormous army with only barricades for protection. So under the cover of darkness the fairy army withdrew to take up positions behind the solid stonewalls of the city.

'Izzy, are you sure you want me to do this?' asked Neave.

'Yes,' replied the brownie, 'we can't keep him under your spell forever and I think now is the time to give him a chance to redeem himself. He has no idea about our plans or our defences and unlike Caledonia he doesn't know the surrounding area so I don't think he can do us any real damage.'

'I can't argue with your logic, 'said Neave, 'it's just that I'm not sure that I would be as forgiving as you are.'

'He is my cousin and a member of our royal family and maybe even next in line to our throne so what else can I do?' Izzy asked herself more than the fairy wizard, she then added, 'I'm just hoping that with Liz out of the way he will see the error of his ways.'

Neave looked over to Murray who stood obediently behind Izzy magically bound to do his cousin's will. The wizard spoke a few words of magic and released Murray's magical bonds.

Murray's first instinct was to draw his dagger and attack the women before him. The only thing that stopped him was he didn't know which one he wanted to kill the most. While he tried to decide who to strike first he realised the sheer folly of the idea. Neave could probably kill him with a word and Izzy was far more skilled with a blade than he would ever be. He decided now was not the time to act but he knew his time would come and when it did he would make the most of it.

Izzy looked at Murray and said, 'don't disappoint me and more importantly don't disgrace our family.'

With that Izzy and Neave left Murray alone in his room.

Murray lay on his bed and waited until he was sure the two women were long gone. Once he was sure he was alone he strapped on his sword and headed towards the city gates. Along the way he stopped often to talk to any brownies he passed telling them Izzy had sent him to supervise the brownie withdrawal. He walked unopposed all the way to the now almost deserted frontline.

Again he waited until he was certain he was no longer being watched and slipped over the barricade and into no mans land. He then bent down, picked up a spear that had once belonged to a fallen troll soldier and tied a large white rag to its shaft. Once he had completed this small task he headed towards the pixie lines waving the spear from side to side so anyone ahead of him could see his 'white flag' of surrender. Within minutes he saw a small patrol of five trolls appear out of nowhere.

'You there,' he called, 'take me to your,' he never finished his sentence as a troll's spear pierced his chest. Murray started forwarded for an instant and then toppled forward dead before he hit the ground.

Izzy and her friends, who had been stalking the trolls for five minutes, were just about to launch their attack when they heard Murray call out to the trolls. As the troll nearest to her threw its spear directly toward Murray she took advantage of its distraction, as did her companions and the troll patrol was quickly dispatched with ruthless efficiency.

The livid brownie walked over to her fallen cousin determined to end his life if the troll's spear had not already done so.

It had been sheer chance that the four warriors had happened upon the scene of the brownie's demise and Izzy was tempted to leave him where he had fallen.

Finn however had other ideas and bending down lifted Murray up and placed his dead body over his shoulder and said softly, 'your people cannot know their prince was a traitor so we will tell them he died a hero, carrying out hit and run raids on the pixie camp.'

'You are right,' said Izzy, 'although he doesn't deserve the honour.'

The four friends cut short their raid on the enemy camp and returned to the city carrying the body of the fallen brownie 'hero' with them.

The city's defenders watched as the pixies and trolls of Rupert's army tore down the deserted barricades. It was a task that would take them most of the day. The attacking army now believed nothing stood between them and the city.

Llewellyn's longbow men on the city wall picked off any troll or pixie unfortunate enough to stray inside the range of their mighty weapons but for the most part the fairies and their allies sat back and watched the pixies work throughout the day.

The morning after the barricades had been destroyed, it dawned grey and overcast but very warm. The occupants of the city were greeted with the sight of six large siege towers heading towards the city.

Under the cover of darkness Rupert's army had moved its catapults to positions from where they could fire into the heart of the city. It was obvious to all in the city that the real battle was about to begin.

Inside the hollow hills that the ellyllon miners had constructed as part of the city's defences, archers and wizards waited for the order to fire on the enemy who now surrounded them.

A cheer rose from the city as one siege tower crossed one of the concealed pits and toppled forward, crashing to the ground. The pixies replied by sending a flaming barrage from their catapults into the city.

Every fire started by the inbound missiles was hastily doused with water ending any threat they may have caused. Sir John had insisted that the fairies set up what he called 'fire brigades' because he had expected the pixies to use these tactics. If the fairies had not been prepared for this eventuality it could have caused havoc inside the fairy city.

Finally the order came for the hidden archers to open fire. The wizards cast spells on their arrows that caused them to detonate on impact. By the time the last archers and wizards withdrew through their escape tunnels they had destroyed six catapults and more importantly two more siege towers.

Troll soldiers charged the hills but arrived well after they had been vacated. The trolls managed to gain access to some of the hollow hill only to be buried underneath tons of soil as they set off the booby traps left behind by the former occupants.

The commanders of the city watched as their enemy continued to close in on the city. The advancing army had lost three of their six siege towers and hundreds of men to hidden archers and to the traps that Llewellyn and his miners had set but to the disappointment of those on the wall none of this seemed to even slow the army's steady advance.

Arrows rained down on the attacking army as they reached the city wall and they positioned siege ladders. As the pixie archers provided covering fire intended to pin the city defenders down, trolls and pixies began to climb towards the ramparts.

All along the ramparts fairy soldiers pushed ladders back into the swarming troops below trying to climb into the city but there were simply too many and eventually the hand to hand battle for the city began.

Finn watched as the trolls and pixies parted to reveal a massive battering ram that was heading straight for the city's main gate.

'Wizards to me now!' cried the fairy prince, then turning to Adam and Liam who along with Izzy, Cameron and Dylan were standing beside him, said hurriedly, 'Adam, go and find Dougal and Derry and have them join the troops positioned behind the gates. Liam you go down there and take command, it is vital they don't get inside the city.'

As his two friends departed, six fairy war wizards arrived answering Finn's call.

Finn, seeing the wizards arrive, turned to them and ordered, 'stop that battering ram before it reaches the gate.'

The wizards ran to their positions and sent balls of magical fire towards the approaching battering ram and the trolls pushing it forward. They watched in despair as their spells seemingly hit an invisible barrier and bounced off harmlessly. They then tried several other spells but all to no avail, nothing they did penetrated the magical defences.

The leader of the wizards cried out in frustration and Finn asked anxiously, 'what's wrong?'

'There is a defensive spell on the ram sir,' explained the wizard.

'Can't you penetrate it?' replied Finn.

'No my lord we have tried every spell at our disposal but we are not powerful enough to break through,' explained the wizard.

'Find Neave and find her fast,' ordered Finn and the wizard nodded and quickly departed.

Finn looked over at the ramparts and saw that things were not going well on his left side.

'Izzy, Cameron, Dylan, I think you are needed over there,' he said pointing, his three friends nodded in agreement and drawing their weapons charged towards the enemy. As Izzy left her post she signalled two dozen waiting brownies to follow after her.

While his friends watched the approaching army from behind the stone walls, an invisible Phil had been doing as much damage as he could. He had initially tried to pick up and then knock over one of the siege towers but it had simply been too large for him to do either. So after a quick sweep of the pixie army but in a failed attempt to locate Rupert, Phil turned his attention to the pixie catapults.

When Phil saw the hundreds of pixies and trolls climbing ladders into the city he decided to leave the catapults for now and spend some time clearing the walls.

By the time he reached the walls large numbers of Rupert's men had reached the city's ramparts and were now fighting hand to hand with the fairys and their allies manning the walls.

In a single sweep Phil sent ten ladders (complete with the soldiers climbing them) crashing to the ground. He turned around to make another sweep when out of the corner of his eye he saw the large battering ram heading towards the city's gates.

Even from this distance Phil could sense the magical protection placed on the battering ram and he knew it was unlikely that the fairies would be able to stop it before it reached its destination. Forgetting the pixies and trolls climbing the walls, Phil now turned his focus towards the battering ram.

He flew directly to the gate and then turned into the direct path of his prey so he could intercept it before it reached the gate. He flew higher to gain enough height to swoop down on the approaching ram but before he was a quarter of the way up he felt a searing pain in his left wing and felt himself tumbling towards the ground unable to stop himself.

Izzy and those who followed hit the trolls and pixies on the rampart like a tidal wave knocking many of their enemy off the rampart, either back over the walls from where they had come or into the city itself. The fairy soldiers, who were waiting below, quickly dispatched any pixies who survived the fall into the city.

Then, for no apparent reason, ten of the attacking armys ladders fell into the troops waiting below allowing the fairy and brownie soldiers to momentarily drive the last of the enemy off this section of the wall.

Izzy turned and was about to order her followers to follow her to another defensive weak spot when she was knocked to the rampart by what felt like an earthquake. She dragged herself to her feet, looked over the wall and saw the crumpled form of Phil lying not far from the city gates. From what seemed like every direction, trolls surged towards the fallen dragon that had become visible the instant he hit the ground and who was struggling in vain to rise to his feet. Izzy stared helplessly at the dragon praying that Phil would be able to protect himself but it soon became obvious to her that he was not going to be able too.

From his position just inside the gate Dougal felt the shock waves caused by Phil's impact with the ground.

He then heard Finn cry, 'Phil's down!'

'Open the gates now!' demanded Dougal.

'We cannot,' answered the gate guards.

'If you don't,' said Dougal, his voice as cold as ice, 'I will and I will, kill anyone who tries to stop me.'

The fairies responsible for the gates simultaneously opened them believing that if they didn't the leprechaun would actually kill them and they would be unable to stop him.

Dougal ran towards his friend not even sure if he was still alive. Finn and the archers on the wall fired their arrows at the trolls charging towards the dragon momentarily holding them back.

Dougal knelt down and with strength borne out of necessity, he lifted Phil who weighed at least as much as the leprechaun and carried him as gently as he could back into the city. The gate guards closed the gates behind Dougal and Phil as soon as they entered the city.

'Send for the healers,' cried Dougal as he gently placed Phil on the ground still not certain if the dragon was even alive.

Then to Dougal's absolute joy he heard Phil whisper, 'you have saved me again my friend.'

The dragon then lapsed back into unconsciousness and Dougal forgot his instance of happiness which was quickly replaced with real concern for his friend.

It was not long before two healers, both with experience of treating fairy dragons, arrived to examine Phil. Dougal watched as they examined his friend the battle momentarily forgotten.

'He's very lucky,' said the elder of the two healers, 'he is severely concussed and his left wing is badly broken but he will live and may even fly again.'

Dougal relieved picked up his friend once more and placed the dragon in the back of a large wagon that had arrived to take him to the infirmary. He watched until the wagon, Phil and the healers disappeared from sight, then Dougal drew his sword and turned to face the gate and anyone who breeched it.

Finn, like Dougal, watched as the wagon carried away the valiant dragon and then turned his attention to the battering closing in on the gate directly below him.

'Where is Neave?' he said to himself now believing she was the only one who could stop the approaching ram.

'Wizards boil the oil,' ordered Finn although he didn't believe for a minute that it would work.

As soon as the ram was in range of Finn and his archers' arrows, they fired at it but like the wizards' spells before them they just bounced harmlessly off the ram's magical protection.

Finn felt the whole gatehouse shake as the battering ram struck the gate for the first time.

'Pour the oil!' he shouted and then watched as the oil did what he had expected, nothing.

'Where are you Neave?' he asked himself one more time looking around desperately wishing that his friend was at his side.

Dougal watched the gate before him shudder under the impact of the battering ram. When he saw it begin to buckle he ran forward trying to brace it by adding his weight but it soon became clear that with or without his added weight the gate was going to fall so he moved away from the gate and prepared himself for the onslaught.

The gates weakened with each blow, finally shattering. Within seconds pixies and trolls began to stream into the city. The leading ranks of the attacking army were cut down quickly, many falling to fairy archers before they even reached the first rank of defenders.

Dougal took a deep breath and threw himself at a charging troll. All around him the sounds of metal on metal could be heard as leprechauns, pixies, fairies and trolls fought for their lives.

Dougal lost track of time, at one point he heard Liam call out for some of his men to follow him. He quickly glanced over and saw Liam and half a dozen fairies running after at least a dozen pixie knights heading into the city. Dougal tried to follow but could see no way through the masses of friend and foe that surrounded him.

Finn's archers fired volley after volley into their enemy on both sides of the city wall. He watched as Liam broke away from the battle at the gates to chase after a group of pixie knights that had broken through the defensive lines. He would have fired at the knights himself but they were already out of range when he first saw them, so he turned his attention back to the pixies and trolls that he could fire on.

'Finn,' he looked up when he heard Neave call his name, 'I'm sorry it took me so long to get here.'

'Can you seal the gate?' he asked almost desperately.

'There's only one way to find out,' said Neave, 'I'll need someone to cover me while I cast the spell.'

Finn, Neave and two other fairy guards left the gatehouse and headed into the fight at the gates. While Finn covered her back and the two guards stood infront of her, Neave closed her eyes and began to mutter words while making strange gestures with her hands.

Finn, at first, thought his friend had failed but then soon realised that no more of the enemy troops were entering the city, infact he was almost horrified to see that three trolls seemed to be trapped inside an invisible barrier.

Neave then spoke a couple more words and then pointed to the battering ram. The ram burst into flame and within minutes it had burnt away to nothing.

Ten minutes later the battle for the gate was over, for the time being at least.

Dougal looked around to make sure the risk was over and then said, 'I'm going after Liam.'

Dougal ran off in the direction he had last seen Liam heading. Finn signalled for a dozen of the gate guards to follow the departing leprechaun. Finn, his men and Neave then returned to their places on the battlements.

Liam and his followers finally caught up to the pixie knights in a small courtyard after the knights had taken a path that led them to a dead end.

'Cut them down where they stand,' ordered a knight.

Although the knight wore a helmet that covered his entire face the moment Liam heard the pixie's voice he knew it was Sir George.

'I have waited a long time for this Sir George,' said Liam evenly, 'now I'm going to make you pay.'

'The mouthy one is mine,' said the knight coldly as he wondered how this fairy he was sure he had never seen before, knew his name.

So focused on the pixie before him Liam never saw Dougal arrive at the site of the small conflict. It was not until Dougal approached Sir George from behind that Liam even knew the leprechaun was there.

'No Dougal, I will finish this one myself,' said Liam firmly.

Dougal stopped in his tracks and nodded instantly realising who the knight Liam fought was.

'Who are you?' asked Sir George.

'A friend of Sir Arthur and Sir John's and your executioner,' answered the fairy woodsman.

The confused knight decided it was time to finish this and attacked Liam with renewed vigour.

After Adam (who had decided that at the moment Derry would be of most use putting out any fires that still burned inside the city) had sent Dougal to reinforce the gates, he searched the city walls to see where he was needed most.

Seeing a weak spot on the wall on the right hand side of the gate house he ran off in that direction. By the time he arrived at his destination trolls and pixies outnumbered the fairies on that part of the wall and were beginning to take control.

'To me!' he cried rallying the fairies around as he charged towards his enemy. After ten minutes of bitter hand to hand fighting Adam had reluctantly started to give up ground to the ever increasing enemy force.

Just when Adam thought he would have to withdraw his men and regroup, Izzy and her followers hit the pixies and trolls from the rear throwing them into total disarray. Adam, always quick on his feet, charged forward finally securing the battlement.

'You have no idea how happy I am to see you guys,' said Adam hugging his little brother.

'Glad to be of service,' said Izzy, 'but the fight is not over yet,' she added pointing to the next wave of trolls who were attempting to gain access to the barricades from their newly erected ladders.

'Arrgh nooo, don't they ever give up,' said Dylan as he wiped the sweat from his brow and re-entered the fray.

In what was normally Strahan's throne room but was currently being used as a command centre, the fairy king, his daughter and the commanders of the fairy army, were trying to organise the defence of their city. It had become clear to Amber from the very beginning that none of the fairy officers had any idea what they were doing. If it hadn't been for the quick thinking and actions of Finn and her friends the city would have already fallen. The fairy officers had repeatedly ignored any advice Sir John had given them and eventually the knight had left to fight fires caused by the pixie catapults.

Amber did not blame her father, he was a peaceful man who left the military decisions to the commanders of his army. The problem with this was that none of these men had ever actually experienced battle before. They all believed that they had learnt more from their text books than Sir John had through years on the battlefield fighting in the army of their enemy.

Amber walked over to a fairy runner and handed him a note she had written moments before.

'Take this to Finn,' she ordered, the fairy nodded and ran from the room.

Finn watched as a troll phalanx (an almost impenetrable wall of shields) tried to protect a small band of pixie wizards as they tried to nullify Neave's spell so that Rupert's army could re-enter the city through its broken gates.

Finn fired arrow after arrow into the phalanx but to no effect.

'Don't worry Finn,' said Neave, 'I doubt if even William could break that spell and from what I know about William, he's not likely to risk his life to even try.'

Finn nodded and was about to turn his attention elsewhere when a messenger from the fairy high command ran up to him and handed him the missive.

'What does it say and who is it from?' Neave asked.

'It's from Amber,' answered Finn, 'and she wants us to ignore any orders we disagree with. In short she wants you to take control of your order and for me to take over the army. She thinks we will be able to do this without the 'fools' as she calls them even realising. If they do she says she will take full responsibility.'

Neave smiled at Finn and said, 'I thought we already had.'

Just before nightfall horns sounded from behind the troll and pixie lines and the attacking army broke off the attack for that day. They had held the city walls this time but Finn wondered whether he would be able to say the same thing again tomorrow. The pixie catapults still fired flaming missiles into the city but Finn was confident that Sir John's fire brigade would be able to keep the damage to a minimum.

CHAPTER 24

DOUGAL'S PLAN

After Rupert's army had withdrawn for the night all the members of the small group who had gone in search of Amber weeks before went to visit their fallen friend.

They found Phil in surprisingly good spirits, if a little drowsy, his left wing was in plaster and his head bandaged. The healer on duty informed the worried friends that the other healers' first impressions were indeed correct and that Phil would make a complete, if slow, recovery. Phil was particularly pleased to hear Dougal's description of how Liam had dispatched the evil Sir George. Liam for his part was remarkably quiet on the matter.

One by one the friends left Phil's bedside heading off to get something to eat and whatever sleep they could before the battle continued the next day, until only the twins and Neave remained. The three waited until Phil drifted off to sleep and the healer suggested that now would be a good time for them to leave.

As they walked from the room Dougal said, 'this has to stop and it has to stop tonight.'

'If only there was a way,' Derry replied.

'There is, I have a plan,' said Dougal obviously proud of himself.

'Well let's hear it then,' said Neave.

'I'm not sure we want to,' groaned Derry worried it would be as bad as one of her brother's other hair brained theories.

'Neave,' said Dougal ignoring his sister, 'can you make yourself invisible?'

'Yes,' was her simple reply.

'Good. This is what I think we should do. Make ourselves invisible, walk into the middle of the pixie camp, find Rupert and the wizard. Once we've found them we bring them back to the city and then we force the weasel to call off his army.'

'That's not a plan Dougal,' said Derry rolling her eyes towards the heavens, 'it's a suicide mission.'

'I'm up for it,' said Neave, 'and I think there is no time like the present so let's get going.'

Derry shook her head in resignation and followed her brother and their friend towards the city gates.

'Neave, you and Derry can cast spells that let you see us even though we are invisible, can you cast one that let's me see the two of you as well?' asked Dougal.

'Yes,' said Neave, 'I can.'

The three conspirators faded from sight as Neave and Derry cast their spells well before they reached the broken city gates. It took Dougal's eyes several minutes to adjust to his new heat seeking vision. He now not only saw his sister and friend with a strange red glow but all the fairies and brownies who manned the city walls as well.

When they reached the city walls Neave magically transported them all to the other side so she didn't have to disturb the spell she had placed on the city's ruined gates earlier that day.

Working their way through the enemy camp the three invisible friends searched for their elusive prey. After an hour they were all starting to think that the king might not even be in the camp.

'Let's grab a pixie and question him on Rupert's where abouts,' whispered Dougal as soon as they reached an area free from enemy soldiers.

'Great idea,' said Neave, 'it certainly beats wandering around all night for nothing.'

They then headed back to the perimeter of the camp and waited until they found a single pixie that was walking aimlessly back and forth on some sort of sentry duty. As Dougal walked towards him the pixie turned as if he heard something and stared directly at the invisible leprechaun. Seeing nothing the guard shrugged his shoulders, turned back around and started to walk away. The pixie got about four feet before Dougal lifted him off the ground while placing a hand over his mouth.

Dougal nearly dropped the pixie when he felt a sharp pain in his hand as the pixie sank his teeth as deeply as he could into Dougal's flesh. Before Dougal could threaten his prisoner the pixie threw his leg back with all the power he could muster hitting Dougal in the midriff. Dougal doubled over as the air was knocked from his lungs but managed to retain his grip on the feisty pixie.

When Dougal was able to speak he said, 'if you don't stop wriggling I'm going to crush the life out of you.'

The pixie's reply to Dougal's threat was to bite down even harder on Dougal's hand.

Followed by his sister and their friend, Dougal carried the still struggling pixie to a place that he was sure would be safe enough to question his prisoner.

'Right, 'said Dougal removing his hand from the pixie's face, 'I'm going to ask you a couple of questions and you are going to give me some answers.'

'I don't think I am,' said the pixie with a calmness that shocked Dougal.

'Where is King Rupert?' Dougal demanded.

'Don't know, never met the man,' answered the pixie almost cheerfully.

'Look,' said Dougal trying to remain calm, 'we can do this the hard way or we can do it the easy way, I don't care which.'

'Stop, stop you're scaring me,' replied the pixie sarcastically, still sounding totally unimpressed.

'Let's just feed him to the dragon and be done with it,' said Derry.

'The dragon's dead, I saw him fall with my own eyes,' said the pixie, 'actually I even felt sorry for the proud beast.'

'Enough of this,' said Neave materialising before the pixie, 'kill him Dougal, I'll just get the answers from his corpse.'

'You can't do that,' scoffed the pixie but it was obvious to all present he was now not quite as calm as he had been.

'What I can or can't do is of no concern to you,' said Neave so coldly it sent a shiver down both the twins' spines. 'Dougal, kill him.'

'All right, all right, I'll talk,' said the pixie as he felt Dougal's grip start to tighten around his throat, 'but not because I'm scared of you, it's just that I find the thought of someone using my dead body as a tool somewhat distasteful.'

'Where's Rupert?' Neave asked.

'In a small camp about two miles behind the main encampment,' said the pixie obviously reluctant to tell.

'How many guards?' she persisted.

'I have no idea,' replied the pixie, 'I've never even seen the king. I wasn't lying when I said I had never met my esteemed king and I've never been near his precious camp. All I know is he never travels anywhere without at least twenty knights and his wizard advisor.'

Neave nodded to Dougal who then knocked the plucky pixie unconscious and placed him on the ground.

Dougal then bent down and picked up Neave saying, 'we'll get there much faster if I carry you.'

Neave vanished from sight again as Dougal began to jog towards the king's camp.

It did not take the two leprechauns long to jog the two (Connaught) miles to reach the kings camp. The invisible twins and wizard had no problem avoiding the hundreds of pixies and trolls who guarded the camps perimeter. In the centre of the camp stood a huge silk tent easily large enough to house at least half a dozen leprechauns comfortably.

As soon as they entered the tent William said, 'your highness we are not alone.' He then began to make intricate gestures with hands.

Neave who had already cast a silence spell on the inside of the tent to stop any of the guards outside hearing whatever happened inside the tent, quickly threw up a magical wall to protect her and the twins in an attempt to deflect whatever spell William was in the middle of casting.

'So, at least one of you is a wizard,' sneered William as his spell bounced harmlessly back to him and as he prepared a more powerful spell added, 'are you that weak that you are afraid to show me your face?'

'I am certainly not afraid of a wizard of your limited ability,' Neave taunted as she appeared at the opposite end of the tent to William.

'So it's you, the fairy witch, I thought you were still hiding somewhere in Caledonia,' said William who was doing his best to hide his mounting fear as he raised his hand and threw a ball of fire directly at Neave.

'Is that the best you've got,' taunted Neave as she doused the flame with magical water before it was halfway to her.

She shook her head and smirked saying, 'I was really hoping you would provide me with a challenge.'

Derry, stunned, watched enthralled as the two wizards hurled spell after spell as well as the odd insult at each other. It was the most amazing display of power the young leprechaun had ever seen. She knew her friend was powerful but almost could not believe how powerful she actually was. Derry was starting think her friend was toying with the wizard. She was reminded of a time when she was much younger and had watched her cat playing with a frightened mouse.

With Neave busy and his sister distracted Dougal went after Rupert who was making for the tent's door screaming for his guards who could not hear him.

Dougal caught the fleeing king only feet from the door lifting the king off the ground. Unlike the defiant pixie who had fought Dougal all the way, Rupert simply past out in sheer terror as he felt himself leaving the ground.

Dougal turned as he heard William screech, 'how is one so young so powerful,' and then he was gone.

'Where is he?' asked Derry.

'I'm not sure,' said Neave, 'either my last spell got him or he transported himself out just in time. There's too much spell residue to tell for sure but even if he did get away I don't think we will see him again any time soon.'

'Right let's get out of here,' said Dougal.

Neave nodded her agreement, muttered a few words and before the twins knew it they stood in the middle of the fairy storerooms that they were using as prison cells.

'I wish you could have used that spell to take us to Rupert in the first place,' said Dougal tiredly.

'If I had known where his camp was rest assured that is exactly what I would have done,' said Neave. 'We should all go and get a couple of hours sleep and then meet back here with the others a couple of hours before dawn.'

'Not quite as much fun when you're the one who's being held captive is it?' mocked Amber.

Rupert looked at her but said nothing in reply.

'It's over Rupert,' said Finn, 'call your army off and we'll let you live.'

'You know as well as I do that within two days my army will take this city,' said Rupert.

'Yes it will but it will do you little good if you're dead,' snapped Finn.

'If you kill me you lose your only bargaining power and I don't think you'll do that,' the pixie king replied.

'He might not but I will,' shouted Dougal as he tore the king from his chair and thrust him towards the door.

'Dougal wait!' cried Amber.

'No let him go,' said Neave who then followed Dougal and the pixie king out of the room.

'I order you to let go of me now giant!' screamed the king in a tone that reminded Dougal of a spoilt two year olds tantrum.

'I don't take orders from a cowardly rag doll,' sneered Dougal who then added, 'I think it is time you realised weasel that your days of ordering anybody to do anything are over unless I choose otherwise.'

Rupert didn't know what to say and for the first time in his life he was truly afraid. He had no idea what this insane giant was planning to do and seemingly no way to control him either.

With the exception of his sister who had little trouble keeping up with her brother's pace, Dougal's friends had to run just to keep up with the leprechaun. Only Derry and Neave knew what Dougal planned to do and the others, although shocked by their friend's actions, were still keen to find out. Dougal slowed his pace slightly to allow the others to keep up.

Of those in the city who watched the strange sight of one of the giants carrying an unknown pixie through the city while being followed by Princess Amber, Prince Finn and their closest friends, only Sir John and his knights knew the true significance.

Sir John, Sir Arthur and Sir Oliver ordered the followers to remain at their posts and then they ran off to join the procession.

'Amber what's he doing?' asked John, 'and how in the nine hells did he get hold of Rupert?'

'He, Derry and Neave walked into his camp last night and bought him back, as for what Dougal's doing now, your guess is as good as mine,' explained Amber.

'What happened to William?' asked Arthur.

'Neave,' was Amber's simple reply.

Both John and Arthur nodded in understanding. Sir Oliver who was yet to see Neave in action looked over at the small fairy in wonder.

By the time Dougal reached his destination the first rays of sunlight had just begun to light the morning sky. He stood on the gatehouse and watched as the first of the pixie and troll soldiers began to walk towards the city. He wanted to take a deep breath to calm his nerves but he didn't because he didn't want the pixie king to know he was not totally in control. He took one last glance at the approaching army and silently prayed that his plan would work.

'I'm going to ask you nicely one last time,' said Dougal, 'call your army off.'

When it became clear to Dougal that Rupert had no intention of answering him he took hold of Rupert by his ankles and then held him upside down over the city wall.

'You can't treat me like this, I'm a king!' Rupert screamed.

'I think we have already established that I can treat you anyway I want,' said Dougal bluntly.

'Let me go!' continually screamed Rupert with more than a little fear now evident in his voice.

'Call off your army and I'll think about it,' said Dougal almost casually.

'I'll see you roasted alive for this,' Rupert tried to roar but now sounded more like a frightened kitten.

'No you won't and what's more you know you won't,' said Dougal who was now almost certain that he had won.

Dougal then went on to add, 'even if by some fluke you live through this and your army wins this battle let me assure you that the victory will be short lived because if my sister and I don't return home to our people within the next two weeks my father will return with an army of giants and they will tear your puny little empire apart piece by piece, but if you call your army off now you might live to rule your little country for a little while longer with a few conditions of course. Oh and by the way my arms are getting just a little bit tired,' he added loosening his grip on Rupert's ankle.

'All right, all right!' screamed Rupert desperately, 'I'll call them off.'

'Good for you,' said Dougal, 'and then you're going to dismiss your troll and esprit follet mercenaries. Once you've done that you're then going to order the rest of your army to return to Tudorland. That includes your occupation armies in Caledonia and Gwyllion as well as freeing all of your brownie and ellyllon slaves.'

'That would mean surrendering half my empire,' said the shocked pixie king, 'I won't do it.'

'Half an empire is better then none at all, is it not?' asked Dougal again slightly loosening his hold on Rupert's ankle.

'Yes,' Rupert agreed reluctantly but secretly vowed to get even with this upstart giant.

'Good, it's settled then,' said Dougal pleasantly, 'oh and by the way, you and your men will bury the dead and you will remain here as our guest until all of our conditions are met.'

Rupert was going to protest but realised it was pointless. He knew he was in no position to argue with the obviously stubborn giant so the pixie king simply said, 'your terms are acceptable.'

It took Rupert's army three days to bury those who had fallen in the attack of the fairy capital. It had been the troll mercenaries who had suffered the greatest losses and in comparison the fairies and their allies' losses had been fairly light. Everyone in the city knew however if it had not been for Dougal, things would not have ended as they did.

Dougal had searched for the old fairy soldier who had sung to him and Derry on the eve of the pixie invasion but no matter where he looked he found no sign of the old fairy. The thought hit Dougal that perhaps the old soldier did not live to see another sunset. Dougal realised sadly that even in victory there is sorrow.

The night at the victory celebration Dougal found himself thinking more about the old soldier and others like him then he did about the victory which he had played a major part in.

Izzy, seeing Dougal's expression and understanding how the young leprechaun felt, took him aside and said, 'Dougal, you are right to grieve for those who have fallen but you should also celebrate what we have achieved. In defeating Rupert we have saved far more lives than we lost and you my friend are the main reason for our victory. This is your moment Dougal, enjoy it and remember we do this to honour those who have fallen as well.'

Dougal thought about what the little brownie had said. She, more than anyone, knew about loss for she had been fighting a futile war for years trying to drive an enemy from her homeland. Most of her family had been dragged away to work as slaves in the pixie mines. Her cousin had betrayed her and her people, yet no matter what hardships she endured she had kept fighting and had finally seen her enemy defeated. Yes, he thought, Izzy did have a reason to celebrate and in helping in her victory so did he but first he had something far more important to do and he was sure the banquet would still be there when he returned.

Dougal left the main hall and walked into the kitchen, picked up the largest side of raw beef he could find and went to visit Phil. He spent several hours with his friend talking more about the things he and Phil had done before they had arrived in Connaught. He stayed with Phil until he was chased away by an overly vigilant healer.

By the time he returned to the celebrations Dougal was in a far better state of mind to enjoy them.

two weeks after the pixie withdrawal, Llewellyn and his ellyllon miners left the fairy city all keen to return to the hills and green valleys of home.

Llewellyn was particularly eager to assist any pixies that still remained in Gwyllion in their departure from his beloved homeland.

Before he left Llewellyn promised to return when his people had established a stable government so a formal alliance could be signed between the two nations.

Izzy and Cameron watched as the miners marched out of the newly repaired main gates and Izzy knew her time to leave was also approaching.

Already reports of the pixie withdrawal from Caledonia were starting to reach the city and during that morning Izzy had heard the thing she wanted to hear most of all. Several of her cousins had been found in pixie work camps and mines, so the happy little brownie was no longer the next in line to the Caledonian throne.

Izzy knew she, Cameron and their followers would be heading home soon because like the ellyllon they had a country to rebuild but she knew that the friendships she had made since she had freed Amber would last a lifetime.

Yes, she would be leaving soon but she would be back.

The fairies kept Rupert locked in their cells until all their demands were met.

As soon as the last pixie troops had withdrawn from Caledonia and the slaves had been freed the fairies kept their word and released the pixie king.

Sir John made the most of his king's absence by meeting with others like himself who had had their lands confiscated by the king, gathering the numbers to allow him to stand against the king if it became necessary.

On his return to Tudorland, King Rupert was met by a delegation of knights led by Sir John. No longer fearing their king, the knights demanded the return of all their estates and lands.

King Rupert, who was now a shadow of his former self, granted their request.

The Pixie Lords were not however satisfied with these concessions and forced Rupert to sign a charter that gave them control of their own destiny which was far greater than they had ever known in the past.

A knights' council was set up to 'advise' the king before he passed any new laws or sanctioned any military action. Sir John, First Lord of Huntington, was appointed as the first, First Knight of Tudorland. It was fair to say the balance of power had shifted in the pixie kingdom.

Rupert was seldom seen after he signed the knights' charter and on the few occasions that he left his private chambers it was only to call his pet raven but sadly for Rupert the bird never answered his call.

With autumn fast approaching it was now Dougal and Derry's time to depart. Although Phil was recovering faster than his healers had expected, it would still be at least two months before he would be fit enough to make the journey to his new home. The dragon had decided that in future he would now divide his time between the two worlds so he could keep a protective eye on all of his friends.

Dougal and Derry said goodbye to the injured dragon (this was particularly hard for Dougal who had spent many hours with his friend following the battle) and then walked outside to join those who would escort them to the portal that would take them home.

They were met halfway by Amber who had come to say goodbye to the twins. The fairy princess had never been good at saying goodbye and thought it would be easier to do it privately with only the three of them present.

Everyone had noticed that a change had come over Amber since the departure of Sir John and the other pixie knights. The normally focused princess seemed to be somewhat distracted as if she was somewhere else at times.

It was still well before dawn and Dougal and Derry wanted to slip out of the city as quietly as possible. Waiting outside for them was the small band of fairies that had earlier bravely travelled in search of a fairy dragon named Phil.

These brave fairies had been rewarded for their actions in the recent events.

Finn had been promoted from Captain to General with Adam and Dylan his new captains. As for Liam he was given the task of organising a new order called Druids. The Druids were to study the plant and wildlife of the fairy realm and record them in journals.

Neave was offered the command of her order but turned it down. She retired from her post in the fairy army and set up a small school to teach the most magically gifted fairy children.

They took their time enjoying the three day journey to the small hill that would take them home but they soon arrived and it was time to say goodbye. It was fair to say they all found this incredibly difficult and tears flowed freely as the twins promised to return.

Dougal said, 'Go n-eiri an bothar leat,' (may the road rise with you) as he turned and walked into the hill.

It was with a strange mixture of sadness and joy that Dougal and Derry looked at the trees of their own world.

'It's always good to be home,' said Dougal, more to himself than his sister.

'We're not quite there yet little brother,' said Derry smiling at Dougal.

From the portal Dougal and Derry travelled to Phil's hidden cave where they stored their fairy armour and weapons and then began the last leg of their journey home.

As Dougal pushed his little barrow through the gates and into the lane and headed for the flourmill, he thought about the reaction of his father, mother and brother to his and his sister's return home the night before.

The twins had wanted to tell their family the truth about their adventure but realised it was probably better if they didn't so they told them they had travelled the countryside living off the land and playing music and doing odd jobs for people who needed their help.

Derry was right, although their father was not happy about his children running off like they did, he believed it had been Derry's idea and Dougal did his duty by going with her to make sure she was safe. No matter how hard he tried, Connor could never stay mad at his daughter for long.

Although she didn't say so out loud both of the twins got the impression that not only did their mother understand why they left for the summer but that she was secretly proud of them. Aedan for his part said he was only happy to see them back because he was sick and tired of doing all of their chores.

Dougal was shaken from his thoughts when he heard someone call, 'Dougal, you've come home.'

He turned and saw Cait walking quickly towards him and to his surprise, although he could not believe how happy he was to see her, he no longer had the fear he used to have whenever he saw her.

'Hello Cait,' he said confidently, smiling at the beautiful leprechaun as she approached.

Cait examined Dougal as she approached him. He's changed, she realised. She no longer saw the shy, quiet boy who had disappeared from Caer Gorias months before. No this Dougal seemed older, far more self assured, there was steel in his gaze. No longer did he avoid looking her in the eye, his voice no longer shook as he spoke to her. He's filled out as well, she realised seeing forearms larger than she had ever seen before. He was still only average height for a leprechaun but he was obviously far stronger then most and as much as she liked the old Dougal she was certain she was going to like the new one even more.

'Where have you been?' Cait asked as she caught up to him.

'You wouldn't believe me if I told you,' Dougal replied.

'How do you know I won't believe you?' she asked.

'All right, come for a walk with me,' he said as he picked up his wheel borrow and started forward again, 'if you promise not to tell anyone, I'll tell you the whole story.'

'I promise,' she said as she slipped her arm inside his and rested her head on his now broad shoulder as they walked towards the flourmill.

THE END

(For the moment at least)

Printed in the United States
71815LV00006B/91-96